JOYCE
The Sci-fi Thriller

Galvanized Group Inc.

1

This story is a work of fiction. Any similarities to people dead or alive, mummy or zombie or anything in between, is purely coincidental.

TABLE OF CONTENTS

The dark and twisted life of scientist, Dr. Joyce Picard, begins sometime in the not so distant future ...

THE BLACK GLOVES OF DEATH

Joyce was a lighthearted, ten-year-old girl, looking forward to what each day would bring. Little did she know, that the events of *this* day, would forever change her life...

It was a bright, sunny morning and Joyce was peacefully sleeping in her warm, cozy bed. Her mother, Adora, came in to wake her for school. They played a fun game every morning, "Tickle time baby! It's time to get up princess!"

"Oh, Mommy, stop!" Joyce giggled.

"I have a perfect breakfast, for my perfect girl."

Joyce jumped out of bed, quickly dressed, and prepared for another fun-filled day. She went happily into the kitchen for her always-wonderful meal.

"Mommy you're the best cook in the world!" Joyce enthusiastically declared.

"Well thank you honey, that's quite a complement!"

Joyce happily ate, taking her time and savoring every bite.

"I'm so glad to see that you cleaned your plate babe. Now Joyce, you finish getting ready and don't forget to brush your teeth."

"Okay Mom, I'm on it," Joyce said, and she quickly jumped up from the table.

It was taking Joyce longer to get ready, than it usually did, and Adora could smell hair spray, all the way in the kitchen. "Joyce, are you fixing your hair?" she asked.

Then Joyce came into the room smiling with pride. "Yes I did, Mommy, and I look lovely!" she bragged.

"Very fancy hairdo!" Adora said, trying hard not to laugh as she looked at the "fancy" hairdo. "Joyce you're so creative. You could have a career in hairdressing!"

"Mommy, I do like to design hair, but just for fun. I'm not serious about it as a career," Joyce said, as she checked out her masterpiece in the hall mirror. "I want to be a supermodel!"

"With that beautiful face, and the natural confidence, that you inherited from your Daddy; you'll be the best at anything

6

you put your mind to."

"Thanks Mommy," Joyce said, and then asked, "Daddy had confidence too, huh? Sometimes I miss Daddy. Does he see me from heaven?"

"He sure does baby, every day," Adora answered sweetly, while masking her pain. "Oh my, look at the time! We better get going!"

Adora and Joyce headed for the bus stop. The two of them walked hand in hand, swinging their arms as they went.

"Mommy, I know why you're named Adora. It's because you're so adorable!"

Adora smiled at Joyce lovingly as the school bus pulled up. "Now don't forget Joyce, Mommy loves you more than life itself." Adora gave Joyce a big hug, and a kiss on the cheek, just before she boarded the bus. "Have a great day, and learn something."

Joyce joined her friends at the back of the bus, (where the cool kids sat). And she and her mother waved to each other as the school bus pulled away.

The bus made a few more stops and then Joyce and the other clamoring students arrived at the schoolyard.

Joyce's first class was Science, and she was thrilled to find that she had received an A+ on the big test! It was a great accomplishment and she and her classmate Tommy were both given stars to put up on the "Super Student" wall. Joyce had a crush on Tommy, and she seized the opportunity to let him know. She gave him a flirty smile and Joyce was delighted when Tommy smiled back. "It must be my fancy hairdo," she concluded.

At lunchtime, Tommy asked Joyce to go to the candy store with him after school. She wanted to go, of course, but decided to play hard to get. "Sorry, Tommy, not today, but can I have a rain check?"

Not really knowing what Joyce meant by a rain check, Tommy quickly agreed with a nervous grin.

This was akin to a steamy romance, at the grammar school. And Joyce's girlfriends were all giggling and whispering about

Joyce and Tommy having a date.

The day seemed to fly by, for Joyce, and it wasn't long before the bell rang. School was out, and the student's rushed from the building and boarded the buses. Tommy rode the same bus as Joyce, and he was quite the Casanova. He boldly sat next to her and then held her hand. Joyce felt her face flush, and wondered if Tommy wanted to marry her. The two sat in uncomfortable silence during the entire trip; it was thrilling for Joyce, yet terrifying at the same time.

By the time the bus arrived at Joyce's stop, she knew that she was in love. She waved goodbye to Tommy and the rest of her friends and got off the bus. She was excited to have a boyfriend and couldn't wait to see him again the next day.

Joyce looked around the bus stop, and was surprised to find that Adora wasn't waiting for her there, as she usually was. "Where the heck is Mommy?" she wondered.

Joyce was anxious to show her mother the A+ science test. "I'm not waiting for her, this is too important! Mommy will be so proud, she needs to see this test right away!" Joyce decided to go home by herself. She ran down the hill, from the bus stop, tightly holding the A+ paper in her hand.

When she arrived home, she burst through the kitchen door. "Mommy! Mommy! I got an A+! Mommy!" she shouted.

Suddenly, Joyce felt the violent grip of a man's strong arms clench her. He squeezed her so tightly that he forced the air from her body. She looked down and saw huge hands wearing black gloves. Joyce was completely helpless, she couldn't move, she couldn't even gasp for air.

Then she heard the man's low rumbling voice, "Don't scream and don't look back." Then he threw Joyce sharply to the floor, and scrambled out the door.

Joyce laid flat on the floor and listened to the dogs next door barking wildly. When the dogs quieted, she leaped to her feet and ran through the house franticly searching for her mother. "Mommy where are you?!"

Joyce finally reached Adora's bedroom, at the back of the house. The door was closed and she burst into the room and saw her mother. "Mommy I found you! Are you okay?"

But, there was no response; Adora lay motionless on her antique brass bed. Her beautiful, long, dark hair was tossed about her shoulders, and the delicate white lace bedspread, beneath her, was drenched in blood.

Joyce slowly approached the bed. She placed her tiny hand on her mother's shoulder, gently turning her, to see her face. Adora's head rolled off of the pillow, and fell to the floor with a thud. Joyce knelt down beside the dismembered head, holding her science paper in front of its face, "See Mommy I got an A+!"

THE PERFECT NARCISSIST

Thirty years later....

We find Joyce seated at a table in a small, sterile, white room. She is now wearing black glasses and her hair is dark brown with a bit of gray. She is unassuming, but has a sense of honor and strength. She is waiting, somewhat frustrated, but hopeful at the same time.

An attractive woman finally enters the room. She shuffles across the floor and sits in the chair across the table from Joyce.

"Hello Tammy, I'm Dr. Joyce Picard," she introduced herself. "How are you feeling today?"

"Okay, I suppose."

"Are you comfortable?"

"Not really, but I'll be fine."

"Tell me Tammy, are you having any anger issues or do you feel sad?"

"I feel better this week than I did last week," Tammy responded.

"That's good to hear."

"I get depressed once in a while, when I think of all that I've been through," Tammy said sadly while looking at the floor.

"Were you abused when you were a child?"

Tammy was defensive, "No Way!" she quickly replied. "My parents were very good to me. They made sure that I had everything that I wanted. Daddy took me to work with him sometimes. He was always proud of me, and everyone in the office loved me. Mom and I liked to shop, and she always bought me beautiful things. We played games together every night, just the three of us. Monopoly was Mom's favorite, and mine too, of course." Then Tammy chuckled, "Daddy just put up with it and went along with whatever I wanted to do. What a wonderful life we had together, my wonderful family!" she said with a smile.

"Well, tell me Tammy," Joyce asked confused, "if things were so wonderful, why did you kill them?"

"I had no choice, there was no other way. Things got so bad that I just couldn't take it. I tried to talk to them, but they were both against me."

"My goodness Tammy, what did they do to you?"

"Can you believe that my parents were so cruel, that they wouldn't let me date until I was sixteen? All of my friends were dating, and I had become a social outcast. Obviously, I couldn't put up with it, so I did what I had to do."

Joyce was shocked at Tammy's reason, for killing both of her parents. But she didn't let it throw her, and went on to her next question. "Okay, now that we've got that cleared up, let's talk about the men that you killed. Were you dating them?"

"Not always," Tammy replied, thinking deeply. "Well, one man in particular comes to mind; his name was Dirk, a lawyer from a well-known firm. He was a very, good-looking man. I met him for the first time in his office building. I was there meeting my friend, Kimberly, to take her to lunch. As we rode down the elevator Dirk's eyes met mine, and wouldn't you know, that we ended up at the same restaurant! Eventually, he approached our table and asked if he could sit with us.

We had a lovely lunch, and I know that I had impressed Dirk. He was absolutely crazy about me, but he had to leave early to get back to court. When I acted disappointed, he invited me to dinner, that night, to make up for it."

"After work, that day, I went home and prepared for my date. It seemed like forever until I would see Dirk again. I must say that I was definitely in love with him."

"He finally called me and I decided to meet him in the lobby of my building. I didn't want him to get the wrong idea by inviting him up to my apartment; after all, I am a lady."

"At eight o'clock sharp, Dirk pulled up in a long, sleek limo! He had a smile that was amazing, and he gave me a bouquet of flowers. I remember it well, a nice mix of roses. We had champagne, on the way to the restaurant. I took just a few dainty sips, not too much, because I wanted to be aware of every detail of this magical night. And it was magical; Dirk was mesmerized by me and clung to my every word and movement. The chemistry between us was incredible and Dirk couldn't resist me. When the evening came to an end, he tried desperately to talk me into letting him come up to my apartment. But, I stood my ground and left him pouting in the car."

"The next day, at work, I couldn't get Dirk off of my mind. I called him from my office every chance I got … just to say hi. When I finally did get him on the phone, he had to cut our conversation short because of his stupid meetings. It was driving him nuts, not being able to even talk to me on the phone! I felt bad for poor Dirk, I know that he wanted to see me and he didn't even have the time to lunch with me."

"Near the end of the work day, I called Dirk's office again and his secretary told me that he had already gone home. I couldn't believe that he hadn't returned my calls before he left, and I knew that his stupid secretary hadn't given him my messages. I asked her for Dirk's home number and she refused to give it to me! I was shocked; surely Dirk had told everyone in his office about our date and how much he loved me. This woman must have been insanely jealous or something, that's the only explanation that I could think of. Finally, I lost my patience and went to the office to confront her. I wasn't playing games with this bitch and she knew it; one threat and she gave me Dirk's home phone number. I told her not to mention it to Dirk, because I wanted to surprise him and she told me that she wouldn't breathe a word of it to anyone. Apparently, it was against the rules for her to give out the home phone numbers of the attorneys."

"I was driving home from Dirk's office, when I remembered him mentioning that he had a gourmet kitchen. Right then, I realized that, in his cute way, he was hinting and wanting to check out my cooking skills. I'm a great chief, by the way."

"When I got home I called, Dirk, right away. He was very surprised that I had phoned, and asked how I had gotten his home number. Being a woman of my word, I didn't tell him that the secretary had given it to me. I simply told him that I wanted to come over and cook for him. At first Dirk said no, I'm sure that he didn't want to impose. It took a while, but after some coaxing, and a little sweet talk, he agreed to let me come over."

"I went through my recipes, and decided to make a standing rib roast. Getting my ingredients together, I prepared my special marinade. I also mixed my secret sauce, especially for Dirk; my insurance in case the dinner didn't turn out exactly as I had planned."

"I wore my hair up and slid into a stunning black dress with shoes to match. I put on my best jewelry and then my most exotic perfume. When everything was perfect, I packed my car and left for my new man's home.

I knew exactly where his house was. I had once admired that very area and thought that maybe I would marry Prince Charming, and live there myself someday. And now it was actually happening, my dream was coming true!"

"Before long, I pulled up to Dirk's security gate and the guard asked me who I was. I was a bit miffed, surely he should have been expecting me, but I played along and told him my name. The guard went into the shack to check, and then told me that I wasn't on the guest list. When I protested, he called Dirk and then waved me through. Incompetent ass! I felt like a criminal or something! But, I wasn't about to let it ruin my special evening with Dirk, so I decided to let it go.

I pictured my beautiful dashing Dirk standing outside of his perfect home waiting to greet me. But, when I arrived, no Dirk; that wasn't like *him*! He wasn't waiting to help me out of the car and carry the bags in for me. I quickly concluded that he must have been caught up on the phone with that stupid guard; probably scolding him for treating me so horribly. I kept my composure and waited in my car for Dirk. It was about twenty minutes later, when I realized that he wasn't coming out. I decided to press on alone, and gathered the bags from the car by myself. There was a long winding staircase that I had to climb; and it was quite difficult with the heavy groceries. Thank God for the lights, or I may have tripped!"

"After my struggle, I finally arrived at the front door and rang the bell. It seemed to take forever, and I nearly dropped a bag, but Dirk finally opened the door holding two overly-full glasses of wine. He smiled, and said that he was happy that I had called."

"Dirk showed me to his huge kitchen and directed me to put the grocery bags on the counter. He didn't lift a finger to assist me and I felt like the hired help! As soon as I put the bags down, good ol' Dirk shoved the wine glass in my hand. I put it down, on the counter, and asked him if he would help me with my coat. At this point, I was surprised that he took it and hung it in the closet. I almost expected him to point a finger at the closet and grunt, or maybe even toss my coat on the floor!"

"Somehow, I held it together and decided to get to work. The kitchen was amazing, everything sparkled and shined; a real pro's kitchen. As I put items, in the refrigerator, I noticed how empty it was. Dirk must be lonely; it was obvious that no one ever came to visit! Poor Dirk, of course he didn't have any idea how to respond to a women coming into his domain. He didn't know how to entertain; it would simply take some training, on my part, to show him the way."

"As I put the last item in the refrigerator, Dirk stumbled back into the kitchen, and again handed me the glass of what I believe to be a burgundy. 'Come on baby, take a drink,' he said with a slur. 'How would you like a tour of my palace, you beautiful princess?"'

"My heart melted once again, my adorable Dirk was back. He gave me a tour of his impeccably decorated home; very rugged, masculine colors, of course. I knew that I would have to redecorate after we were married."

"When we got to the bedroom, passion got the best of Dirk. He couldn't resist me, and tried to push me on the bed. I certainly couldn't blame him, I did look ravishing. But, being a lady, I politely pressed past him and told him that I needed to get the dinner started. He protested, it was darling, but he knew that he was being a bad boy."

"Once I was back in the kitchen, it was time to impress Dirk with my cooking skills. You know what they say, 'The way to a man's heart is through his stomach!' And cooking in this kitchen was a dream, everything was at my fingertips."

"It wasn't long before Dirk came in. He hugged me from behind and kissed my neck; the sweet thing. He asked if he could help me with anything, but knowing that he would just be in my way, I suggested that he set the table. I didn't think he could do much damage that way! Ha! Was I ever wrong! What a disaster! Dirk didn't even know where to place the silverware! Oh well, that's a man for you! At least he gave it a good college try! I finally had to come into the dining room to help him with the setting. He was getting frustrated; he was so intent on pleasing me. Dirk thanked me for the rescue with a kiss."

"Things in the kitchen were under control. I was just waiting on the roast, so I let Dirk pull me to the sofa for a chat. I finished my glass of wine and then, much to my shame, I gave Dirk an extra-long kiss! After that, I quickly suggested that we save the rest of the wine for dinner; that it would pair well with the meat. I certainly didn't want the alcohol to cloud my head. I wanted to be one hundred percent aware of Dirk's every move and every smile. My God, I was in love!!"

'"Not a problem,"' Dirk boldly declared, 'there's plenty more where that came from.' And he happily opened another bottle. Dirk was getting drunk, which was definitely not in my plan; lack of self-control on his part, not very dignified."

"I was a bit disgusted, so I went to the kitchen and finished cooking the meal. It was perfect, if I do say so myself. The roast was pure genius and I decided not to use the special sauce that I had made for Dirk. I went to call him for dinner, and found him in the living room with a cozy fire burning in his lovely marble fireplace. He was cradling a brandy in his hand, in a crystal tumbler. I then announced that it was time for dinner."

"Dirk got up and slowly approached me with a dazzling smile. He held me in his arms and gave me a passionate kiss. I knew that things could quickly get out of hand, he was so passionate and he wanted me so badly, but I broke away and suggested he have a seat at the table. I walked into the dining room and pulled a chair out for him, but Dirk took my hand and led me back into the living room. He pushed me down on the couch, and then climbed on top of me. I told him that we had plenty of time for that later, but he wasn't taking no for an answer. It was a bit difficult to push him off of me, but I managed to, and then got up and fixed my dress. Dirk was getting much too direct with me. What made him think that I would allow this kind of behavior? What did he think that I was, some bimbo?"

"I went back into the dining room, and Dirk followed me. He finally relented and sat down at the table. I gave him the famous fake Tammy smile, then, I proceeded to the kitchen. I put the final additions on the plates and decided to use the special sauce on Dirk's meat after all. Dirk perked up when he saw the incredible meal and told me that he had never seen such a magnificent feast! Of course, he told me that I was a feast for his eyes, as well, but by this time, I was a bit aloof as I placed the plate in front of him."

"I sat down at the table, anxious to enjoy the delicious meal with Dirk. He ate one bite and I waited for his reaction, but he said nothing. He merely gulped down his wine, then excused himself and left the room. I thought it a bit rude, but I waited politely for his return. I was growing impatient; I didn't want the food to get cold, so I decided to go ahead and start eating. And let me tell you, it was amazing. It was my best roast ever and I was right, the wine did pair nicely with the meat. As a matter of fact, I was so involved with my wonderful meal that, I had nearly forgotten about Dirk's rude behavior. But suddenly, I felt something pushing into the side of my face. I was stunned and quickly turned my head, to see Dirk's hardened penis aiming right at my mouth. He was glaring at me, like a ravenous dog, and spoke to me in a very rude tone. 'You want a big, juicy, piece of meat? I got it for ya baby, right here!'"

"That's what he actually said to me! And in the middle of dinner, can you imagine?" Tammy asked Joyce.

"No I can't. "Joyce agreed.

"Dirk had ruined my evening; after all of my hard work and planning, he didn't even eat! I still can't believe that all he had taken was one bite, with no mention about how perfectly it was prepared! Dirk made me so angry, that I actually lost patience with him!" Tammy said gritting her teeth.

"What did you do next?" Joyce asked.

"The only thing I could do, of course!" Tammy answered. "I sliced his penis clean through with the steak knife and added it to my plate. I must say that I was greatly impressed with the cutting ability of Dirk's steak knife. I checked the brand name, it was an Orto. I bought a set of them for myself the very next day."

"And what did Dirk do after you cut off his penis?" Joyce asked concerned.

"You ask what he did after I cut off his penis? Nothing! I

16

know if my penis got cut off, I would do more than lay there like a baby and cry. He just watched me cut into it, eating his penis, one small bite at a time. It complemented the roast perfectly, but I wasn't sure about the wine pairing. What goes well with penis? The red wine didn't seem to enrich the flavor enough, so I got up from the table, carrying the wine bottle with me. I stepped over Dirk and went into the kitchen. I dumped the red wine down the sink and then looked for the recycling bin. Of course I assumed that Dirk recycled, but I was shocked, at his total disregard for the planet, when I found that he didn't. I was still holding the wine bottle in my hand, when Dirk started crawling toward the phone. I was amused; the wimp was actually trying to do something. I wrapped the bottle in a towel, and holding it by the neck, broke it on the edge of the sink."

"Now, I turned my attention to Dirk, and with the broken bottle in hand, I went after him. It wasn't much effort, he was moving like a snail, and when he saw me, he started the whimpering again and he even begged me for mercy! What nerve he had; after all he had put me through that night, he actually had the audacity to expect me to be nice to him again. Well, that certainly wasn't going to happen. I had taken all I could stand and I cleanly ripped through his neck with the broken bottle. I'm sure that I cut his juglar ...um... jugular...whatever it's called... I had to jump out of the way to avoid the blood. I did get smudged, but who could tell? I was glad that I was wearing black."

"I wiped the blood from my shoes and then went to look for the perfect bottle of chardonnay. I knew that Dirk would have the bottle that I wanted. It wasn't hard to find and I poured myself a glass and let it breathe just a bit. Yes, the wine was the perfect fit for the penis."

"Dirk's moaning had stopped by this time, and I was actually able to finish my meal in peace; what a pleasure. After eating, I drank the rest of the chardonnay and cleared the table. As I picked up Dirk's plate, I realized what a waste it was that he had left that beautiful meal, the way he did. I didn't have the room in my tummy for it, but believe me; I packed it up to take home."

"What did you do next Tammy?"

"I did the dishes, of course! Dirk had a great dishwasher very expensive, too rich for my blood! I then went into the living room and sat by the fire and enjoyed the view. The lights of the city were incredible at that time of night. Yes, it's just too bad that it didn't work out with Dirk; I could have really seen a future with him, but he had to ruin everything. Who wants a penis in their face when they are trying to enjoy their dinner?"

"Not me," Joyce said.

"I never wanted to go through that pain again! After such a horrible experience, I certainly didn't trust men anymore. It was just too heartbreaking for me."

Joyce decided to change the subject and took another look at Tammy's record. "Let's see here, Allen Jones, another date gone badly?"

"No, he was a great friend after the, "Dirk thing."

"Why did you kill him?"

"He wanted to end our friendship! Can you imagine that? I needed a shoulder to cry on and he was cutting me off!"

"How did you do it?"

"You mean, how did I kill him?"

Joyce nodded, and then Tammy happily explained. "Oh it was poison, much too easy, not enough of a challenge. But, it was exciting when I killed a random waiter after he got off of work one night."

"Oh, that must be Barry Dent."

"I don't know what his name was, he was just a rude waiter, a very rude waiter. When I want water, I want it now! And extra napkins ? Yes ma'am! It was actually fun wasting him. I jumped out from behind the shadows, just like in the movies! I had it all planned out, I even used one of the steak knives from the restaurant...ha...ha. Ironic isn't it? Or poetic justice, or something? Stabbing was fun!" Tammy said excitedly. "What a rush! I didn't know what I had been

18

missing out on!"

"I like stabbing someone, pushing the knife through their flesh and into their body... feeling the slippery blood on my hands. I tried to avoid the blood with the Dirk episode, but after the waiter, I found out how much I liked it; the blood, I mean. Watching the way the persons' life sort of, runs out of them. Watching their expression and the way that their body feels when they pass from this world ... and then they're dead; and I killed them. I'm exhilarated and powerful, it's a great feeling. But, it was stabbing that got me caught, after the Kimberly thing."

"Who's Kimberly?" Joyce asked, "I don't see a Kimberly listed as one of your murder victims."

"I mentioned her before; she was the girl that I went to lunch with when I met Dirk. We grew fond of each other. She was the only girl that wasn't jealous of me; the only girl that didn't hate me because I'm so beautiful. It's tough being so beautiful, it's hard to find a real friend and Kimberly truly became my friend, in spite of what other women told her about me. She was almost like a sister to me."

"How did she get away from you?" asked Joyce

"Get away? What are you talking about? She loved being my friend. We saw each other almost every day. We would go shopping together, movies, you know, fun stuff. That is, until she married, *Bob*. Kimberly was always busy with, Bob! Busy with, Bob, and too busy for me!"

"One night, Kimberly and I had plans to see a movie. But, when I called her to find out if she was ready to go, she told me that she wouldn't be able to make it! Bob, had surprised her with a romantic dinner. Then, she nauseatingly went on to say that after dinner, Bob was going to give her a full-body massage and that she was looking forward to making love all night. She said she would call me the next day to tell me the details... Eww! I had to get off the phone before I threw up. I didn't want to hear any of the gory details. Just picturing, Bob, naked was enough to make anybody sick. Much less, him humping away on her like a fat snorting pig. Can you imagine that?"

"No," Joyce replied, "I can't."

Tammy smiled at what she thought was Joyce's approval, and then began to tell her a harrowing tale.

"One day, the planets were aligned, Bob was busy and Kimberly finally agreed to meet me for lunch. But, the lunch date was terrible; all Kimberly did was talk about Bob and how much she loved him. I couldn't even eat. And then, came the big news... Kimberly was pregnant with Bob's child. She expected me to be excited, but I couldn't even fake it and I told her, 'That's what you get when you make *love* all the time.' She seemed upset at my comment. But, all I could think about was how much time Kimberly would have to spend with a baby. First Bob and now a baby, I knew that I would never see Kimberly again. A baby! I hate fuckin' babies. The baby had to go, it was going to ruin everything. I had already dropped the ball with the Bob situation by letting Kimberly marry him. It never occurred to me that Bob could get her pregnant. I never even thought that he was capable of procreation! What a dork!"

"This baby thing was a big mistake and I had to stop it. I made my plan and waited until the pregnancy was about six months along before I made my move. Kimberly and I met for dinner at our favorite place. She was ridiculous bragging about her perfect life. I went along with it trying to picture something else in my mind. Perhaps a muscular movie star, tanned and gorgeous, in a hot steaming shower. Water dripping from his dark wavy locks, smiling at me seductively and asking me to join him. Tammy shook her head, wow I have been in prison too long, now where was I?"

"At a restaurant with Kimberly," Joyce quickly reminded her.

"Okay, the long, torturous dinner was finally over and Kimberly and I headed for the parking lot. When we got to my car, I had to open the passenger door for the big bloated whale and even help her in. I can't believe she even fit! Man, that baby was really doing a number on her body.

20

Kimberly looked horrible! We would have to start going to the fitness center again, after this was over with!"

"Kimberly had a big smile on her face and thanked me for helping her. She wasn't aware of it, but I was ready to make her life less complicated. I told her that I had seen the perfect house for her and her family, and that I wanted to show it to her. I parked a couple of miles away from the hospital, just close enough to save Kimberly's life, but not the baby."

Joyce interrupted, "Didn't you think that Kimberly would be angry with you for killing her baby?"

"No! Not really. Well ... maybe at first, but once she got used to it, she would be relieved. It was for her own good. I'm certain that I could have convinced her of that, if I had only had the chance."

"But anyway, let me get on with the story. Kimberly saw a house for sale down the street from where I had parked and asked if that was the one. I said no, then I reached into my purse and grabbed my Orto steak knife. You know, like the one I used on Dirk."

"Yes," Joyce acknowledged.

"I didn't hesitate, I was certain that I was doing the right thing, for both of us, and I tried to stab her in the belly to kill the baby. I don't know how, but Kimberly grabbed my arm. She surprised me, she was much stronger than I expected and she fought back! She pushed me hard and I accidentally sliced her arm. When Kimberly screamed, I told her that I was sorry; that I didn't want to stab her, that the baby was my target. Kimberly was like she was demon possessed or something; she told me that she wasn't going to let that happen! 'Don't fuck with my kid' was what she said, and then she twisted my arm and forced me to drop my knife. It really hurt too! She was really mean to me! Kimberly grabbed the knife away from me and there was nothing that I could do about it. I didn't know that pregnant women were strong like that. Maybe it's the hormones or something. She jumped out of the car and reached into her purse and I

21

wondered what she was doing with my knife. I didn't see it and I wanted it back, it was part of a set! Honestly, was this really happening? Was Kimberly really stealing my knife? I knew that things were getting out of hand, so I got out of the car to try and explain. But, Kimberly ran at me and the next thing I knew I was on the ground. I felt my body spasm and then I peed myself. That damn Kimberly had shocked me with a stun gun and then she kicked me in the head when I was down. The next thing I remember, I was in the hospital, with a guard standing by me. It was totally unnecessary; they had me handcuffed with an I.V. in my arm! Where was I going to go? Everyone was making such a big deal out of Kimberly and her baby and I was the one that got hurt! Of course, you know the rest, now I'm on death row."

"Thank you Tammy, that will be enough for today," Joyce said as she pushed the call button for Stewart, the lab assistant. Stewart was standing by, as he always was, and quickly let the guard into the Interview Room.

When Joyce got up to leave, Tammy started screaming at her, "Where do you think you're going bitch? I'm not done talking to you!" Tammy was struggling, trying to get at Joyce. She was spitting and gritting her teeth. "Get back here now you stupid cunt! You can't just dismiss me like this! I'm gonna kill you Joyce! Blood will be shed!"

Joyce was accustomed to dealing with the Tammy's of the world. She simply looked at her and calmly replied, "Now Tammy that isn't very lady like, is it?"

Joyce had been interviewing serial killers for years, struggling to unravel the nightmare of her childhood. She suffered, listening to each killer as they told her of their horrific deeds. She walked out of the Interview Room exhausted, and slowly headed down the long, cold hallway with Stewart, by her side. "Well, Joyce, how did it go?" he asked anxiously. "Did you glean any new information from Tammy? Anything that we can use?"

"Yes Stewart, it was a very productive interview. Tammy is an anomaly, she's nothing like any of the others. There is still

22

no consistent link between any of them to explain why they repetitively murdered. She's further confirmation that our studies are accurate. The diseased brain must be replaced. Yes, there is no question about it; our Living Artificial Brain is the only cure for the serial killer."

"What do we do now?"

"Now, we go home and start fresh again tomorrow morning."

"Why don't you let me drive you home Joyce? It's after dark and I worry about you living in that bad neighborhood. There's so much crime, and it always seems to be within blocks of your apartment."

"Thank you Stewart, you're very sweet, as usual, but I'll be fine."

"That gosh darn Brian, if he wasn't such a crook and paid us what he's supposed to, you could move into a safer neighborhood."

"I know Stewart, it is difficult watching him drive his Mercedes and lavish himself, and his girlfriends, with expensive gifts, while we struggle just to survive. But Stewart, we venture into the taboo and you know as well as I, that there isn't another laboratory anywhere in the world that will permit our research. They just don't understand and think that we're playing God. So, I'm afraid that we're stuck with Brian until our theories are proven. At least he's too self-involved to pay enough attention to us to try and shut us down. And let's not forget about you, I'm not the only one living in a bad situation. I wish that you could afford a place of your own. I don't think it's healthy for you to both live and work here at the lab."

"I don't mind Joyce, really I don't, my home is here, working by your side. I can think of no better place to be."

"So like you Stewart, hardworking and uncomplaining. No one could ask for a better assistant."

"Thank you Joyce, you're terrific."

At that moment, Stewart and Joyce both heard the guard shouting, "Hey is anybody there? Somebody, please get in here and help me with this nut!"

Stewart hurried along sniffing from his allergies and pushing up his glasses. "Geepers, I'm going as fast as I can," he said softly.

Stewart could hear Tammy's voice getting horse as she begged, "Joyce come back! I'm sorry, don't leave me!"

Tammy's hands were still locked in the restraining cuffs, attached to the interview table. "Come on man, release her from the table," the guard said disgusted.

Stewart quickly went into the Observation Booth. He placed his thumb on the red button; it scanned his print and then unlocked the restraining cuffs.

"Me ... go home," Stewart mumbled. "Me get my own apartment? What a joke. There's always something around here that needs my attention." Then he addressed Tammy, over the intercom, and spoke much louder than his usual subdued tone, "Gee whiz Tammy, Joyce left for home after your nonproductive rants. Why did you have to wear her out like that? Thank Gosh we won't have to see you again."

Then he asked the guard, "Is the prisoner secure?"

"Yeah, I got her!" he answered.

Stewart pushed the button to open the door of the Interview Room.

"Come on, let's go sweet cheeks," the guard said to Tammy, "back to your luxurious suite on death row."

JOYCE AND THE TRANSVESTITE; AN UNLIKELY PAIR

The workday had been stressful, and Joyce was happy that it had finally come to an end. She climbed into her old hatchback car, and sat there for a moment, relieved that the interview with Tammy was over.

"I just want to relax tonight, no cooking for me," she said to herself, and then headed for her favorite Chinese restaurant. The restaurant was located a block from her apartment. She found a parking space, and then bought a big, beautiful

24

bouquet of flowers from an old lady who had a flower stand in front of the restaurant. "A bright splash of color at the table will be cheerful tonight," she said to the nice lady. Joyce stood for a moment and gently rubbed her nose on the soft flower pedals and enjoyed the fragrance before she went inside to order dinner. Yes, soon she would be home and could close the door to the stress of the day.

As Joyce paused for that brief moment, she spotted a beautiful tall woman, with dark glowing skin. The woman wore bold but tasteful make up, a stunning dress and high platform shoes. Joyce admired her, thinking how she could never be so daring and wear such a glamorous outfit. As Joyce was admiring the eye-catching woman, a man pulled up beside her, in his car, and began to yell and curse at her. Joyce couldn't hear what the woman said to the man, but after she had spoken, he screamed even more viciously and then sped off in his car, screeching the tires as he went. The attractive woman put her head down and Joyce noticed that she was crying. But then, with quiet strength, she lifted her head and patted her tears away with a silky orange scarf. She began walking down the sidewalk in Joyce's direction and when she was close enough, Joyce asked her if she was okay.

The woman answered with a small chirp, "Yes I'm fine," and then she managed a smile. "What can I do for you?" she asked.

"How about a cup of coffee?" Joyce suggested and then she gave the woman her flowers."

"For real?" the woman expressed with glee. "No one has ever given me flowers before! And I could sure use a cup of coffee."

Joyce smiled, and then the two ladies decided to go down the block, to Mays Coffee Shop. As they walked along together, Joyce got a closer look at the woman and found that her features were rather masculine. Her hands were large, she had broad shoulders and spoke in a falsetto tone. Joyce then realized that this woman had once been a man.

Being a scientist, who studied human behavior, Joyce was intrigued and wanted to know more about this mysterious and unusual person.

"I'm sorry miss, I didn't introduce myself; I'm Joyce."

"It's a pleasure to meet you, Miss Joyce, they call me, Tache".

"Well Tache', it's a pleasure to meet you too."

The two, entered the Coffee Shop together and sat down at a table. There was an awkward silence and Joyce began to feel uncomfortable. She had spent nearly her entire life studying or working in a laboratory. The only people that she interacted with were either scientists or serial killers and she found herself lacking in social skills. So, without adieu, she got right to the "interview". "Tell me your story Tache'," she abruptly said.

Tache' got right to the point, "I suppose you want to know why I'm a hooker."

Finding out that the beautiful woman, was a lady of the evening, was a complete surprise to Joyce. She was caught off guard and immediately apologized, "I'm sorry Tache', I didn't mean to be so blunt, it's just that I find you a fascinating person. I hope that you're not offended, but I would like to know all about you. That is, if you don't mind."

"Oh it's very simple, prostitution is the only way that I can make a living, but I don't like it. It's not what I had planned for my life, that's for sure. My pimp, Tyrone, was absolutely dreamy at first, but now he's very demanding and he terrifies me. He's always angry at me for not making enough money and always pushing me for more. No matter how much I bring in, it's never enough. In fact, Tyrone, may show up again at any time. He makes me so nervous." Tache' began to wring her hands, "I can't stay long," she said.

"Don't worry Tache', I'm paying you for your time, consider me a customer."

"Paying me to have coffee with you? That's crazy! You must want something from me, don't be shy, everybody wants something. Why don't you just get to the point and I'll take care of business."

"You're right Tache', I do want something, I want you to tell me more about yourself. Like I said before, I find you a fascinating person."

"Well, there ain't nothin' fascinating about me, but I've had stranger requests. Okay, it's your money honey! What do you want to know? Kinky sex acts? How to please your man?"

"No, no, nothing like that, I want to know about you, about your life."

"Do you want me to tell you some hot steamy stories about my sexual escapades? Maybe something to masturbate to?" What turns you on honey? Just let me know, I've got plenty of 'em."

"No Tache', I'm truly interested in your life. Why don't you start from the beginning. What was your early childhood like?"

"For real?"

"For real."

"Well, whatever floats your boat, baby," Tache' said and then thought for a moment about what to tell Joyce. "I went from foster home to foster home. Is that the kind of things that you want to hear about me? The truth?"

"Yes Tache, that's exactly what I want to hear, the truth. Why were you in foster care, what happened to your parents?"

"They were both murdered. My dad was shot and my sweet mom was beaten to death."

Joyce's mind flashed back to her own childhood and the horror of finding her mother's dead body. "Oh how horrible for you, I'm truly sorry," she told Tache', feeling deep compassion for her.

"They were both in the military," Tache' went on to say. "The robbers must have caught Daddy by surprise and they killed him right away. Mom fought them, that's what I was told anyway, she had a lot of defensive injuries."

"A devastating thing for a child to go through," Joyce said, "please, go on Tache'.

"I was spending the night at a friend's house when it happened. Everyone said that I was lucky that I hadn't been there. But, I was angry that I hadn't been there; thinking in my childish mind that I could have prevented it somehow." Tache' paused and then became emotional, "But, you want to know the truth, I'm still angry that I wasn't there, because my life would have ended too. I would have died with my parents and been spared my terrible existence on this Earth."

This woman seemed on the verge of suicide and Joyce was concerned. "Do you want to hurt yourself?" she asked.

"Oh no, I would never kill myself, I promised Mama. She didn't die right away, she lingered for three days. When I knew that Mama was going to heaven, I told her that I wanted to go with her, but she made me promise to go on without her. She told me that killing myself would be the same as murder, and that she couldn't rest in peace thinking that I might kill myself."

After Tache' had told Joyce about her parents, the floodgates burst open and she bared her soul, to the stranger named Joyce.

"It was tough after my parents were dead. My friends' family took care of me for a few weeks, but you know how it goes, it's always the same old story, 'Oh you'll be happier in this new home, they're a very nice family.' Yeah right, as I got raped and beaten over and over again."

"After being passed from foster home to foster home and being raped by men and abused for nearly my entire life, I was confused and not sure what my sexual orientation was. Then there was a new abuser, a woman. All I knew was that I had a dick and that my new foster mother, wanted it. She said, that if I didn't fuck her, she would tell the police that I raped her. I was a young teen by this time and much bigger than she. There was no doubt in my mind that the police would believe her. This craziness went on for years, forced to have sex with both men and women."

"Then the day that I had been waiting for finally came and

28

I turned eighteen. I was happy that I could leave all of the insanity behind me, and I joined the army. I loved the army, everything about it. I liked the structure and I felt like I finally belonged someplace. I always did the best I could and never got into trouble. Everyone liked me and respected me and when I finished my term, I was out in the workforce with a degree. I got a job right away, at a law office, as a paralegal. I worked hard and I was quickly promoted. Things couldn't have been better! I had an outgoing personality back then, and I fit right in with the girls. Even though I was a big black man in an office filled with skinny blonde women, we were the best of friends. "The Blondes" as I used to call them, and I, went out together on Friday nights after work. I didn't drink alcohol, but the girls would get pretty drunk and I usually ended up acting as body guard and designated driver. I kept myself in excellent physical condition and I was rarely challenged."

"One night, it was getting late and I was rounding up the blondes to go home, but I couldn't find Shirley. The girls told me that she was with a guy and to go ahead and leave without her. But, Shirley was drunk and I felt responsible for her, so I kept on looking. When I couldn't find her anywhere in the bar, I went outside. I walked down the alley and heard screams coming from a downstairs apartment. It was Shirley! I ran down the stairs and burst inside. A man had Shirley down on the couch and was on top of her trying to rape her! I was furious; I grabbed the guy, pulled him off of Shirley, and as I scuffled with him, I told her to get out. Shirley stumbled as she ran, but I could hear her climbing the stairs outside, and I knew that she was safe. I just wanted to get out of there, but the man kept on fighting with me. Finally, I shoved him and knocked him down then, I ran out the door. I knew that he couldn't catch me and I thought I had it made, until I saw his roommates standing at the top of the stairs, blocking my way.

Seconds later, the guy came charging up the stairs after me. He took a swing at me, lost his balance and then fell backward. He hit his head on the cement and broke his skull;

I could tell right away that he was dead. Everyone there was in shock for a moment, but soon a crowd of people gathered and then the police showed up. I didn't run; I had nothing to hide, but I found that the fact that I was innocent didn't matter. All of the witnesses were friends of Joe, the dead guy. The story they told wasn't even close to the truth, painting me as the aggressor who went crazy and killed the sainted Joe. But, the cruelest blow of all, was the blondes; they just stood by and watched as the cops handcuffed me and took me away. They didn't try to help me, not even Shirley. Even at my trial, she wouldn't testify on my behalf. She said that her husband didn't want her to get involved. She even told my attorney, that if he subpoenaed her she would deny even being there. I guess that they put more stock in risking their marriages, than sending me to prison on a false murder rap."

"When I went to prison, I lost all hope. I had the shit beat out of me and I was gang raped the very first day. And things only got worse from there; being abused, it was like my childhood all over again. Seems no matter how hard I tried, I couldn't escape physical and sexual abuse. I finally gave up and didn't care anymore. I used to lay in my bunk at night and think of all the violence and meanness in the world. I was depressed, more depressed than anyone could ever be, and there was no way out. That was, until I met Candy. Candy lived as a woman in the men's prison. The prison doctor even provided female hormones for her and she grew breasts. Candy had the run of the place and no one ever beat her up. Even the guards were kind to her."

"Candy told me that I didn't have to keep getting the shit beat out of me anymore, 'They're going to take your ass anyway you look at it honey, you might as well get the benefits. It's easier to be a woman, in the joint. Look at my life, you don't see me suffering. Do ya?'"

"I realized that Candy was right, I had already had the man beat out of me, and I followed her lead, but I never took hormones. I used the name, Tache', and everybody treated

30

me great. Candy and I ran freely around the prison, passing notes and doing favors for the other prisoners. Of course, there was sex involved, but strangely enough, I felt in control of myself."

"When I got out of prison, I didn't know what to do. I was still living as a woman and it was impossible for me to get a job. I was discouraged and was walking down the street, to this very coffee shop, when Tyrone pulled up in his fancy golden Cadillac. I know that sounds so typical, but he was the only one that cared. Tyrone was friendly and sweet and he set me up with a job. I know it's disgraceful, but it was my only option. What else could I do? And I was already used to it; it was basically the same thing that I had been doing in the joint anyway, and at least I get some money out of it, not much though. Tyrone can be nice sometimes. Oh, but when he gets angry, get out the way!"

"Tyrone and all of us girls live in a big house together; kinda like a family, if you stretch your imagination a little. Tyrone takes care of everything and I get to keep some of my cash. I never do no dope. The young girls he gets hooked on the dope; that's all they work for, he don't pay them nothing, just dope. I wish I could get a real job, but my life is so twisted and messed up, I just can't anymore. But, things could always be worse, right Joyce?"

"Yes they could," Joyce quietly agreed, but she struggled to think of a worse situation.

Noticing that Joyce was upset, Tache' quickly tried to comfort her, "Now don't you go feeling sorry for me Miss Joyce, my life will get better, I know it will," she said with an unconvincing smile. "I do have some happiness in my life, my little chubby-cheeks, Qunitsha, she's my hope and joy. She's not my baby, she belongs to Shawna, one of the other girls, but we all chip in and she has five mothers. She's Tyrone's baby and he loves her."

Tache' started to get restless. "I better get going, Tyrone's got to be looking for me by now. It was so nice talking to you Joyce. And you were right, talking really did help, I feel much better."

Joyce tried to stuff a handful of cash into Tache's hand, but Tache' pulled away. "No way I'm taking money from you," she strongly objected. Then she reached into her purse and pulled out some cash and tried to give it to Joyce, "I should be the one paying you!" she said with conviction.

Tache' had an adorable personality. She started teasing Joyce and Joyce actually began to laugh. This was unusual behavior, as she was generally very serious around other people.

Tache' was truly a hidden treasure and Joyce wanted to see more of her, so she gave Tache' her phone number. "I'd like to get together again sometime," she told the big flashy transvestite. And call me if you ever need anything, I care Tache', I really do."

Tache' welled up with tears, but quickly brushed them away. "Gotta go now. God bless you, Miss Joyce." Then Tache' rushed out the door of the coffee shop and ran across the street.

This had been a special meeting, and both Joyce and Tache' knew it.

Joyce sat at the table in May's coffee shop, completely stunned. For some reason she felt a kinship with Tache' and it was strange. Ever since the murder of her mother, it was as though she was dead inside. Joyce wondered what it was about this unusual person that made her feel alive again.

When Joyce finished her coffee, she went to the Chinese Restaurant and got her take-out dinner. She headed home, surprised at what the day had brought.

BIZARRE AND ASTONISHING; WHO IS DEREK?

When Joyce arrived at her apartment building, she entered the lobby and one of the neighborhood children ran up to her with a box of kittens. "Hey, Dr. Picard, do you want one? They're real cute."

32

Joyce smiled kindly, "Oh they are all very adorable, but I have to say, no thank you, sweetie. Why don't you try Mrs. Anderson, I heard that she's been wanting a kitten."

"Gee thanks Doc," the boy said and then walked down the hall to Mrs. Anderson's.

Joyce went up the stairs to her unit. She opened the door and in a cheerful voice called out, "Derek I'm home!"

Joyce's apartment reflected her obsession … research. By the front door, stood stacks of science magazines, piled all the way to the ceiling. The bookcases along the walls were filled to overflowing with medical journals and models of brains. Books were stacked on top of the papers, and papers stacked on top of books. There were several desks with computers and rows and rows of files. A large human skeleton stood in the corner, a bit dusty, but useful just the same.

Joyce entered the dining room, she put the bag of takeout food on the table and then went into the kitchen. "Derek honey, would you like a martini? I certainly need one after the day that I've had! I got takeout for dinner, shrimp and egg rolls, your favorite! Go ahead and help yourself while I get our drinks."

Joyce could hear the take out bag rustling in the dining room and when she walked in with the martinis, Derek was already nibbling on a shrimp. "Here's a plate babe," she said. "And I put two olives in your martini, just the way you like it."

Derek took a sip of his drink and then ate one of his olives. "Now Derek, don't be in such a hurry silly, you need to leave the olives in the drink for a little while to get the flavor."

Derek gave Joyce a heated look. "I know, I'm sorry, I'll quit nagging, I promise. Now let's have a nice dinner together, shall we?" Derek seemed to feel relieved considering the apology.

"These are the times that I cherish," Joyce said as she sat back with her drink in her hand, "the time I spend with you."

Derek kindly offered Joyce a shrimp. "Oh isn't that nice,

thank you, Derek."

"Oh Derek, you'll get a kick out of this," Joyce said chuckling. "One of the neighbor boys tried to give me a kitten. They were cute, but I had to say no. I didn't think that you would warm up to the idea! I know how you *hate* cats!"

Derek looked at Joyce, not convinced that it was funny.

"Not amused? I'm sorry honey, but you have to admit, it was humorous, you, trying to live with a kitten."

Derek soon left the table and Joyce watched him from the dining room. He went down the hall, into the bathroom, and got himself cleaned up.

Joyce collected the take out bags and cartons and threw them in the trash. "Thank goodness, no dishes tonight, I'm exhausted."

When Derek was through in the bathroom, Joyce washed her face and then changed into comfy pajamas. She was in the mood to knit, and sat on her worn cozy couch, and went to work on her current project. Derek helped her, as he always did, keeping the yarn tangle free. He took a break from time to time to brush off the lint.

"My goodness Derek it never ends, this consistent grooming, stop worrying, you look great. Your black hair is incredibly shiny." But Derek didn't listen and kept primping anyway.

"I think that this may boarder on Obsessive Compulsive Disorder!"

After that comment, Derek grabbed the knitting from Joyce and ran under a desk, behind some stacks of papers.

Joyce went after him, "Derek I'm sorry! Don't unravel it; it's a sweater for you!"

Derek peeked out through the papers and then pushed the knitting out to Joyce.

"Thank you! Come on out now, let's see your face."

Derek poked his head out, then quickly pulled it back in.

"Okay, I'm not going to stand here and beg you to come out; I'm going to finish knitting your sweater!" Joyce sat back down. "I had no idea that *rats* were so overly sensitive."

34

Joyce kept knitting and waiting, and a little while later, Derek came out from behind the papers. He shimmed up the couch to Joyce, and gave her a kiss on the cheek. "Now that's better," she said, and sweetly kissed him back. "I love you Derek."

Derek snuggled on Joyce's lap and soon fell fast asleep. After finishing her knitting, Joyce picked Derek up and carefully walked into the bedroom and placed him on the bed on the satin pillow, right next to hers. Derek awoke, but stayed put and watched Joyce get into bed. Joyce leaned toward him and whispered, "Derek, the happiest day of my life was when I met you for the first time, going through my trash in the kitchen. When you looked up at me, I knew that my life would never be the same." Derek gave a soft squeak in agreement and then they both snuggled into their cozy down pillows and fell fast asleep.

In the morning, when Joyce awoke, she climbed out of bed and did her stretching routine. Derek was already in the bathroom, using his litter box.

When she was through stretching, she passed the bathroom, on her way to the kitchen and said good morning to Derek.

Joyce started the coffee brewing and got the morning paper from her front door. Even though it was considered outdated to read a newspaper, Joyce liked the smell of the ink and the way that it felt in her hands. When her coffee was done brewing, she poured herself a nice big cup and then poured Derek a small glass of apple juice. She placed the beverages on the table and put Derek's special supplements in a shot glass. Derek joined her at the table and she began to read the newspaper. A few moments later, Joyce peeked to see that Derek was taking his supplements. She had created this special formula especially for him. They extended his life and enhanced his brain and physical abilities.

"I don't have much time this morning Derek. It's going to be a busy day and I have to go to the lab a bit early. Will bagel and cream cheese suffice for breakfast this morning?"

Derek was lapping up his juice then he paused and looked up at Joyce. "Okay, okay, a big breakfast it is, but I'll have to hurry. Bacon, eggs and hash browns as usual. I can read the paper tonight. I know, I know, you're right, it's a good idea for me to have a hearty breakfast."

Joyce quickly rushed into the kitchen to whip up the big breakfast while Derek patiently waited. When it was ready, she placed a plate in front of him with care, and then bowed, "Your breakfast, my liege. Derek squeaked with delight.

When Joyce and Derek finished eating, Joyce cleared the table and put the dishes in the sink for later.

"Shower time Derek!" she announced and then she picked him up and headed into the bathroom. "Oh my, you're still gaining weight, but it's solid muscle. That formula of mine is working great!"

Joyce entered the bathroom and put Derek in the shower, on a non-slip shelf that she had made especially for him. Then she turned on the water and climbed in herself. She put shampoo on her own hair, and then she squeezed a little on Derek and the two of them scrubbed together. Joyce was singing and she and Derek enjoyed the fresh clean scent of the shampoo and the tingling shower spray. When Joyce finished shampooing her own hair, she helped Derek rinse and then laid him on a clean fluffy towel on his grooming table. "Now Derek, I'll be finished washing in a minute and then, I'll dry you off, you stay right there," she instructed.

Derek enjoyed his showers and he always waited patiently on the grooming table, but Joyce never failed to tell him to wait there for her, it was the order of things.

When Joyce had finished her shower, she quickly dried off and put on her robe. "Okay Derek, the blow dryer's plugged in and I've got your brush, are you ready?" Derek quickly sat up, he loved to be brushed and Joyce started blowing his thick black fur on the lowest setting of the blow dryer. As Joyce brushed through Derek's coat she examined his old injuries. "I'm so happy that your battle scars are starting to fade. I wonder how many fights you were in, from your life on the streets? I'd bet that you won them all; you're such a bad ass Derek! Derek squeaked and nodded his head, yes.

What a handsome rat you are," she said as she finished his styling. "Okay, all done, you can get down now Derek. Now, I've got to get myself ready."

Joyce rushed through her own blow dry and quickly got dressed in her work clothes. "What do you think Derek? Do you like this look?" she laughed. "Yes I know; the same as every day, no frills."

Joyce went to the kitchen to make lunches, for Derek and herself. Bringing her lunch to work was her daily routine as there were no restaurants near the laboratory. It was located in a secluded place, on the edge of town, near the woods.

"Your lunch is on the counter, Derek, have a great day. See you tonight." Joyce stepped out of the apartment and then closed the door behind her.

The neighbors always heard Joyce talking to someone in her apartment. They all knew that she lived alone and didn't know what to think of her. Most of them believed that she was crazy and steered clear of her.

THE DEVIL IS FACED WITHOUT FEAR

Joyce made the long drive to work and arrived with new hope. Today was the day that she was to interview an infamous serial killer, Dan the devil. He had killed scores of women and was extremely dangerous. Because Joyce was a woman, the prison had refused her many requests to interview, Dan the devil, as he became completely unmanageable in the presence of any woman. But, Joyce's persistence finally paid off and the interview was granted.

Joyce had a different agenda than the detectives who had previously interrogated, Dan. She wasn't merely seeking a confession and the facts of his crimes, she wanted to know

37

his deepest, darkest secrets and probe into his perverse mind. Joyce was certain that because she *was* a woman, Dan would react strongly to her and she would be able to take advantage of his emotional state and get him talking. Joyce had no fear of this man or any other, fear was something that she had learned to control, or perhaps even lost, a long time ago.

All that Joyce intended to focus on, was collecting information. Information, that could possibly solve the turmoil of her past and help her to achieve her goal, finding the cause and cure to the serial killer epidemic.

Joyce entered the Interview Room, just seconds before the prisoner arrived. Before she could get organized, the guard came in and pushed, Dan the devil, down on the chair, across from her. He signaled Stewart, in the Observation Booth, to push the red button and lock Dan in the cuff restrains, attached to the metal table.

Joyce took a good hard look at, Dan. He was huge, like a monster, extremely muscular with a heavy bone structure. He had a ruddy completion and a thick hideous scar slashed across his face. He was the ugliest man that Joyce had ever seen. His eyes were piercing, murderous and filled with lust and hatred. Dan tried to intimidate Joyce, right away. He locked eyes with her, and it was as though they aimed for her very soul. Joyce could feel the presence of pure evil, but still, she was unshaken.

"How are *you* feeling today, Joyce?" Dan asked, trying to take control of the interview. "Wet and juicy, I'm sure," he said in answer to his own question. Then he laughed and laughed at himself as though he had made an hysterical joke.

Joyce didn't react the way that Dan had expected her to. She waited for him to stop his hideous laughter and simply started the interview. "Dan, in answer to your question, I'm feeling hopeful today."

"Hopeful huh, hopeful that I'm going to stick my cock in your mouth, you mean! Oh I'm having some evil thoughts about you Joyce."

Dan started breathing heavy and became agitated; he violently tugged at his restraints. "If I wasn't locked up to this table, why I'd…"

"What would you do Dan?" Joyce curtly asked. "Tell me about it."

Dan was taken back that Joyce actually wanted to hear the gruesome details of his fantasy. Surely she knew that he was a serial killer. Did she want to hear how he would murder her? He paused for a moment and then it was as though he entered into another world and began to describe what was in his evil mind. "You live alone Joyce, I know you do, and one night when you come home, I'll be waiting there for you. I'll grab you by your throat and squeeze while I push you down on your bed. I'll keep squeezing until you nearly pass out, but not all the way out, I want you to know exactly what I'm doing to you. Then I'll strip you down, I'll take off every piece of your clothing, accept for your panties; that I save for last. The best part will be when I take down my pants and you see MY ENORMOUS HARD COCK! Then when I reach to take off your panties; that's when your terror builds to the next level. God I love it, feeding off of your emotions, fear and terror, they penetrate me, excite me!"

Dan began to squirm in his chair. It was revolting, but Joyce found that she could lock minds with him and be just as hardened as he, this notorious, merciless murderer.

"Then, down come the panties," Dan said panting. "I could just rip them off of you, but I want you to feel it as your panties come slowly down; slide past your thighs and calves and then completely off and over your feet. I'll hold them up to my face and breathe in the aroma, the aroma of fresh pussy! Oh, it's been such a long time since I've smelled a woman like you, Joyce. I can smell your pussy from across the table."

"I know about you Joyce, you've never broken away from your obsession long enough to have a man and your pussy must be real tight, I know it is! Oh I can feel it now, a tight wet

39

hole squeezing my throbbing hard cock. Then I'll choke you, Joyce, it's a rush and you'll actually like it at first. I'll take my time with you, because you're special. I'll choke you, let you breath; then choke you again while I'm fucking you, fucking you real hard. Yeah, it'll be sweet; I'll keep fucking you and choking you, AND FUCK YOU UNTIL YOU'RE DEAD!!"

Joyce looked down at her notes, "Yes I read here that your M.O. is strangulation." Then she looked up at Dan, "How does it feel to kill, Dan? Do you enjoy it?" she flatly asked.

"It's not the killing that I enjoy, killing is just a means to get what I want. It's fear and terror, that's what I'm after. It feeds me and makes me strong; to have control, complete control over life and death, gives me a sense of exhilaration. I'M A GOD!! And then after the death I feel relief. I'm okay for a few weeks, but then I start to hunger and I want to experience it again. I actually feel like I'll die if I don't feed the devil inside of me. It takes complete control of my mind and everything I think and do. I'm not the one in charge, Joyce, it's the devil, it dictates everything, every rape, every murder; I just do what it tells me to. I'm an addict; killing is a rush to me, like a drug. It drives me to seek out more and more powerful women to consume, women like you Joyce."

"Were you taking drugs at the time that you committed any of your crimes?"

"Nope, I never take drugs, raping and killing, are my drug."

Joyce was surprised that the interview was going so well, she certainly didn't expect this hardened killer to open up so quickly. She was pleased to find that she had been right in her assumption that Dan would respond to her, because she was a woman. But, it was just too easy and she suspected that perhaps he had an ulterior motive.

"I'm like you Joyce," Dan declared, "I'm driven to rape and murder, just like you're driven with your experiments and research. You have no control over it, it controls you. You have no life, no life at all accept your laboratory. You're forced over and over again to deal with sick fucks like me. You can't control yourself any more than I can control myself.

Joyce if anyone can understand the sickness of compulsion; the helplessness and the control that it has... it's you. There's a reason that I asked to see you Joyce, to talk about your mother's death."

Joyce didn't discuss her mother's death with anyone, not even Stewart, but for some reason she was compelled to discuss it with this murderer. Perhaps he could give her some insight into the death. "Okay Dan," Joyce reluctantly agreed, "let's talk about my mother."

"She was decapitated, and you found her," Dan said. "She was decapitated, and you found her!" he repeated, raising his voice.

"Yes that's true," Joyce calmly replied.

"They never caught the man that murdered her, did they?"

"No they didn't," Joyce confirmed. "it's still and open case."

"Is that when you snapped? Is that when you became obsessed?"

"If you mean, if that is when I dedicated my life to the study and cure for killers, I'd have to say yes."

"How would you feel if I told you that I knew who killed your mother?"

"Okay Dan, I'll bite. Who killed my mother?"

"Dan paused and then he said loud and clear, "It was me, I'm the one, I'm the one who killed your mother, Joyce! I'm the one who destroyed any chance you had for a normal life. It was me!"

Joyce sat in disbelief momentarily; this wouldn't be the first time that she had experienced a false confession. Dan was scheduled for execution; this could merely be a way for him to buy more time and galvanize another investigation. "Okay Dan, if you killed my mother maybe you can answer a few questions for me."

"Joyce, it was me, I'll tell you anything you want to know. But, please believe me when I tell you that I didn't know that the woman had a daughter. I was on my way out when you came bursting in through the kitchen door. I was as surprised

41

as you were when I grabbed you from behind and threw you on the floor."

"That's common knowledge Dan, it doesn't prove anything."

"You were wearing a polka dot dress and your hair was a mess, all ratted up and full of hairspray. It was the A+ school paper that got to me, you came in the house shouting about it and I saw it in your hand. You were so proud, and I knew what you were going to find, when you went into the bedroom looking for your mother. It was the first time that I ever felt remorse. The first time that I realized that my actions had an effect on someone else beside me. My victims were never human beings to me, they were simply things, a means to make me feel good. I felt ashamed and I tried to quit killing after your mother, Joyce, I really did, but I couldn't, the compulsion was much too strong. But, I never decapitated another woman, I could never bring myself to do it again. If I couldn't stop killing all together, I could at least do that for you. I always knew that my actions would affect the little girl, who found her mother decapitated. But, I could have never realized that it would come to this someday; that I would be facing her and voluntarily telling her about it. I hope that my confession can give you some closure, Joyce."

Joyce said nothing, both she and Dan sat in silence. It was true, Dan was the killer, he knew things about the case that hadn't been released to the media. And Joyce had never told another soul that she had been holding the A+ science paper in her hand.

"Aren't you going to say anything? Go ahead, go crazy, hit me, beat me to death, I'm helpless strapped here to the table. Now's your chance for revenge!"

"I believe you Dan," Joyce said with complete composure. "What made you decide to come forward, at this time?"

"Oh my God, Joyce, don't you feel anything? Don't you have any emotions? I've created a monster! You're as fucked up as I am!"

"Like I said Dan, I believe I *am* fucked up, just as fucked up

42

as you are, twisted, but in a different direction. Now let's test the truthfulness of another part of your statement. You said that you have no control and that you're driven to feed on fear and terror. We'll see about that."

Joyce got up from the chair, she walked across the small room and closed the blinds. Immediately, Stewart shouted from the Observation Booth, "Joyce, what are you doing!"

Joyce ignored Stewart and moved to the camera and turned it off.

"Joyce, answer me," Stewart said a little louder.

Dan sat quietly, wondering if Joyce was preparing to kill him.

"Release the restraints Stewart," Joyce commanded.

"No way," Stewart sharply refused. He was fearful of even being in the same building with, Dan the devil, and he wasn't about to release him.

"Stewart do you trust me?" Joyce asked.

"With my life," Stewart affirmed, and then he pushed the red button and released, Dan the devil.

The second that his restraints unlocked, Dan lunged at Joyce and grabbed her by the throat. He pushed her down on the metal table and began to choke her, but he stopped before she passed out, just as he had described earlier. Then, he ripped off Joyce's lab coat. Dan was so strong that Joyce was completely at his mercy, she knew that struggling was futile as he removed all of her clothing, all but her panties. Dan pulled down his pants and exposed his raging hard on, then he reached for Joyce's panties, but before he pulled them down, he looked for the fear and terror on her face, but there wasn't any. Nothing, no fear, no terror and he experienced no rush or exhilaration. The devil in Dan wasn't being fed. Dan's penis went limp and he slowly released Joyce's neck.

Joyce took in a deep breath and looked Dan directly in the eyes, "Go ahead Dan, kill me. You might as well; I've been dead inside ever since the day that you killed my mother."

43

Dan pulled up his pants, and sat down with his head in his hands, totally defeated.

"Dan, I notice that you've lost your erection," Joyce said as she sat up and reached for her tablet. "This confirms that you were telling me the truth. We have just experienced a major breakthrough. Now explain to me what you're feeling."

"Empty," Dan said, "empty, alone and ashamed. I didn't want to do that to you, Joyce, but I couldn't help myself. It's the devil, I tell ya, the devil, I have no control!"

"Joyce I've followed your career through the years, as if you were my own child. I want to help you in some way before I'm executed, it's the least I can do. I know about your research; that you've created the Living Artificial Brain. I think your right, the only cure for the serial killer is to remove the source of the disease, the brain, start from fresh and implant a new psyche. Can I help you Joyce? Is there any way? I'm sorry for everything I've done, and especially for what I've turned you into."

"Dan, as a matter of fact there is something very important that you can do for me."

"Anything Joyce, you just tell me what it is."

"I haven't been able to get a volunteer for the brain transplant. Would you be my first brain transplant subject?"

"Of course I will, just tell me how."

"First, I'll have to get, Brian, onboard," Joyce said as she put her clothes and lab coat back on. "He's the head of the department and I'll need his approval before we can move ahead. Would you be willing to talk to him and convince him that you're a willing participant?"

"I'll do my best."

"When is your execution scheduled?"

"In twenty-eight days."

"Okay, we'll have to move fast. You wait here and I'll see if I can get the meeting set up."

Joyce told Dan to place his hands back into the restraints, on the table, and then she opened the blinds to the Observation Booth. Stewart was standing by. "Lock the wrist restraints," Joyce instructed.

"All right," Stewart responded, and quickly pushed the red button. Joyce walked across the room to turn the camera back on, but then decided to leave it off, just in case a problem arose with Brian.

Brian, was a good looking, celebrity scientist and a dyed-in-the-wool narcissist. Although he had actually contributed to science at one time, he was now nothing more than a walking prescription pad. He received large kickbacks from the drug companies, enough that it had made him a rich man.

Brian, held press conferences from time to time, announcing the great strides that his research was making to solve the serial killer epidemic. He released the uncontroversial information, regarding Joyce's alternative remedies, and she made him look good. But, Brian wasn't about to let Joyce succeed with her drug-free solution; it would spoil his gravy train with the drug companies. So, he interfered and tried to slow her down, every chance he got.

Convincing Brian to approve the brain transplant on a live subject would be difficult. But with a willing volunteer, perhaps he could be pressured into it somehow. Joyce was determined, and she decided that she would not take no for an answer. This was her big chance to move ahead and do the first brain transplant with a living human being.

Joyce was pumped up, and she burst out of the Interview Room. "Stewart, is Brian in his office?" she hurriedly asked.

"Yes he is," Stewart answered, "but his wife is in there with him. I think they're fighting again, that poor woman. His mistress, Jody, was here earlier today. That man can't keep his *you know what*, inside his briefs."

Joyce walked quickly down the hall with Stewart gliding alongside her, sniffing and trying to keep up. "I don't know what's going on Joyce, but I want you to know that I'm behind you all the way. All I ask is that you don't send me in the room with, Dan the devil, I'm scared of him."

"It's okay Stewart," Joyce told him as she approached

Brian's office, "just wish me luck with Brian, I'm going to need it!"

Joyce's excitement got the best of her, what she had been working for her entire life was just a breath away. The only obstacle was Brian and she didn't have time to be polite. She boldly walked into Brian's office without knocking, "Brian I need to talk to you, now!"

Brian was angry at the interruption. "I don't have time for this, Joyce. Can't you see that my wife and I are having a discussion?"

"It can't wait Brian, we have a willing subject!"

"Oh you women and your emotions, I've had about all I can stand! I'm surprised at you Joyce, I thought that you were more like a man, and had better control of yourself."

Then Joyce noticed that Brian's wife, Peggy, was crying. Joyce liked Peggy and she tried to console her, but Brian kept right on yelling at her.

"Damn it, I can't take this crying anymore! Go home Peggy, we'll finish things up when, and if, I decide to come home!"

Peggy didn't say a word and ran out of the office, with tears flowing down her cheeks. Joyce wondered how such a sweet woman had gotten involved with an asshole like Brian.

"I'm glad that's over with," Brian said. "I wish that she would quit complaining and just be grateful for the time that I *do* spend with her. The only reason I married the bitch, in the first place, was because her father was loaded and funded me to get this lab started. I don't love her and I never will."

Brian shook his head, "I don't know why I'm telling you all this. Well, one bitch down, one more to go. Now tell me Joyce, what's so important that you have the *nerve* to come busting into my office? Did you break a *nail*? Do you need a *new test tube*? This better be a *big* emergency!"

Joyce ignored Brian's insults and got on with her agenda, "I have a subject in the Interview Room and he has volunteered for the brain transplant."

"Well good for him!" Brian said sarcastically. "Too bad I'm

cutting off your funding, no more fooling around with your *toy brains*."

Brian's words hit Joyce like a punch to the gut, he had just told her that her research was coming to an end and that everything she had worked for was over.

Joyce felt as though her life was on the line and she became even more determined. She held herself together and bravely went on, "I already have five brains ready to go sir. We won't need additional funding to do the surgery, there's already an account designated for it."

"Forget it Joyce, just give the bastard some medication and send him on his way. The drugs work. What you want to do is *unethical*. I'm sure that you're violating *his* rights, or *someone else's* rights, or the rights of some *insect out in the woods!* Just get the hell out of my office. I've had all I'm going to take from you women today!"

"Brian, please just talk to Dan. He only has twenty-eight days until his execution. There isn't much time."

"There is no fuckin' way that I'm going in that disgusting Interview Room, it stinks. I'm not talking to some bum about his *feelings*. Who gives a fuck about this piece of shit?"

Joyce knew that arguing with Brian wasn't the answer, it was going nowhere, so she decided to try another approach and appeal to his vanity. "You know Brian, it would look real good if a video were released of you in the Interview Room, talking with the condemned man. Think of the publicity, it might even create a media frenzy. You would probably get another award!"

Brian thought about it for a few seconds and then nodded his head in approval, "Okay, I'll indulge you, for now Joyce, but just the video, nothing more. Don't think that I'm going to get behind you and your crazy theories."

"Thank you Brian you're the best!" Joyce managed to force out. "It's Dan Harris, you'll be talking to, just give him a chance."

"You must really want this Joyce, I hear desperation in your voice. Maybe you can give me a blow job afterwards, that is, as long as I don't have to look at your *face*."

"We'll see Brian, just follow me," Joyce said, feeling like she might throw up. The thought of giving Brian a blow job was revolting, but Joyce was willing to do anything to achieve her goal.

Brian followed Joyce down the hallway. "Wow Joyce, I never noticed what a great ass you have! Too bad you're such a plain Jane, or I'd fuck you."

"Wonderful," Joyce responded and just kept on walking ahead.

"Yeah the media will eat this up alright," Brian said straightening his tie. "It's good for my image to show how committed I am to my work. I might even pretend like I give a shit. It could even mean another grant for me."

Brian and Joyce arrived at the Interview Room and stood by the door. Before she could even open it, Brian was already complaining, "Come on Joyce I don't have all fuckin' day."

Joyce quickly placed her thumb on the door lock button. The security computer identified her and opened the door to the Interview Room.

Dan was sitting with his hands locked in the restraints, looking up at Brian. Even though he was trying to be friendly, he still looked menacing.

Brian just ignored him and sat across the table. "Okay let's get this thing over with. Is the camera on? Get it in close, this is my best angle. Be sure the volume's up high enough to hear the great questions that I'm going to ask. I want to get it right the first time, and get out of here … no retakes."

Joyce pretended to adjust the camera, but left it turned off. Then she joined Stewart in the Observation Booth.

Brian started the interview. "Well hello, Don."

"That's Dan, my name is Dan."

"Oh that's right, *Dan*. Cut!" Brian shouted. "Take two… Hello Dan, how are you feeling today?" Brian kindly asked.

Dan turned and looked through the window at Joyce, "Is there a script?"

"Okay cut!" Brian screamed. "This isn't working, Joyce, this guy's a smart ass."

"You just got off on the wrong foot," Joyce said, over the speaker, trying to calm Brian. "Just give it another try, it will only take a few minutes and don't forget about the great publicity!"

"No, this has gone far enough," Brian said as he began to stand up. "He isn't co-operating."

"Dan please, just answer Brian's questions, nothing more."

"Okay Joyce, I will," Dan agreed, "I'll just answer his questions."

"Dan will be fine now Brian," Joyce promised, "let's keep on going."

"Okay, I'll go along with this for a *little* bit longer, but it's hard to look at this guy. My God you're ugly."

Determined to help Joyce and get the brain transplant, Dan ignored Brian's abuse and answered the question. "I'm feeling a little depressed, sir."

Brian sat back down, pleased at the response. "That's quite normal, considering that you're facing execution. What medications are you currently taking?"

"None, I never took drugs my whole life."

"Well that's the problem Dan, if you had been on medication, you wouldn't have committed murder, and this whole thing wouldn't be happening to you. Drugs can stop *all* violent behavior. That's what I'm working on so diligently here at the lab. Better drugs mean a better society. Why don't we start you off on a mild sedative and increase the dose until the end. Does that sound good? It will make your life a little easier. I understand Dan, that's my job, to cure the violent offender. I know that it may be difficult for you to talk about the past. But, what was your childhood like, any bad experiences?"

"My old man used to beat me, sometimes knock me out."

"Oh that's a shame, I understand," Brian said sadly.

"You understand… come on man, cut the shit. I want a new brain and Joyce has agreed to do the transplant. I'll

49

sign any papers that you want."

"Cut!" Brian shouted again. "He's not supposed to talk about your stupid *toy brains!*" Then he turned to Dan, "You really don't want to get involved with this brain transplant charade Dan. The brains are a piece of shit, just like Joyce and that disgusting sniveling Stewart. Joyce won't have a job in about five minutes anyway. How's she going to do the brain transplant when she doesn't even *work* here?"

Joyce began to cry, she felt like her life had just ended. It was as though Brian had stopped her heart from beating. All hope was gone. "That's it Stewart; it's over," she sobbed, "everything we've worked for ... finished."

Dan didn't like what Brian had said about Joyce, and his murderous devil wanted to be unleashed. He was seething with hatred for Brian, "You're dead asshole," he said lashing out. "I'm going to break you in two, pencil neck! Nobody talks about Joyce like that!"

"Oh do we have a little love affair going on here?" Brian said mocking. "Well it makes sense that the two ugliest people would have such an attraction."

"She's not ugly, she is perfect, and you're going tell her so!"

"What are you planning to do about it, Mr. Death Row? All locked up and helpless... Wah wah!"

Brian curtly walked around the table and slapped Dan across the face. Yeah, what are you gonna do about it... Loser?"

Joyce was near hysteria, Stewart was trying to calm her, but he was still keeping an eye on Dan and Brian. "Now that's enough of that Brian," he told him as firmly as he could.

"What's the matter Joyce, why aren't you defending your lover boy yourself?" Brian asked. "I don't give a shit about this. This interview is over! I'm getting out of here!"

Stewart looked at Joyce for direction, but Joyce just sobbed and looked back at him with helplessness in her eyes. Realizing that his leader was down for the count, Stewart decided to take matters into his own hands. "Don't worry Joyce, everything will be alright." And then Stewart made a bold move and he pushed the red button to release Dan the devil!"

Immediately, Dan jumped up. Full of anger and rage, he grabbed Brian by the neck, threw him on the interview table and held him there. "Not so tough now, are ya pencil neck? Say it! Joyce is perfect! Say it!" Dan screamed violently in Brian's face.

Brian was pinned, he was at Dan's mercy and he fearfully choked out the words, "Joyce is perfect." He was so terrified that he peed his pants and then began to cry and plead with Joyce. "Joyce I was just kidding! I'm not cutting off your funding, I'll give you whatever you want! Just get me out of here!"

"What do you want me to do with this wimp?" Dan asked, looking in the direction of the Observation Booth.

"Hold him as you are," Stewart said quietly and then he pulled a hypodermic needle from his pocket.

Joyce didn't make a move or say a word, she just sat there in quiet desperation. She didn't try to stop Stewart, she couldn't, he was now the one in control, and Joyce let him do the thinking for her.

Stewart stood in the Observation Booth with Joyce, holding a needle that he intended for Brian. But he was afraid to go in the Interview Room with Dan. "Joyce, Joyce, get it together and do what needs to be done," he said, touching her shoulder. Joyce looked up at Stewart and he handed her the needle. Joyce took it from him and then slowly walked toward the Interview Room.

Stewart spoke over the speaker to Dan," Dan just keep holding him down, Joyce is coming in."

"Don't worry, this piece of shit ain't going nowhere," Dan said and pushed down harder on Brian's chest.

When Joyce entered the Interview Room, she was still in a daze. She looked at Dan and he nodded, to give her the go ahead.

"Okay Joyce, do it, give him the shot," Stewart spoke over the speaker.

Joyce responded as though she had no mind of her own, she shot Brian in the neck and he quickly went limp.

Once Brian was unconscious, Stewart spoke to Dan from the Observation Booth and politely asked him to sit back down with his hands in the restraining cuffs. When Dan obliged, Stewart pushed the red button to secure him.

Seconds later, Stewart entered the Interview Room with a gurney and loaded Brian onto it. "Come on Joyce," he said, "we've got to get him into surgery, right away!"

Joyce followed behind Stewart, she was beginning to pull herself together and realized what Stewart was intending to do. "Stewart, stop! We can't do the brain transplant on Brian, he hasn't given his consent. He isn't a serial killer! We're crossing the line, we have to stop."

"Joyce listen to me," Stewart said, still wheeling Brian on the gurney. "We've already gone too far and we can't stop now. Turning back is not an option. And why is it such a stretch to do the surgery on Brian? He's standing in our way and the fate of the entire world hangs in the balance. It all depends on this surgery. If we don't transplant Brian's brain, our research will end, and we'll both go to prison. We can't go to prison Joyce, how many innocent people will be killed if we don't find the cure? This move is for the greater good, come on Joyce, get onboard, you're just minutes from achieving your dream!"

Stewart had a good argument for transplanting Brian's brain. He was just one man and an asshole at that. Surely Joyce and Stewart didn't belong in prison and that's exactly where they would both end up if they let Brian come to, he would see to that. The choice was now obvious ... Joyce would perform the first brain transplant!

"Stewart, you're right, there is no other choice; we're too close to let anything stand in our way! Prepare Brian for surgery, and I'll go take care of Dan."

"Yes ma'am," Stewart said with a salute, thrilled that Joyce had given the go ahead.

Joyce headed back to the Interview Room; she went inside

and sat across from Dan. "I'm sure that you know what's going to happen here Dan. You just return to your cell and keep your mouth shut."

"Nobody listens to me anyway." Dan bulged out his eyes and made a silly face, "I thought you knew, I'm crazy. You don't need to worry about me Joyce. You're the greatest, and with all due respect, I still want to stick my dick down your throat and choke ya!"

"I'll take that as a complement," Joyce said, and sent for the guard to take Dan back to his cell.

Once Dan was out of the facility, Joyce scrubbed for surgery and then joined Stewart in the Operating Room. "Sorry for losing it back there Stewart," she apologized, "but I'm fine now, let's get to work."

"You didn't lose it Joyce, you're brilliant and I'll follow you forever, until the end of time."

Such devotion had to be treasured.

JOYCE CROSSES THE BLOODY LINE
BETWEEN SCIENCE AND MURDER

Joyce and Stewart began the surgery. It was something that they had performed together on cadavers, time and time again. So much so, that it was almost second nature to them.

Stewart began the anesthesia. All of Brian's vitals were perfect and Joyce made the first incision and opened up his head. She worked feverishly, preparing to extract the brain.

Stewart was getting nervous, the brain extraction was taking longer than it should. He was relieved when he heard Joyce say, "We're ready for the Living Artificial Brain. Let's use brain number five, it's contains the most agreeable program. Brian must be the perfect boss."

Joyce had plans to use Brian as her puppet and sign off on everything that she needed. It would expedite her research and make life much easier.

53

Stewart agreed, "Brain number five it is." He left the room and came back with brain number five.

Joyce was ready, she pulled Brian's brain from his open skull and placed it in a gel solution. "This should be an interesting study," she said with a laugh, "when we dissect it, we'll find out what an assholes' brain looks like. How's he doing?"

"All vitals are within normal range," Stewart reported.

"Okay Stewart, this is it, activate the Living Artificial Brain."

Stewart placed the brain into the activation chamber of the Brian Activation Machine and turned it on. The machine wasn't much different than a paint mixing machine, as all the artificial brain needed was a good thump to begin functioning.

Joyce had developed special nerve endings, in the artificial brain. Clinging tendrils, that reached out like slim vines, searching for, and then attracting the nerve and blood vessels of a living subject. Once the nerve and blood vessels were located they attached.

Stewart removed the activated, Living Artificial Brain, and carefully carried it across the room. He and Joyce watched as the brains' nerves and blood vessels moved, stretching and reaching out; the clinging tendrils searching for a living subject to latch onto. When it got closer to Brian, the nerves and blood vessels in his open skull began to respond and were reaching for, and attaching to the artificial brain.

"Joyce, Joyce, it's working!" Stewart exclaimed.

"Hold on now Stewart, this is touchy," Joyce said as she worked to complete the brain insertion. Hours passed and Joyce was definitely feeling the strain. Dealing with a live subject wasn't the same as working on a cadaver and she had to make adjustments, hoping that they were the right ones. Finally, Joyce breathed a sigh of relief, "Okay Stewart, close."

Stewart joined the incisions and Joyce carefully monitored Brian. The brain was working perfectly. All tests were normal and soon, it was time to take Brian off of life support. Stewart

54

and Joyce stood by holding their breath, this time their subject would come to life.

"Okay Stewart, this is it, go ahead and disconnect the life support."

Stewart moved slowly and deliberately, he disconnected Brian from life support and Brian immediately flat lined. Joyce wasn't thrown; she and Stewart had learned to expect the unexpected. They worked quickly, trying to get Brian's heart to beat on its own, but no response. Brian was dead! He was still flat lining! No matter what procedure they tried, he wouldn't respond.

"Brian, why are you always such a problem? Can't you ever cooperate with anything?!"Joyce screamed at the lifeless body and pounded on its chest. "It's useless Stewart," she said, "hook him back up, we need to buy some time and find out why his body won't function with the brain."

Stewart reengaged the life support, and then he and Joyce sat on the floor defeated.

"I just don't understand it Stewart, everything looks perfect."

"I don't know either Joyce, there's no explanation; the situation is bleak."

After sitting there for quite some time, Joyce finally got up, "We'll keep him under lock and key while we review every experiment, every procedure and every single note that we've ever written! There just has to be an answer!"

Joyce checked Brian's vitals, then she turned off the light and left him lying in the darkened Operating Room.

"Let's go to Brian's office and have a drink," she said, "I know where he keeps his scotch."

"I don't drink alcohol Joyce," Stewart stated.

"Yes, Stewart that's right, just come along anyway."

Joyce and Stewart both sat in Brian's office on his fine leather chairs and Joyce reached into the drawer, where he kept the scotch. She got out two glasses and thoughtlessly poured a shot for Stewart.

Stewart hesitated, but said again, "Joyce I don't drink

alcohol."

Joyce was thrown for a moment before she responded, "That's right, Stewart I'm sorry." She threw back her shot and then sipped Stewart's. "I was certain it would work, I just don't understand it," she said.

"I don't understand it either Joyce, the brain is functioning perfectly, but Brian's dead and that's a fact."

"We'll take a few days to review and hopefully figure out where we went wrong. I've got some ideas, more things that we should try." Joyce finished the scotch and then got up. "I'm going home to get some rest and you should do the same. It's been a big day for both of us. We'll start fresh in the morning."

Joyce and Stewart knocked off for the night and Joyce was back at the lab first thing the next morning. After reviewing the situation, she had an idea and called for Stewart. "Stewart, we didn't upload Brian's memories and responses. The brain may need to be personalized before the body will respond to it."

"That makes sense," Stewart agreed, and then the two of them worked to implant Brian's memories and responses.

Joyce sat at the main computer and set up a program for Brian. When she entered Brian's name she accidently spelled it as Brain. Stewart was looking over her shoulder and he snorted, "BRAIN Jones!" Joyce, quickly started to correct her mistake, but Stewart squealed, "No, leave it BRAIN!"

"Okay Stewart," Joyce agreed, "it is apropos, and what do we want to enter for his personality? D..I..C..K?"

"I want him to be nice to his wife, Peggy," Stewart said with honor, "she deserves to be treated like a queen."

"Okay Stewart, we'll make him a gentleman, Peggy will think that she's married to a prince."

"Now, as far as his reactions at work, he should just stay out of our way."

"Yes, I agree of course," Stewart said, "but remember he still has to have a certain amount of charm to get the funding that we need."

56

"Yes, you're right, he'll be the perfect politician; gets things done, and then stays out of the way. Brian will obey me, sign papers with a smile, and make everything a lot easier around here."

"What about me Joyce? Will Brian listen to me too?"

"Stewart, you're second in command around here, of course you'll have power."

Joyce finished programming Brian's brain and rose to her feet. "Let's see if Brian's body responds to the programming. Disconnect the life support!"

Stewart disconnected the life support and then held Joyce's hand. They quickly found that the programming wasn't the answer when Brian flat lined again. Luckily they were able to stabilize him, and then they both went back to the drawing board.

Three days went by, and Joyce and Stewart were still trying unsuccessfully to find the reason why Brian's body wouldn't respond to the functioning brain.

On the fourth day, Peggy called Joyce, "Joyce, I haven't heard from Brian and I'm worried. He usually calls me by now, even if it's just to tell me a lie. Do you know where he could possibly be?"

"I'm sure that there's nothing to worry about Peggy," Joyce told her, "he was here at the lab this morning."

"Joyce, you don't have to try and cover for him, I know what I'm married to. I was putting up with Brian's philandering long before you met him. But even so, I still worry."

"I'll try to have Brian call you the next time I see him," Joyce promised.

Stewart was standing by and tapped Joyce on the arm. "Joyce what are you telling her that for, Brian's not going to be calling her. He may end up in the incinerator."

"I know Stewart, I just didn't know what to say."

It was day seven and Joyce and Stewart were at wits end. "There's just no explanation for it Joyce!" Stewart said in frustration. "We've tried everything and nothing's changed,

Brian hasn't improved. It may be time for us to face the fact that the brain transplant won't work."

Just then, there was a loud pounding at the main door to the laboratory. Joyce and Stewart looked at each other alarmed. "Answer it Stewart," Joyce instructed and Stewart checked the monitor, and saw three policemen and a big angry man.

"Can I help you?" he meekly asked through the intercom.

"Where's my brother you freak?!" the angry man shouted.

Then one of the policemen held up a paper. "We have a search warrant, open the door."

"Let me get the supervisor, she'll be right with you."

Joyce was standing beside Stewart, "They're here to look for Brian. I'll stall them as long as I can and you get Brian in the incinerator!"

Stewart panicked, "Joyce, we're going to prison! O.M.G., I knew that this was going to happen!"

Joyce grabbed Stewart by the shoulders, "Stewart, get Brian to the incinerator! Now!"

Stewart ran for the O.R. and wheeled Brian out and then down the hall, while the police banged loudly on the door. Once Stewart was out of sight, Joyce opened the door and let the men inside the lab. "What is it gentlemen?" she calmly asked.

"Listen you freak, I'm Bill, Brian's brother, and I know all about you. He was going to fire you and Igor and you've done something to him! I know it!"

"Mr. Jones, calm down, or we'll have to remove you," one of the officers told him.

"You don't understand officer," Brian's brother pleaded, "these two are a couple of ghouls, they do experiments with brains and dead people! They've probably put one of their toy brains in my brother's head and have him locked away somewhere!"

"If your brother's here, we'll find him, Mr. Jones," the officer assured Bill.

"Now, Dr. Picard, you stay out of the way and let us search

the premises."

"Officer, you don't understand, this is a laboratory with sensitive material and experiments. Some of it can be hazardous, even deadly without proper handling. You better let me guide you through to insure the safety of your men."

"Yeah sure, you'd like that," Bill shouted, "hide every clue so we can't find Brian!"

The officer gave Joyce the go ahead and she began to slowly guide the men through the lab. She did her best to stall the search at every turn, trying not to be obvious, but the policemen weren't falling for it.

"Here, here!" Bill shouted, "the incinerator! Hurry, they probably have Brian in there right now, trying to destroy all the evidence!" Bill began pounding on the door to the Incineration Room.

Joyce did her best to turn the men in another direction, but one of the officers agreed with Bill and demanded that Joyce let them inside.

"Why certainly gentlemen, I'd be happy to let you in, but we've been having trouble with our identification lock pad and it might take some time.

"You better get this door open lady or I'll knock it down!" Bill threatened.

At that moment, Stewart opened the door and came out of the Incineration Room, and the men quickly burst inside.

"Stewart, did you get it done?" Joyce whispered.

Stewart discretely shook his head no, and Joyce felt a heavy weight pressing down on her, what she had feared was actually happening. It was over, she and Stewart were going to prison for the rest of their lives, or maybe even facing execution.

Suddenly, Joyce heard a familiar voice, "Hello gentlemen, what's all the ruckus?" It was Brian! He was alive!

Brian spoke to the police and then they left, relieved that they had found the person that they had been searching for.

But, Bill stayed behind to talk to Brian. "Listen bro, I've got a bone to pick with you."

59

"Alright Bill, let's go to my office."

The two men went into Brian's office and they didn't close the door. Joyce and Stewart were happy at their good fortune and stood by, listening. They wondered if Brian would react properly, or if he would arouse Bill's suspicions and do something out of character.

"We're not out of the woods yet," Stewart said quietly to Joyce and she nodded in agreement.

"You sure made a fool out of me," Bill said angrily, "me charging in here with the police. I just couldn't believe that my own brother would fuck me over. I thought that you'd have to be dead or held hostage by the ghouls before you'd fuck me over, but obviously I was wrong. You've been missing a whole week, and with my money! Whatever happened to our weekend at the lodge with the Chinese hookers? I can't believe that you did this! You have all the women and money in the world, and it's still not enough. You don't give a shit about anybody but yourself. I hope that your good time was worth it, because you're dead to me! Don't ever contact me again!" With that, Bill stormed out of the office and then Stewart let him out of the building.

"Good thing that we used brain number five," Stewart commented. "With any aggression present, that could have been a disaster."

Joyce didn't respond, she was still grossed out about the Chinese hooker weekend at the lodge.

Finally the enormity of what had happened set in, "Joyce! Joyce!" Stewart said in jubilation, "Brian's alive! We did it Joyce! We did it!"

"Yeah, Stewart, what in the world happened in the Incineration Room?"

"O.M.G. Joyce, it was crazy! I had Brian lined up and I was ready to push him into the furnace, when I heard someone coughing. I stopped and looked around the room, thinking that someone had gotten in, but there wasn't anyone there. When I looked back at Brian, he was already trying to sit up and talking to me. By this time, the police were pounding on the door and Brian was sitting there in nothing but a hospital gown. I didn't know what to do, but then I remembered an old pair of scrubs that I had left in there last week and I helped him put them on … just in the nick of time."

"Amazing," Joyce said, "simply amazing. The answer was that simple … time, the brain and body simply needed an adjustment period."

THE EXECUTIONER
PREPARES A DEATH MOCK FORMULA

Once Stewart and Joyce had recovered from the shock of the police search and Brian coming back to life, it was time to get on with the plan … Dan.

"Dan's execution is in three weeks Stewart," Joyce said concerned. "There's probably not enough time for us to get the brain transplant approved, but I'll still give it a try. Brian seems to be able to act normal enough to get by. I'll go with him to see the warden and attempt to get him to cut through the red tape and push the approval through."

"May I offer an alternate plan?" Stewart asked.

"Yes, of course Stewart."

"As you already know, it's most likely that you won't get the brain transplant approved, but there should be no problem getting Dan's organs donated. With me being the prison executioner, I may be able to switch the death drugs with a formula that will only mock death. It's risky, and could still be fatal if we don't revive Dan in time, but it may be the only chance we've got."

Joyce agreed with Stewart and then made an urgent appointment for Brian to meet with the warden.

They decided to take Brian's car to the prison, as he normally would. But not being sure if he was capable of driving, Joyce planned to drive. When Brian and Joyce were ready to leave, Brian insisted on driving the car himself.

"Well Stewart," Joyce said, "If he thinks he can do it, let's give him a chance."

"I don't know Joyce, it could be dangerous."

"Nothing ventured, nothing gained," Joyce replied and then she bravely got into the passenger seat.

Brian started the engine and smoothly pulled away.

"So far so good," Joyce shouted to Stewart and then she waved good-bye. "Wish me luck!"

"Good luck Joyce!" Stewart said. "You're going to need it!"

All went well, Brian was able to safely drive the car and he and Joyce arrived at the prison. When Joyce entered the warden's office, with Brian, she was tense. Not just that she wouldn't get approval for the brain transplant, but just as much so, that Brian would "short circuit" or something would go wrong with his programming. "Oh why am I taking such a risk?" she questioned herself.

Stewart had carefully coached Brian as to what he was to say to the warden, and then he was to defer to Joyce.

"Hello Professor Jones," the warden said holding out his hand, but Brian just stood there, not moving. Joyce quickly stepped ahead and introduced herself. The warden didn't seem to take notice that Brian was "off" and he offered them a seat.

"Now Brian, why don't you tell me what's so urgent. You've never requested a meeting with me before. As a matter of fact it's usually quite difficult for *me* to get a meeting with *you*."

"Thank you for seeing me sir," Brian said, "but perhaps my colleague, Dr. Picard, could explain it better than I."

Joyce took her cue, "Yes sir, Professor Jones and I have been working very closely on the Living Artificial Brain. The condemned man, Dan L. Harris, has volunteered to be the first subject and I was hoping that you could somehow cut through the red tape and get approval for the surgery before his execution."

"Yes Dr. Picard, I've heard about your experiments at the research lab, very controversial, yes *very* controversial indeed. I'll be honest with you and not waste your time or mine, the answer is NO, plain and simple. And I doubt very seriously that anything as bizarre as a brain transplant will ever be permitted under any condition. This isn't Nazi Germany where we experiment willy-nilly on human beings, not even the condemned ones. A man facing the death penalty will agree to anything if he thinks that it will prolong his life or give him the opportunity to escape. And I'm afraid that Dan the devil, agreeing to this surgery is nothing more than that, the act of a desperate man. Besides that, the governor will never sign off on it. It's an election year and he's taking a hard stand against crime. Releasing a notorious criminal, such as Dan Harris, to a couple of scientists, just won't fly. The public demands justice! This man has committed heinous crimes! Your request is completely outrageous!"

Joyce knew that it was useless for her to try to change the warden's mind. And besides that, there was no way that he could have pressed through all of the barriers, even if he had wanted to. By this time, she was afraid that he might even make a stand to stop the brain transplant experiments all together. So, Joyce simply asked for the donation of Dan's organs, and the warden agreed. "Yes most definitely Dr. Picard, the executed donating their organs to science is always smiled upon. Let me have the paperwork and I'll sign off on it."

Joyce pulled the paperwork from her briefcase and handed it to the warden. "Sir, I know that it's an unusual request, but could I see Dan and get his signature myself?"

"Yes, it is unusual, but since you and Professor Jones are scientists, I'll approve it."

Joyce was happy that Stewart had seen to it that the paperwork was in order. The warden signed and within minutes she and Brian were going through a strict security search to enter death row.

Joyce and Brian weren't allowed to be in the cell with Dan. The guards all hated him and were looking forward to his execution, so even though Joyce adamantly requested it, they wouldn't take Dan into the visiting area where she could talk to him.

One of the guards took the papers from Joyce, he instructed her to stand back and then he passed them into Dan's cell for his signature. When Dan reviewed the papers, he looked at Joyce confused. "What the fuck is this shit? I thought that I was getting a new brain?"

"Yes Dan I know, the transplant wasn't approved, but *trust* me."

Dan quickly scribbled his signature in the appropriate places and handed it back to the guard. "Fuck you Joyce!" he muttered discouraged. But then Dan noticed Brian standing there with a goofy smile on his face. "Hey, why isn't fuck face acting like his usual ...." Then he stopped and smiled at Joyce. "You crazy fuckin' bitch," he said shaking his head in disbelief.

Joyce left the prison happy; she had won a small victory. When she and Brian reached the lab, Stewart was waiting for them. He wasn't surprised at the outcome of the meeting and had already started to prepare the death mock formula.

"Should we do anymore testing on Brian?" Stewart asked Joyce.

"No, he's good enough; he can drive and talk, just send him home for the night and let Peggy be the judge. I'll be the first one she calls if he does anything strange. We can do additional testing another time, if need be. For now, let's just observe."

"Yes, Peggy's harmless, she won't ask any questions of Brian, she'll just be happy that he's home at all," Stewart agreed.

After Brian had left the building, Joyce found that she was in need of some rest. She asked Stewart if she could lay down for a little while in his room and Stewart kindly agreed. Joyce slowly walked down the hall and into Stewart's room. She laid down on his starchy clean bed and tried to nap, but she couldn't. Her head was spinning with ideas and thoughts and she found herself tense and staring up at the ceiling. Actually, she was staring at a picture of Einstein posted to the ceiling above the bed.

"Stewart you're such a freak!" she whispered. Joyce sat up and looked around the room. It was clean and uncluttered, just like the laboratory. One dresser and one bed, no pictures of friends or family. No signs that it was even lived in it. Stewart's room was very neat and organized, unlike Joyce's cluttered apartment, and she liked it. "Just like Stewart, clean and orderly."

Finding herself too restless to nap, Joyce decided to go home.

DEREK AND JOYCE GET AWAY

Joyce drove home, but was still anxious when she came through her front door. "Hi Derek!" she said in a cheerful tone, not wanting to let on that she was stressed.

Joyce sat down in her favorite chair and Derek happily greeted her. He climbed up her leg and then onto her lap. Joyce petted him and he rolled on his back for tummy rubs.

"Why don't we have an early dinner tonight Derek, how does spaghetti sound?"

Derek loved spaghetti and when he heard the word spaghetti, he quickly ran to the kitchen.

"Okay, spaghetti it is!" Joyce said as she got up and followed Derek.

Dinner was soon prepared and Joyce and Derek enjoyed the delicious meal. After the dishes were washed, Joyce took a long hot shower. She decided to put on a sweater that Peggy had knitted her for Christmas. "Yes, Peggy is certainly a wonderful person," she thought as she slipped the sweater over her head. "I hope that she's having a nice time with Brian."

When she was dressed, Joyce joined Derek on the couch and tried to pick a movie for them to watch together. After viewing the selection, she was disappointed, "Looks like there's nothing new, we've seen all these." Then Joyce turned off the television and sat quietly with her eyes closed, trying to rest. But her mind was still racing. She wanted to call Peggy to see how things were going with Brian, but decided not to. "Peggy couldn't talk about Brian, with him there, anyway." Then there was all of the work that needed to be done at the lab. Over and over again, she thought of something else that needed her attention. The death mock formula, Dan's brain transplant, her head was spinning.

Derek began to get restless too, he had been alone all day and he wanted Joyce's attention. "Well, since there aren't any good movies on, why don't we go bye-bye, Derek?"

Joyce didn't have to say bye-bye a second time. Before she could even get up from the couch, Derek had climbed into his carrier. "Good boy Derek, I don't want you to scare the cats!"

Derek was a big river rat, fierce and strong. He was larger than most cats, and the cats in the neighborhood always gave him a wide berth. Because of this behavior, Joyce concluded that Derek must have tangled with a few of them before she adopted him.

Before Joyce closed the carrier, she leaned over to Derek and rubbed noses with him. "My good boy is such a bad ass," she said, and then she closed the carrier and they headed out the door.

Joyce placed Derek in the back of her car and then opened the carrier. Derek climbed out and was waiting for her in the front seat when she got inside. Joyce smiled, and gave him a pat on the head. "Let's get out of the city tonight Derek, nothing like fresh clean air to clear a person's head." Joyce pulled out of the driveway and into the street. She passed the Chinese restaurant with the flower cart. "Oh look Derek, your favorite, the old lady has lilies on the flower cart tonight. We'll stop and get a bouquet on the way home."

Joyce drove the car and Derek rode on the passenger side with his head out the window, the wind blowing through his silky black fur. They went to a place in the country where she

66

and Derek had spent many special days together. Joyce spread out a sleeping bag, and laid down and peacefully gazed at the stars, while Derek climbed the nearby trees, enjoying the cool summer breeze. Joyce finally relaxed and she and Derek had a wonderful time.

PIMP, WHORES, CRACK AND QUNITSHA

Meanwhile.....Tache' was enjoying her evening as well. It was her night off and she was babysitting little Qunitsha.

"Well, Qunitsha, do you want to play with the baby doll, or the teddy bear?" Tache' asked as she held up both toys in front of the tiny baby. Even though Qunitsha was too young to even sit up yet, Tache' swore that she had pointed to the toy that she wanted. "Oh you're so smart suga', the baby doll it is! This little doll's bigger than you are ... you sure?"

Qunitsha's eyes got big, and she smiled and kicked her chubby legs in jubilation. She grabbed the dolls hair with a strong determined grip, and then she started putting it into her mouth.

"Oh my, I don't think that this is a good idea after all,"Tache' said trying to take the doll from the baby. She soon realized that Qunitsha wasn't about to release it, and she decided to distract her with the stuffed dinosaur. "To the rescue!" Tache' laughed, as she animated the dinosaur. It seemed to take on a life of its own as it galloped up the baby's leg.

Qunitsha loosened her grip on the doll's hair and then grabbed the soft plush toy.

"I think we'll put this doll away until you get older!" Then Tache' placed the doll on a high shelf.

Playtime came to a halt when Qunitsha became fussy. "Are you hungry sweetheart? Come on, let's get you some formula. I'm so glad you like it honey."

Tache' gently picked Qunitsha up and headed for the kitchen to get a bottle from the refrigerator. As the bottle was warming, she went into her bedroom, with Qunitsha, in her arms, planning to get a clean hand towel to use as a burp cloth.

Tyrone heard Tache' in the bedroom with his daughter and screamed loudly from the kitchen, "You get my baby out you room! You know I want her in that livin' room. She ain't allowed in the be'rooms. Who knows what shit you bitches have layin' round. Member who's in control here, you fuckin' ho!"

"I know, you in control, Lil' T., I just had to get a fresh towel for your baby."

Tache' quickly grabbed a towel and then walked back into the kitchen where she found Tyrone sitting at the table, smoking crack. Qunitsha began to cry and rub her eyes when she smelled the irritating smoke.

"Would you shut that baby up!" Tyrone shouted. "Fuck, get her outta' here!"

"Tyrone you shouldn't be smokin' in the house with Qunitsha, it's not good for her."

"Did I really hear you talk back to me bitch!? Qunitsha my baby and she might's well be gettin' used to this shit. Crack ain't gonna hurt her none. Shit, my pops smoked it when I was growin' up, and look at me!" Tyrone pounded his chest, "I be a b'ness man! I got somethin' goin' fo' me! I ain't gonna be no worthless crack head like he be!"

Tyrone took another drag from his crack pipe and then he stood up. He walked toward Tache' with Quintsha in her arms and Tache' was frightened. She was certain that Tyrone was going to slap *her*, as he usually did, so she turned away from him to protect the baby. But when she didn't feel a blow, she thought it was safe and turned back around.

"Gimme my daughter!" Tyrone demanded, then, he took Qunitsha and held her up facing him. Tyrone smiled a big toothy smile and Tache's fear lessened. Even high on crack, Tyrone was still kind to the baby. After all, he was her father.

"I'm so fuckin' lucky I had me a girl," Tyrone said, smiling.

Tache' was happy that Tyrone was pleased, "That's so

68

nice honey, most men want sons."

"I don't want me no son. Havin' a boy is diff'nt, a boy be challenging his pops, tryin' to take over the b'ness, yo. Ya feel me Tache'?" Tache' reluctantly forced a smile. "Girls, they be better … ya know? They be nice to their pops, she do what I say! Feel me?" Tache' just stood there and didn't respond.

"She my little ho in trainin'! Ain't you my little ho in training Qunitsha? Ain't you?" Tyrone gently shook Qunitsha back and forth, "Ha, that funny," he said. Then Qunitsha started giggling. "See, she know! She know! Yeah, and Tache' here, she the one to learn from. She know all the tricks how to satisfy a man, or a skanky bitch, she a real freak. Right Tache? Fuck, you a freak in bed! Never liked me some mens befo' I met you! Yeah, glad I had me a girl."

Even after Tyrone had said such horrible things, in front of the baby, Tache' decided to try to keep him in a good mood. "Tyrone honey, what do you think about spending the evening together, like a real family does. I bought a nice big roast and we could have dinner and spend time with the baby. You should see Qunitsha playing with this dinosaur, it's so cute! Let me show you."

Tache' took Qunitsha from Tyrone and smiled happily at the adorable baby. "Yes, this is my favorite day of the week, when I can spend quality time with my little one."

"Your lillle one? Your little one? I don't remember your dick goin' all up in Shawna's pussy! Don't fuck with me bitch! That's my blood not yours, and don't you forget your place 'round here, ho!"

"You high, that's all," Tache' said quietly. Then she walked into the living room with Qunitsha, in her caring arms, while Tyrone continued to rant. "And what makes you think that you my family? I got better things to do then spendin' time wit' you. And I don't want no fuckin' roast neither. You stay outta this kitchen, ho, I gots b'ness to conduct!"

Tache' was used to Tyrone's abuse and she simply sat down on the couch. She started feeding Qunitsha her bottle, trying to put everything out of her mind, but the beautiful baby.

"You're such a good girl, and so quiet because all of your needs are met. You'll always be well taken care of, as long as I'm around. I love you sweetie."

The baby gently held Tache's finger as she enjoyed her bottle. Tache' rocked her, and burped her, as well as she could, without a rocking chair. And when Qunitsha fell asleep, Tache' carefully placed her into the old, hand-me-down playpen and covered her with a soft pink baby blanket.

Tache' would have loved to buy Qunitsha a crib, but Tyrone objected. "If that cage was good nuff fo' me, it's good nuff fo' her," he said. But, at least he had allowed Tache' to buy the soft baby blanket for Qunitsha. It replaced the old tattered sleeping bag that he had idiotically flung into the playpen, after she was born. Tache' felt bad that Tyrone wouldn't let Qunitsha stay in one of the bedrooms, where it was more quiet. He said that he didn't trust the ho's with her in their rooms. He wanted Qunitsha in the living room, where he could keep an eye on her. Tache' guessed that it was his awkward way of trying to be a father and protect his daughter. After all, some of the girls *were* drug addicts.

"Well, it looks like you're sound asleep for the night, my little angel," Tache' said as she gave Qunitsha a kiss on the forehead.

Qunitsha was very tired and so was Tache', the two of them had been laughing and playing all day. Tache' could never get enough time with the precious child, and she took advantage of every minute that they had together.

Tache' was lying quietly on the couch next to Qunitsha's playpen, when suddenly, Tyrone broke the silence, talking and laughing loudly on the phone. Tache' was startled, but then she closed her eyes again, relieved that he wasn't speaking to her. The noise didn't bother the baby, Qunitsha, was a very sound sleeper and accustomed to the racket in the house. With so many people living there, it was common

70

for there to be screaming, laughing, and doors slamming, all hours of the night and day. It was amazing that she got any sleep at all.

An hour passed, and Tache' hadn't eaten that day. She was hungry and thirsty, but Tyrone was still in the kitchen. "Damn! Why does he have to be in the kitchen all the time? It's not like he's cookin' or eatin', he's just sittin' at the table like an idiot, smokin' crack and talkin' on the phone. Maybe he won't notice me if I'm quiet. I'll grab something and get out real quick. Here I go!" Tache' crept into the kitchen and quietly got some leftover chicken, from the refrigerator. But, Tyrone noticed her and quickly hung up the phone. "Had a good day with my daughter, did ya?"

"Oh yes Tyrone, I love taking care of her."

"Well, I gots other peoples for you to "take care" of tonight. New clients, big bucks baby!"

"Oh Tyrone it's my day off, can't one of the other girls handle it? What if the baby wakes up?"

"None of the girls can handle this job, it be too ugly. The bitches don't have your special talent, if you know what I mean? Wit' these clients I need someone strong and someone wit' da right equipment. Ya feel me? We be makin' hell ah money tonight girl! Whooo! That's what I'm talkin' 'bout Tache'. You need be earnin' you keep 'round here!

"But Tyrone, what about Qunitsha?"

"Don't you be worryin' 'bout Qunitsha. You let Shawna do the worrin'. She be home the minute you get you fine ass out on the street. You ass be my big money maker. You be ge'in' too attached to my baby. Yeah it be costin' me way too many dolla's. It a distraction, and I don't likes it! You keep yo' ass on the street, where it belong, not all up in my b'ness. Get goin', and don't be comin' back 'til I calls you. Ya hear me? You gonna' make me some moneys tonight! Shawna take care of her own baby. Now get fuckin' goin'! Bitch! Qunitsha taken up way too much a yo time. Time be money and money be time! Can I get a amen? Whooo!"

Tache' was disappointed, she had wanted to stay home and rest and watch her angel sleep, but she knew that she had pushed Tyrones' buttons. It wasn't wise telling him that she was happy watching the baby. Being a sadist, it had made him angry.

Tache' felt that she didn't deserve to be happy, and Tyrone used it to manipulate her. Tyrone got his way, or Tache' paid, so she agreed to do what he wanted. "Okay," she said, completely defeated.

"Okay? Okay?" Tyrone shouted. He jumped up from the table and slammed Tache' against the wall. "You be actin' like I axked you!" he screamed viciously in her face.

Tache' was stronger than Tyrone, but even so, she was completely paralyzed with fear. It wasn't physical strength that Tyrone used to control her, it was a powerful psychological hold that had her bound. The years of abuse that Tache' had suffered made her easy fodder for a manipulative user like Tyrone.

"I'm sorry Tyrone," she managed to squeak out, "it'll never happen again."

"That right bitch! Sometime you bitches gots to be reminded who in control 'round here!"

Tache' walked out of the kitchen and headed to her bedroom to get ready for the night. She loved her room, it was her own private oasis. She was privileged to have one of the two large master bedrooms in the house. Tyrone said that he gave it to her, because she made him the most money. Tache' was tall, and the space made it easier for her extensive grooming, not to mention shaving twice a day. Tyrone had offered to get all of her facial and body hair permanently removed, but for some reason she could never bring herself to do it. Tache' really didn't see it as being a problem, keeping herself perfectly shaved, was something that was a part of her. The daily ritual helped to keep her sane in some strange way.

Surprisingly, Tache' still thought of herself as a soldier and maintained much of what she had learned in the army. She

72

was disciplined, and kept herself in excellent physical condition. She could count, on one hand, the days that she hadn't done her vigorous exercise routine. The army had taught her to be organized, neat and clean, and she kept her room in tip-top shape. The closets and drawers were arranged according to color, and there were many colors in Tache's wardrobe. The closet was a big walk in, with plenty of room for all of her dresses and shoes, hats, wigs, coats and so on. The wigs were a sight to see. Tyrone spared no expense when it came to his girls having the best wigs, especially Tache'. She had short blonde wigs, long silky wavy wigs, and hot pink for when she was feeling sassy. One of her favorites was her jet black wig that fell down her back and cascaded around her shoulders. It made her feel like a real woman. This was the wig that she would wear tonight. With such important clients, she had to look and feel her best.

Tache' sat down at her dressing table to remove her makeup and the blonde wig that she had worn around the house that day. She never let anyone see her without her makeup and wig; it was part of the charade that she called her life. She felt safe and comfortable in her role as Tache', she had played it for so many years that it was like second nature to her. Being a man was something that she had given up many years before. Tache' never desired sexual reassignment surgery, it just wasn't her. She told herself that she had the best of both worlds, the physical strength of a man, and the sensitivity of a woman. It was how she survived, it was who she was, like it or not.

Tache' looked at her face in the mirror, without the thick foundation and shading, she looked masculine. With her shortly cropped hair, she could still see a glimmer of the man that she had once been, a soldier in the army. The army had been there for her when she was young and needed help. It gave her an education and a chance, before everything fell apart.

Tache' had grabbed a tissue to wipe her face, but ended up using it to blot a tear from her eye. Just one tear, one lonely tear.

"Okay, get yourself together girl. Pull yourself up by the bootstraps solider!" Tache' shook her head, then stood up and walked into the bathroom to take her shower. The shower was extra-large and very extravagant and Tache' enjoyed the time that she spent getting clean. She turned on the water, undressed and then slipped into her own personal waterfall. It was one of her few relaxing times and she appreciated every minute of it.

When she was finished with her shower, she began to dry off with a big fluffy, white towel. She liked white towels because she felt as though she could bleach the sin off of them. When she dried herself, her relaxing thoughts came to an end. She thought about what she was facing; another night of depravity and danger, a night like she had faced, so many times before.

She bravely moved on, to her dressing table. It was time to become Tache'.

"Well, we can't make any money looking like this, get to it girl!" she coaxed herself. Tache' sat down on her soft pink chair and pulled a cap over her hair, to help keep her wig in place. She taped her eyebrows up, to make her look more feminine. Then she moisturized before applying heavy foundation and powder, carefully contouring, shading and highlighting. Next, was the glittery eye shadow for a dramatic effect and Tache' always did a flawless job. Eyeliner, extra-long eyelashes and then blush. Tache' looked herself over, and was happy with what she had accomplished. "You go girl!" she said with a snap of her neck, then she jumped up from the chair and headed for her closet. Tache' began to dress; she put on her large bra with silicone gel pad inserts and then selected her dress for the evening. She decided to go with a short pink, skintight number, stretchy for easy on, easy off. Tache' slid her fishnet stockings over her sleek smooth legs. She decided to wear her new shoes; extra high platforms. The shoes were difficult to walk in, but she loved the way they looked on her. She had just shampooed her favorite wig and it smelled fresh and clean. She pulled it on her head and, as always, it looked incredible. Tache' checked herself out in her full length mirror and said, "Pink lipstick and I'm ready to go!" Tache' had beautiful full lips and the bright pink accented them perfectly. "Oh wait now Tache', don't forget the glitter cream!" Tache' massaged soft glittering cream onto her arms, and her dark vibrant glowing skin glistened in the light. "Time to go!" she said, and then grabbed her purse as she exited her bedroom.

Tache' headed straight for the playpen to check on Qunitsha. "Still sound asleep, praise God," she said. "Your mama will be here any minute, baby girl. You have a good night."

Tyrone came out of the kitchen and sat down on the couch. Immediately, he started watching a porno and smoking his crack pipe. He looked Tache' up and down, "Ooo yeah, Tache'! You be lookin' good enough to eat! Yo! Get over here mama!"

Tache' reluctantly walked over to Tyrone and he firmly grabbed her crotch. He turned her around and then slapped her on the ass. "That's what I'm talkin' 'bout, go make daddy some money. Oh, and remember what I said, don't you be comin' back 'round here, or callin' me. I call you, when it be time to come home. I gots things I gots to do 'round here, and I don't want you in my way. I got lots a phone calls to make, tryin' to get mo' bu'ness for us. See I always lookin' out for my girl."

Tyrone handed Tache' a slip of paper. "Go to this corner they be lookin' for you. Oh fuck you smell good too, now get outa here girl, or you might not be leavin'!"

Tache' put on a brave smile, "I know you love me Tyrone. Bye honey, be careful not to smoke too much. I love you baby."

Tyrone took another defiant hit from his pipe, and then he turned his head from side to side, blowing smoke and filling the room with it. "Less talkin', more fuckin'!"

Tache' left the house and walked down the street with her

beautiful new shoes on. But, it had turned out to be more of a challenge than she had expected. It was very difficult for her to keep her balance. Every piece of gravel, or crack in the street twisted her ankle. She had to be especially careful, either that, or end up with a broken ankle.

"I'm sure glad that I don't have to run in these things!" she thought.

Tache' was happy that the street corner that Tyrone had picked, for her to meet the new clients, was close to the house.

When she arrived at her destination, there was a long stretch limo waiting for her there. As she approached, the chauffeur got out of the car, and opened the door for her.

Tache' didn't know what to expect, she braced herself and looked inside to find five Japanese businessmen dressed in fine suits. It was then that she realized that it was going to be a longer night than she had anticipated.

The men were very excited to see Tache'. She smiled kindly and then entered the car. Immediately, two of the wanton men grabbed her and pulled her down on the seat between them. One of them lifted her skirt, and then they all looked, to check out the merchandise that they were paying so much money for. All of them beamed with delight at what they saw, smiling and bowing their heads up and down in approval. Two of the men had invasively small cameras and began to take pictures from all angles.

"Let the freak show begin!" Tache' shouted, assuming that they didn't understand English. And even if they had, she wasn't concerned; it certainly wasn't going to slow them down!

The chauffer drove around the city for a while, and then stopped in a secluded area. The fancy-suited, perverted men, enjoyed their sick pleasures for hours, ravaging Tache' and taking pictures of every depraved act. When the Japanese businessmen were finished with their fun, they all smiled and bowed their heads again. The chauffer pulled up to the same corner where Tache' had been picked up. He stopped and walked around to open the door for her and then handed her a gold envelope.

"Thank you mister!" she said.

"You earned every cent of it," the chauffer said with a grin. "Hey babe, maybe the two of us could get together sometime? How do I get in touch with you?"

Tache' knew that Tyrone would be happy that she had drummed up some new business. "I'm usually on Fourth Street West, near May's Coffee Shop."

"Oh yeah, I know where that is. I'll see you around!"

"Not tonight though darlin', try me tomorrow night, okay?"

"You bet sexy!" the chauffer said greedily and then got back in the car.

Tache' was a good actor, she waved good-bye with a phony smile and then turned and painfully walked away. She stopped for a moment and took a peek in the envelope. She found that the Japanese business men had paid her much more than the usual take. Knowing that Tyrone would keep all of it, she pulled some out for herself and slipped it into her bra.

Tache' wanted nothing more than to go home. She had definitely put it "all out there" and she was emotionally drained and humiliated. Exhausted and sore, she anxiously pulled her phone from her purse, hoping that Tyrone had called, and that the appalling evening would come to an end. But she was disappointed when she found that he hadn't. She couldn't continue to work in the shoes that she was wearing; they were so uncomfortable that she could barely stand in them. She had to change her shoes if she was to go on, and decided to risk Tyrone's wrath and go home. She only hoped that she could sneak in without being noticed.

Tache' headed for home and had a difficult time even walking the short distance to the house. She decided to go in the backdoor, thinking that it was her best chance to avoid Tyrone. When she arrived, she pressed her ear up against the door, trying to hear if he was nearby. She didn't hear anything and it seemed that the coast was clear. She put her key in the lock as quietly as she could and then slowly turned it, holding her breath as she opened the door. When she stepped inside the house, Tyrone wasn't there and she breathed a sigh of relief. "Oh good, now I'll just sneak in and change my shoes."

Tache' had to pass by the kitchen to get to her bedroom, and she was concerned. "Tyrone's probably in the kitchen, on the damn phone. There's no way that he's in his bedroom sleeping, like a normal person would be. He'll be up all night after smokin' that crack."

When Tache' got close to the kitchen, it was just as she had suspected, Tyrone was in there. But, he wasn't on the phone, and it sounded as though he was cooking! If Tyrone was cooking, Tache' knew that he was in a good mood. Cooking was Tyrone's favorite thing to do when he was feeling kind and generous. "Oh how I wish that I could stay home for the rest of the night," she thought. "With all of the money that I made, maybe Lil' T will let me."

Tache' summoned her courage and slowly opened the swinging door to the kitchen. She saw Tyrone standing at the sink. The roast, that she had bought, was on the cutting board and the garbage disposal was running.

Tache' was thrilled, "Oh Lil' T, that's why you didn't want me to come home. You planned to surprise me and make a special dinner. You're such a sweetheart!"

Tyrone was fixated on what he was doing, and with the garbage disposal running, he didn't hear Tache'.

Tache' was still hesitant, after all, she was disobeying orders, but knowing that Tyrone was in a good mood; she came up behind him, and looked over his shoulder. She was surprised to find that he was cutting the roast into small pieces. He had put one piece in the garbage disposal, but it was too large and part of it was sticking up out of the drain and spinning around in a circle.

"Damn it, I knew I should'a cut that up smaller! Dumb ass!" Tyrone yelled at himself.

78

"What's the matter Lil' T, did the roast go bad?"

The meat was still spinning around in the blades and Tache' reached to turn off the garbage disposal, "Here let me help you," she said. But, when the blades stopped turning, Tache' saw Qunitsha's tiny hand reaching out of the garbage disposal! Tache' quickly looked at what she had thought was the roast on the counter, and realized that it was Qunitsha's tiny body, chopped into pieces. Tyrone was holding a cleaver in his hand and blood was running into the sink.

Tache' was in shock and she slowly backed away from Tyrone. "How could you do this?! Tyrone, how could you do this to my baby girl?! She was your child!!" Tears streamed down Tache's face. Grief and fear struck her to the core of her very soul.

Tyrone turned toward Tache', his eyes blazing with murderous insanity. "What the hell are you doin' here? You ain't pos to be here bitch! I told you to wait 'til I called you, din't I? You gots to understand, I had to do this Tache', she was causin' way too much trouble! She in the way, costin'me too much money yo! I...I wasn't likin' the way you be ignorin' me when Qunitsha be 'round. You too wrapped up wit' this baby, it ain't healthy. Don't you see? I hada do it. I had no choice!"

Tache' kept backing away from Tyrone. She was in utter disbelief and struggling to get her mind back into focus.

"This here was me getting rid of the ev'dence. I had it all fig're' out ... yo. I was gonna tell you, and the rest a da ho's that someone stole Qunitsha, right out da cage. But, you hada come home, di'nt you? You hada come home right in the middle a my work ... di'nt you? I told you not to come home Tache', now you seen all this!"

Tyrone was standing by the sink facing Tache'. He held up the cleaver, dripping with the blood of the innocent baby. "You a good money makin' ho, but now I gotsta fuckin' kill you too!!"

Tyrone lunged at Tache' and slashed at her with the razor-sharp cleaver! She jumped back, the blade barely missing her. Tache' burst through the kitchen door; it swung back hard behind her and hit Tyrone. He stumbled, but quickly ran after her in a murderous, drug-crazed rage.

Tache' got out of the house and sprinted down the street, screaming at the top of her lungs. Her long hair flying; and her platform shoes wobbling back and forth as she struggled to keep her balance. But even so, she was still outrunning Tyrone!

Tache' took a short cut down the alley, toward May's Coffee Shop. She was hoping to get help there, but she tripped and fell to the ground! Tache' tried to get up, but Tyrone was right behind her and he jumped on top of her, holding the bloody cleaver! "I'm gonna' cut you fuckin' head off bitch!!" he screamed, and then swung the cleaver back and aimed it at Tache's neck!

Tache' grabbed Tyrone's arm, trying to stop him, but when she saw the blood of her precious Qunitsha on the blade of the cleaver, she was weakened by deep sorrow. "My baby! My baby! Why Tyrone? Why? Why?"

The pain in her heart was too great for her to overcome and Tache' couldn't fight. She gave up and with the last breath that she had in her, she screamed for the only help she knew, "Lord Jesus, help me!"

At that second, a bright light burst into the alley! Tyrone froze and he and Tache' looked into the light.

Tyrone got to his feet, he pulled Tache' up and held her in front of him, with the cleaver to her neck. "This has now become a hostage sit'ation!" he screamed.

Then from the light, a strange creature appeared and moved in their direction. When it got closer, they could see that the mysterious figure had two heads!

Tyrone and Tache' watched fearfully as the two-headed monster came closer. "Who you be?! Who you be?" Tyrone shouted, but there was no answer.

The two-headed monster approached quickly. When it got close, Tyrone screamed in terror, he shoved Tache' into its clutches, and she fell to the ground before it. When Tyrone pushed Tache', he was thrown off balance and scrambled as he tried to flee from the fearsome creature.

Suddenly, a strong voice commanded, "DEREK TAKE HIM DOWN!" This wasn't a two headed monster that they had encountered; it was Joyce, with Derek riding on her shoulder! Immediately, Derek threw back his head and let out a tremendous war cry! He leapt through the air and landed viciously on Tyrone's head! Derek clawed at Tyrone's eyes with his back feet and then he swung around to the back of Tyrone's neck and bit down hard on a precise spot on his spinal cord. Instantly, Tyrone was paralyzed and fell to the pavement, still as a stone.

Tache' was on the ground, screaming in fear of Derek, "A rat! A rat!"

Joyce knelt down near her and said in a reassuring tone, "You're safe now Tache. This is Joyce, do you remember me? We talked at May's Coffee Shop."

Tache' took a few minutes to respond, but then gained a bit of her composure, "Yes Joyce, I remember you, but please, keep that rat away from me! Don't let him hurt me!"

"I'm sorry that we scared you Tache', but that *rat* just saved your life. His name is Derek, and he won't harm you."

"Tache' looked at the fearsome pimp, Tyrone, lying motionless on the ground, and then at the rat who had put him there. "Are you sure?" she asked.

"Yes Tache', I promise, Derek will never hurt you."

Derek left Tyrone lying helplessly on the ground and came running back to Joyce. Tache' gasped as he jumped onto Joyce's shoulder and then began to clean himself.

It didn't seem that Derek was interested in attacking her and Tache' relaxed a bit. But now, she wondered about Tyrone. "Is Tyrone dead?"

"No, just paralyzed, but we need to get him out of here, before we're discovered. I'll back the car up and we can put him in the hatchback. If you grab his arms, and I grab his legs we should be able to lift him."

Joyce got in the car, turned it around and then backed it

81

into in the alley. When she got out to open the back of the car, Tache' already had Tyrone slung over her shoulder. She threw him in and stood looking at Joyce for further direction. "Well, we'll attribute that to your military training," Joyce said, and then she covered Tyrone with the sleeping bag. "Get in the car, Tache', let's get out of here! Derek, load up!"

THE NEXT VICTIM?

The three of them got in the car and Joyce pulled away. Even though she felt like racing as fast as she could, she was careful to drive the speed limit and not risk getting pulled over by the police. The police were the last people that she wanted to see that night!

Tache' was still in shock, and not sure about what had actually happened. She was crying and struggling to cope. "Tyrone how could you?! How could you?!" Then she paused and was quiet for a moment. She looked at Joyce, with tears streaming down her cheeks, and asked, "Did I kill Tyrone?"

"No Tache' you didn't kill him, Tyrone's not dead. Everything's going to be alright."

"Nothing will ever be alright Joyce!" Tache' said. And then she cried from the depths of her broken heart.

Joyce was driving the car and she couldn't stop to help her, so she looked to Derek. "Derek comfort," she commanded.

With that, Derek moved over and sat on Tache's lap. Tache' was stiff, still scared of Derek. But when Derek gently touched her hand and stared lovingly into her tearful eyes, she was able to calm down a bit.

"Derek is special," Joyce said to Tache'.

"Yes he is, I'm not afraid of him anymore. I feel like I can trust him."

"Yes, you can trust Derek. Now, let me tell you what's going on with Tyrone. First of all, he's not dead. Derek is trained in combat and he used a special technique. He bit Tyrone in a precise spot on the spinal cord that causes temporary paralyses. We have forty-five minutes, give or take, until Tyrone is conscious again. We haven't time to spare!"

Joyce, Tache' and Derek rode on in the old hatchback. It seemed as though they would never reach their destination as they were stopped at one traffic light, after another.

Tache' was extremely nervous, even though Tyrone was covered with the sleeping bag, she still thought that someone would discover him. But most of all, she was terrified that Tyrone would wake up and kill them all!

On the other hand, Joyce was calm, keeping her mind focused on the task at hand … getting Tyrone to the laboratory in time.

Tache' continued to struggle to keep her composure, but suddenly she couldn't contain herself and she exploded with built up emotions from the horrors that had transpired that night. "Joyce, I have to tell you, oh my God! Tyrone killed my baby, Qunitsha! I went in the kitchen and I saw him! He chopped her into little pieces and was putting her down the garbage disposal!" Tache' threw her head back and clenched her chest, "Oh Lord, help me to get through this! Oh the pain that baby must have gone through! What incredible pain! And I wasn't there to stop it! Why did I leave Quinilsha with that pig of a man?! It's all my fault, I believed him when he said that Shawna was coming home to take care of her! Why did I believe him?! Why couldn't it have been me that Tyrone killed?!" Tache, heaved forward and grabbed her stomach, "Joyce, why did you save me?" she grunted, "You should have let him kill me!"

Joyce was shocked to find out just how vile Tyrone really was. She began to have trouble coping herself as the image of the dismembered infant tore at her emotions. Her heart went out to Tache' and she tried to comfort her the best she could. "You're a wonderful person Tache'," she said kindly, "and you don't deserve such pain. None of this was your fault." She gently held Tache's arm, to get her attention, "Look at me Tache', and listen. None of this is your fault! Tyrone's is a sick form of life that needs to be corrected. It's not your fault! You need to say it Tache'. It's not my fault."

Tache' looked at Joyce and tearfully repeated what she had said to her, "It's not my fault."

"That's right Tache', it's not your fault and never forget that. It was quite fortunate that Derek and I happened by. We were on our way home, from the country, when I saw you run into the alley with a man chasing you with a cleaver. We knew that we must intervene. We were there, at the right place, at the right time. Someone was certainly watching out for you tonight. You're safe now, but it will take time for your brain to recover from such an incident. This was a very traumatic event. I'll give you medication to calm your nervous system when we get to the lab."

"The lab? What lab?" questioned Tache'.

"My laboratory, that's where we're going. Just try to hold it together, I'll take care of everything."

Tache' tried, but she couldn't stop herself from crying. It was a heart rendering cry, one of pain and despair.

"Derek," Joyce said disgusted, "you know that I can't stop the car and help her! Why are you just sitting there? Do something!"

Derek, pulled a tissue from the box and handed it to Tache' then he sat in her lap while she wiped her face. Derek rubbed his cheek gently against Tache's arm and then she stroked his luxurious coat while he looked sweetly into her eyes. It was a though Derek had magical powers that pierced through her pain, and Tache' was comforted. She continued to feel better as they rode on together to face the next challenge. Tache' didn't know what awaited her, but she knew, that whatever it was, it would be easier with Derek by her side.

The stressful drive finally came to an end and Joyce breathed a sigh of relief. She pulled the car into the back alley of the lab and backed up to the loading dock. Joyce

84

got out of the car and quickly ran up the ramp, to the big sliding door, and placed her thumb on the lock pad for identification. The door had slowly started to open when Joyce saw headlights coming down the alleyway toward her.

Tache' opened her window and called out, "Joyce, you expectin' anyone?"

"Oh God no!" Joyce said with alarm. "It's the cops! Tache', recline back in the seat, so they don't see you!"

Tache's eyes became large and full of fear, "They're comin' for me! They're coming for me!"

"Shhhh... I don't think so, be calm Tache' just be quiet and try to stay calm."

The police car pulled up, and stopped near Joyce. The driver's side window slid down and Joyce was relieved to see that they were the same officers that had been there earlier that day with Bill, Brian's brother.

The officer on the passenger side, reached in front of the driver, pushing him back in the seat. He called out to Joyce, "Hello Dr. Picard, we were in the neighborhood and thought we should check on you. Is everything okay? Bill Jones was still angry with his brother when we left and I was concerned. Was there any more trouble?"

Joyce nervously approached the squad car, while trying to block the view of her hatchback from the officers. "Oh no, no trouble here. Officer Brady ... isn't it?"

"Yes, Brady, but you can call me George."

"And I'm Officer Sloan, in case anyone's interested," Officer Brady's partner said with a sneer as Officer Brady continued to push him out of the way.

"Hello Officer Sloan it's nice to see you again," Joyce said in a friendly tone, while trying to keep her composure. "Yes, Bill Jones was angry at his brother, that's for sure! But, the whole situation was a simple misunderstanding, on Bill's part. You know brothers, they're fighting one minute, then going to see a hockey game together the next!"

Joyce was so tense that she thought her brain would explode. "Please leave, please just leave! Hurry up and leave!" she thought to herself over and over.

But, Officer Brady was in no hurry to go anywhere, "You certainly do know a lot about men. Are you a hockey fan, Dr. Picard? Perhaps we could go to a game together sometime. I have an extra ticket for Tuesday's game; me being a bachelor and all."

Joyce couldn't believe her ears. Was Officer Brady actually asking her out on a date? All she wanted to do was to get rid of him, "To tell you the truth, I've never researched the game."

"Yes, it may be too violent for a lovely flower, like you."

Joyce tried to keep the conversation friendly, "Well I might surprise you. After all, I am a researcher!"

Officer Sloan rolled his eyes at the awkward flirtation, "Let's get going, we have to make our rounds."

"Just cool it, we don't have a call," Officer Brady said irritated. Then he looked at Joyce and held his business card out the window. "Here's my card, Dr. Picard, my cell number's on the back. If you ever need anything, don't hesitate to call. Maybe we can do some research *together* some time. There's a lot of things about the human body that I find fascinating," he said looking Joyce up and down. "You never know when duty calls!" he said with a wink.

"Will do Officer Brady," Joyce said. She was nearly in shock as men never gave her a second glance.

"Remember, it's George, just call me George."

"Okay George," Joyce managed to choke out, "thank you so much for checking on the lab. I guess you never know when something could happen in this boring old place!" Joyce waved good-bye, "Good night Officers!"

"Good night Dr. Hotty!" George said, and then finally, the police car drove away.

Joyce was relieved and angry at the same time, "I can't believe my luck, a man actually asks me on a date, for the first time in my life, and I'm concealing a hooker and a pimp in my car! Maybe it's their pheromones that George was sensing! It couldn't have possibly been me!"

86

Joyce quickly approached her car and she didn't see Tache'. "Tache'!" she called out frantically. Where are you?!

Tache' answered with a grunt, "Joyce, I'm in the back! Tyrone's awake! He's awake! Help!"

Joyce opened the hatchback just as fast as she could and there, under the sleeping bag was Tache' struggling with Tyrone. Tache' had him in a choke hold, with her legs locked around his body.

"I've been holding him down, the whole time you were talking to those cops! Don't know how much longer ... I ... can keep ... him down!"

Derek was trying to help Tache', holding onto Tyrone's afro with a death grip.

Joyce noticed Tyrone's eyes as he struggled. They appeared as though they were going to pop out of his head, at the sight of his fearsome foe, Derek.

"Hang on to him, just a little longer!" Joyce commanded. "Don't choke him out, I'm getting a sedative."

Joyce ran into the lab and frantically called for Stewart. Stewart responded immediately, "I'm here Joyce. What do you need?"

"A sedative, enough to knock someone out!"

Stewart had a dose with him in his lab coat, for just such an occasion. He was right behind Joyce when she rushed back to the car.

Joyce climbed in the back of the car to help hold Tyrone down. He was fighting and kicking wildly, but with Joyce, Tache' and Derek, working together, they were able to keep him down.

Stewart didn't ask any questions, he gave Tyrone the shot and he instantly went limp.

Tache' pushed Tyrone off of her; she rolled away from him and took a deep breath! "We did it!" she said. Then she pulled herself together and got out of the car. She stood up tall and approached Stewart. As she looked down at him she said in a breathy voice, "Hello, I'm Tache'."

Stewart gulped and stood there in awe at the sight of the

dark, erotic woman towering over him. He turned three shades of red as Tache' smiled, and then held out her hand to shake his.

"Stewart," he said shyly as he glanced up at her. Then he quickly looked down at the ground, pushing up his glasses. "Brown sugar, mmm hmmm," he said to himself.

"Okay, that's enough of the introductions," Joyce said. "Now let's get this man out of the car. Where's Derek? Derek!" Joyce called looking for him. But, she didn't have to look far; Derek had made a nice little nest for himself in Tyrone's afro.

"Derek you're so silly, now get out of there!"

They didn't waste any time and got Tyrone strapped to a gurney. Stewart took the lead and started pushing it into the Operating Room. Joyce hadn't told him that Tyrone was going to get a new brain, but somehow he knew.

Joyce headed for the Prep Room, to get ready for surgery, but realized that she needed to talk to Tache' first. Tache' had been through a harrowing ordeal and she didn't want to upset her further.

"Go ahead and get everything ready, I'll be back in a few minutes," she told Stewart and then she went to find Tache'.

Tache' was standing, just inside of the lab doorway with Derek on her shoulder, nuzzling her neck. She was stiff and confused, but smiled when she saw Joyce approaching. "Hi Joyce, I didn't want to be disrespectful and come inside, everything looks so sterile. What is this place?"

"It's my laboratory," Joyce explained, then she took Tache' gently by the hand and led her into the comfortable lobby. "Have a seat and relax, you're safe here and I'm going to make sure that Tyrone can't ever hurt anyone again."

"What are you planning to do to him Joyce? Are you going to kill him? I'd rather be dead than go to prison again and I don't want anyone else to get into trouble either, least of all you. Let's just turn him over to the police."

"You don't understand honey, I'm not going to kill Tyrone, I'm going to fix him. It's my life's work, the Living Artificial

Brain. A brain transplant will cure his murderous mind."

"He does need a new brain," Tache' said nodding her head in agreement. "It's the crack, it's destroyed his brain. Why one time, I even said that he needed a new brain, but how could I ever know that he could actually get one."

Joyce was surprised that Tache' had believed her so easily, as it even sounded crazy to her as she was saying it. But it was true, and Joyce was anxious to get started. "I hate to leave you at a time like this, Tache'," Joyce apologized. "I know that you're devastated over Qunitsha, but I have no choice, I have to get Tyrone into surgery right away."

"I understand Joyce, the surgery is very important. You go on ahead and don't worry about me, I'll be fine.

"Will you wait for me, while I'm in surgery? I have some other things that I'd like to discuss with you."

"You and Derek saved my life, if there's anything that I can do for you, you just let me know."

"We'll talk more later, and in the meantime, you make yourself at home. The refrigerator's fully stocked, and you and Derek help yourself to anything you want. Derek and I have spent many nights here at the laboratory, it's actually quite homey once you get used to it. The couch is very comfortable."

With that, Joyce started to leave the room and looked back at Derek, "Now Derek, you take care of Tache' while I'm gone." Derek nodded in reply.

Joyce went to prepare for her second brain transplant. This time, it was what she had been working for. She would be transplanting the brain of a sadistic murderer, a man who had butchered his infant daughter and destroyed the lives of many beautiful young women. Joyce was happy to get Tyrone off the streets and stop his reign of terror.

She carefully scrubbed up and then entered the Operating Room. Stewart had everything ready to go and was waiting patiently for her arrival. Joyce looked at Tyrone and suddenly had a rush of excitement. At that moment she realized that her dream was finally coming true. No more testing, no more questions. Brian was under her control, and it was time to get down to business and save the world!

Joyce carefully cut into Tyrone's head; she opened it up and began to disconnect his nerves and blood vessels. She was more confident this time, she felt sure and steady, working to achieve her lifetime goal.

When Joyce removed Tyrone's brain, Stewart was ready with brain number one. It was a brain with limited programming, equipped with only the basics of human functions. As Stewart moved the artificial brain closer, once again the clinging tendrils reached out, searching for a living subject to attach to. And then, just like before, Tyrone's nerves and blood vessels were attracted to the artificial brain, and were quickly fused. Joyce completed the surgery much faster this time and then Stewart closed.

The surgery was complete, everything went smoothly and the brain was functioning perfectly. But knowing the mistakes that they had made with Brian, they left Tyrone on life support to give the brain and body the adjustment period necessary for them to adapt.

Joyce walked out of the O.R. feeling powerful. She took a hot shower and then headed down the hallway to talk to Tache'. She entered the lobby and found her and Derek eating little mini pizzas. "I see that Derek talked you into the mini pizzas."

"Oh yes, there was just no dealing with him, he had to have the little pizzas. I might be going crazy, but I think that Derek's psychic or something. He understands everything, and I even know what he wants."

"Yes I know, Derek has no difficulty getting his point across. And you're not going crazy, he does understand. You see Derek receives a special formula, that I made just for him. He's what I call a super being. He has increased brain power and strength, and his life has been extended to that of a human. "

"Yes, he definitely is super, I've seen what he can do. All I have to say, is that I'm glad he's on my side! Then Tache' got a serious look on her face and asked about Tyrone. "How's Tyrone? Did the surgery go well? Did he survive?"

"Yes the surgery went just fine and Tyrone's resting. But, that's not what I wanted to talk to you about. I'm concerned about you Tache', you've just suffered an attempt on your life and witnessed the horrific death of baby Qunitsha. I want you to know that I'm here for you when you're ready to talk about it."

"I'll never be ready to talk about Qunitsha, never again. And I'd appreciate it if you never mention her name. It's not that I'm a cold person, but it's just my way of coping. It's the only way that I can keep on living."

Joyce was overwhelmed with compassion and she sat next to Tache' and tenderly rubbed her back. "There's no way that I could ever think that you're a cold person," she said. "In fact, quite the opposite, I think that you're the kindest person that I've ever met."

Joyce found herself wanting to care for Tache', to be her friend and to see her every day. She wasn't sure how Tache' would feel about her plans for Tyrone, so she asked her. "Would it upset you if I programmed Tyrone to be nothing more than a drone?"

"What do you mean, drone?"

"He wouldn't be capable of independent thought or action, and be of service here at the lab."

"Of course not, you do whatever you want to, I don't care what happens to him. And if he can be of some help to you with your research, that would be a good thing. Tyrone destroyed everything he touched, and him doing something good, why would I have a problem with that? I don't need, Tyrone, I know the streets and I'll figure out a way to get by without him."

Tache' got up and walked to the doorway, "Miss Joyce," she said, "you and Derek saved my life and I'm forever in your debt. But, if you don't need me anymore tonight, I better be on my way."

"What do you mean?" Joyce asked. "I just assumed that

you would be staying on here with the team."

"You mean that you want me to stay here?"

"Oh yes, most definitely, we could really use someone like you here at the lab. You're intelligent and strong and most of all, street smart, you know how to be discreet."

"Oh I definitely am discreet," Tache' said with a chuckle.

Joyce took Tache's answer as a yes, and before she could change her mind, she took her to the laundry room and picked out a pair of scrubs for her to wear. "They're not as fashionable as what you're used to wearing, but they'll be comfortable, just for tonight."

"Thank you Miss Joyce, you won't be sorry. I'll work hard and be the best thing that ever happened to this place!"

"You already are," Joyce said. "And as far as you working tomorrow, I'd rather that you took a few weeks off and rested, with full pay, of course."

"Oh no, that's the last thing that I want to do is rest. Work is the best therapy for me."

"Okay, if that's the way you want it," Joyce agreed, "you can start work tomorrow. I'm going to get Derek home now and I'll see you in the morning."

"I'll be here, bright and chipper and ready to work."

Joyce smiled and walked out with Derek riding on her shoulder. He looked back at Tache' and she swore that he threw her a kiss.

PERPLEXING PANDEMONIUM

The next day, Joyce awoke excited and happy, looking forward to spending the day with her new friend Tache'. She quickly got ready to go and zoomed to the lab. When she walked inside the lobby, she could hardly believe her eyes. Tyrone was sitting on the couch between Stewart and Tache', and Brian was serving coffee and donuts.

Tache' and Stewart were adamantly discussing what color lipstick looked best on her, and didn't notice Joyce standing in the doorway. But, Brian did, "Well there's the boss!" he said cheerfully. "How are you doing today, Dr. Picard?" and then he handed Joyce a cup of hot coffee.

"Yes, good morning boss," Tache' said, as Brian refilled her coffee cup. "Brian's great," she told Joyce, "he won't stop waiting on us. Sit down now Brian, you're doing too much."

But, Brian didn't listen and kept right on working. After everyone's coffee cup was full, he began to dust the furniture.

"Brian, this is Dr. Stewart Whitehead, sit down," Stewart commanded and immediately Brian sat down. "See I told you, Tache', he does what I tell him."

Joyce didn't ask why Tyrone was awake, and sitting on the couch. For the moment, she was content just to be an observer when Stewart and Tache' quickly went on with their lipstick conversation.

"Brian likes the red lipstick, Stewart," Tache' explained.

But, Stewart strongly objected, "If you wear the red lipstick, you'll have to change to red nail polish. You already have on orange polish, so therefore you need orange lipstick."

"When your right your right Stewart, I can't argue with that logic," Tache' agreed, and then she started applying the orange lipstick.

Finally, Joyce decided to break into the conversation, "Stewart, what's going on with Tyrone? We didn't expect him to be able to come off life support for several days?"

"I don't know Joyce; all I can offer are theories. It may be contributed to the drugs he was on. Or perhaps Tyrone recovered more quickly than Brian, because he wasn't traumatized by taking him off of the life support too soon."

"Perhaps you're right Stewart; flat-lining would be a shock to one's system. Or it could be that the primitive artificial brain doesn't take as long for the body to adapt to. "

"Tache' interrupted, "I love it that he can't talk," she said. "Tyrone all docile and everything. I hate to say it, but I even slapped him across the face and he just looked straight ahead! Straight ahead! Can you believe it? I'm not a

93

violent person, but I couldn't help myself."

"I certainly can't blame you," Joyce said, "he deserved it."

Joyce was happy to see that Tache' was feeling better and that she seemed to be enjoying herself with Brian and Stewart. But, it was time to take care of business. "Stewart, would you start preparing a robot program, on brain assembly procedure? I need to talk to Tache' for a few minutes and I'll check with you later."

"Right away Joyce," Stewart said, and then got up and went to the Computer Room and got to work.

Joyce asked Tache' to come into another room, where they could talk in private. "Seems that you're feeling better today Tache'."

"Oh yes, I'm being very well taken care of. Stewart's a doll, and he gave me the low down on what's going on here and I think it's great! He told me how Brian used to be, and now with his artificial brain ... he's completely different. What a genius you are Joyce, you have the answer to the world's problems."

"I'm glad you're onboard," Joyce said. She paused for a moment and then asked, "Any second thoughts about Tyrone?"

"You kidding? That creep is gonna be forced to do some good, for once in his life, and I think it's great!"

"I'm happy to hear that, I must admit that I was a little concerned that you may have a problem making a complete break from him. Pimps brainwash and control their victims, and sometimes the girls find it very difficult to function without them."

"No way, I'm happy to be off the streets!"

"Will Tyrone be missed by anyone? Does he have any family or friends that we may need to deal with?"

"There's not another living soul who will be crying for Tyrone. He doesn't have any friends and everyone in his family is either dead, or he's dead to them."

"That's good, no complications."

"Now about my new job ..." Tache' interrupted. "Anything

94

you need, you just say the word! I'm ready to get started. What's the first thing on the agenda for today? Would you like me to do the laundry and mop the floors?"

"Oh no, you'll be my assistant. I plan on training you in surgical procedures and brain studies. You will be working in all scientific aspects here at the lab."

"I thought that Stewart was your assistant."

"Stewart is a scientist in his own right. We work together, but I want you to be by my side."

"Wow, assistant to a brain surgeon! I won't let you down!" Tache' promised.

"I'm sure you won't," Joyce agreed. "Now let's go have a talk with Brian."

"Okay," Tache' said, beaming with happiness, then she gave Joyce an enthusiastic hug. Joyce was startled, she hadn't been hugged by anyone for such a long time, that she had nearly forgotten how. But, she did her best, and embraced Tache' in an awkward hug.

Joyce and Tache' went back to the lobby where Brian was still sitting patiently. "Brian," Joyce said to him, "Tache' needs some new clothes. Would you like to take her shopping?"

"Of course, I'd love to. I'd love to take such a beautiful lady out on a shopping spree! Let's go Tache' we'll take my Mercedes!"

Tache' and Brian were leaving for their shopping trip and Joyce called out, "By the way Brian, while you're out, perhaps you might get your wife some nice jewelry? Tache' you can help him out with that, right?"

"Oh of course, something flashy but tasteful. Oh Brian, this is going to be fun!"

Brian waved good bye as he and Tache' excitedly walked toward the door together.

Brian had signed all of the necessary papers for Joyce to keep the lab running. She didn't need him for a while and decided to get rid of him. "And Brian, when you get back, take some time off to spend with Peggy," she shouted.

"Great idea Joyce, I love spending time with my beautiful

wife."

Once Brian and Tache' were gone, Joyce called Stewart back into the lobby, with Tyrone, to fill her in on his progress. Stewart I hate to interrupt you, but you're the one who's been monitoring him. How's Tyrone doing? Is he able to complete all bodily functions efficiently?

"No problems, all of the basic necessities are working properly, with brain number" ... before Stewart could finish answering Joyce, he was interrupted when the phone rang. He answered it, "Dr. Whitehead speaking." ... "Yes, I will be performing the execution on prisoner number J2517 myself." ... "Yes Daniel Lugar Harris" ... "Okay, good-bye Warden." Stewart hung up the phone and looked at Joyce, "By the way, what do you plan to do with Dan after the brain transplant?"

"Dan wants to keep all of his memories; he only wants us to remove the evil part of his personality." Joyce paused thoughtfully and then went on, "Obviously, we'll have to alter the way he looks and of course, give him a new identity. Because of his extremely violent past, we will do extensive testing and observe him for a sufficient length of time. Once we're certain that he's incapable of violence, we'll see how he functions in society."

"Changing Dan's looks would be a good thing according to Brian. Brian thinks that Dan's ugly, but I don't think that he looks that bad, a little rugged perhaps. But, he does scare me," Stewart admitted.

"Good, he can be my bodyguard then, just in case you get any notion of turning on me!" Joyce said laughing.

"Oh yes, I'm so threatening ... snort, snort."

Now Joyce turned the conversation to Tyrone, "Stewart, you're probably wondering why I asked you to begin constructing a robot program on brain assembly procedure. I believe that Tyrone can be programmed in brain assembly. Assembling the Living Artificial Brain is very tedious and time consuming. And as our subjects increase, we could use an extra pair of hands. We can dedicate him exclusively to brain production."

"Making a mindless drone out of him does sound appropriate. It would greatly increase brain production. But what about Tache' does she care what happens to him? Wasn't he a friend of hers of something?"

"No, I don't believe she cares. Pimps do have a very strong physiological hold on their prostitutes, but I don't think that it applies in this case."

Stewart was shocked, "Tache's a prostitute?"

"Yes, she was a prostitute. I guess you wouldn't know that. I didn't tell you."

"Tyrone is a pimp?"

"Yes, a pimp and a murderer."

"I wonder if Tache', actually being a man, has something to do with her ability to sufficiently control her feelings and make the break from Tyrone. It's been proven that testosterone does make one less sensitive. Or perhaps it can be attributed to her turbulent background."

"Tache's a man?"

"Yes, she was born male and became a woman in prison. The male of the species tend to fight more frequently and be more aggressive than the female. It was her way of surviving the violent prison life."

"It's not fair to make such a wide generalization about men Joyce, I've never been in a fight, and I'm a man."

"I'm sure you haven't Stewart," Joyce said with a grin.

Tyrone had been sitting still and silent while Joyce and Stewart spoke, but suddenly he rose to his feet. Joyce gasped and looked fearfully at Stewart.

"Oh, don't worry Joyce," Stewart said, "he's just going to the lavatory. That's funny that you got scared of him ... ha ha!"

"Maybe it is funny Stewart, but even though he's nothing more than a walking corpse, somehow he still seems dangerous." Joyce quickly regained her composure, "Well enough chit chat. How long before the robot program on brain assembly procedure is ready?"

"It's reasonably easy for me to convert. I should be done shortly."

"Let me know when you're ready Stewart, I'm going to take a few minutes for myself.

Stewart agreed, and then headed back to the Computer Room.

Joyce was experiencing success for the first time in her life and she was elated. She walked joyfully around her laboratory, in amazement gazing at the slender vials of chemicals and admiring the colors. She even found the sterile smells intoxicating. Then, she wandered into Brian's office and sat down in the chair behind his desk. She rubbed her hands on the arms of the chair, feeling the fine soft leather.

She reached into the desk drawer and got out the bottle of scotch and poured herself a glass. She spotted some cigars in the top drawer, lit one up and then put her feet up on top of the desk.

"So, this is what it's like to be a big shot," she said out loud. "I have what I want now, and no one can stand in my way! I cannot be defeated! I have the power, and I'm going to change the world ... *ME!!!*"

Joyce was sitting in the luxurious office, reveling in her glory, when the door suddenly flew open and someone shouted at her. "What's going on here?!" It was Jody, one of Brian's girlfriends.

Joyce was startled and she jumped, but managed to pull herself together. "What do you mean, what's going on here? What's always going on here ... work."

"It doesn't look like you're getting any work done to me!" Jody snapped back.

"How do you know what I'm doing Jody? You're not privy to any information about this laboratory."

"Well I do know one thing, and that is that you're not supposed to be in Brian's office! I'm going to tell him what you're doing in here, drinking his scotch and smoking his cigars. You've got a lot of nerve! As a matter of fact, I bought those cigars for Brian on his birthday this year!"

"Oh you did? Very nice choice."

"Where's Brian, smartass?"

"You might as well leave, he went shopping and he won't be back for hours. I'll tell him that you came by."

"I'm not going anywhere, I need to see him and I'm going to sit right here until he gets back."

"I wouldn't advise it," Joyce said, "but it's your choice."

Joyce got up and left Jody in the office, wondering how the hell she had gotten into the building. She checked the main door, and found a lipstick on the floor, stuck in the door jam. "Tache' must have dropped this in her excitement to leave. I'll have to have a talk with her, I can't let this happen again. We can't have breaches in security." Joyce closed the big steel door shut. "Now nobody can get in without notice, and Jody can't get out."

Suddenly, Stewart's voice blasted over the intercom, trying to sound like a D.J. "This is Slewing Stu coming at you from Computer Room A – across from the O.R. First on the hit parade, will be Tyrone the pimp, with his new number – I'm Ready for Implantation. Cha, cha, cha, boom, cha boom, cha, boom, boom! Joyce ... Joyce are you there?"

"Well, this couldn't get any worse," Joyce whispered and then answered the annoying Stewart, "Okay Stewart, I'm coming, you don't have to announce it to the whole neighborhood."

"What neighborhood? We're at the edge of the woods."

"Never mind."

Joyce went into the Computer Room with Stewart, making sure that the door locked securely behind her. Stewart had Tyrone sitting in an office chair beside him, patiently waiting.

"Stewart, let me see what you have so far," Joyce asked.

"The program is complete; Tyrone will have all the skills needed to be our brain assembly robot."

Joyce checked the programming, and then Stewart began to implant Tyrone with a new virtual tool created by Joyce.

"I may need help with this Joyce; I'm not as familiar with it …. Never mind … there, I got it. Do you want him to do anything else besides assemble brains?"

"No, nothing, we need him to be focused."

"Oaky doky."

Then, there was a rap on the door, and someone shouted, "Is anybody in there?"

Stewart jumped out of his skin, as far as he knew, he and Joyce were alone in the laboratory.

"Don't get rattled Stewart, it's just Jody."

"Jody, Brian's girlfriend? How in the world did she get in here? Security breach!! Security breach!!"

"I know Stewart, the door was left ajar with a lipstick."

"Tache's?"

"Yes, she must have dropped it in her haste. Hold tight, I'll try and get rid of Jody."

Joyce got up and opened the door a crack with Stewart standing near, trying to sneak a look at Jody.

"Yes Jody, what is it?" Joyce asked.

"I don't know how long I'll have to wait for Brian, he won't answer my phone calls. Is he with someone else?"

"Yes Jody, as a matter of fact he is, a very glamorous ebony woman."

"I knew it, I knew it! Why can't Brian be faithful to me?"

"How can *you* expect someone to be faithful to *you*, when he is cheating on his wife with *you*?" Joyce said disgusted.

Jody didn't respond to what Joyce had said, she just became more and more angry. "I'm going to scratch that bitches eyes out!"

"I'd pay to see that, Stewart snickered, snort, snort."

"I've just got to see Brian, and tell him that we can still make it work. Oh why do these things always happen to me?" Jody said with her voice screeching.

Joyce just shook her head in amazement at the ranting of the immoral woman.

"I don't even know why I'm wasting my time talking to you, you idiot!" Jody said sharply. "I'm waiting in Brian's office and

100

you better not come in there! Then she turned and marched back to Brian's office.

"If anyone needs a brain transplant it's Jody," Joyce said to Stewart.

"I won't argue with you on that one Joyce ... snort. If she only knew how close she was to getting one, I don't think she would have come back here." Stewart was laughing, but then he hesitated for a moment and smiled nervously at Joyce, not quite sure if she was joking.

When Joyce didn't comment, Stewart went on, "I don't know why a stunning woman like Jody would waste her time on a married man."

"Stunning? Are you serious Stewart? More like slutty."

"Oh, I don't think so. What's so slutty about her?"

"Oh come on Stewart, don't be so naive; the bleached blonde hair and the giant breast implants .... and ...

"I never noticed that her breasts were artificial."

"She has a pretty face, but I'll bet Brian wasn't looking at her face when he met her."

"Joyce, do you think that Brian's good looking?"

"I don't like him, but he's good looking, according to everyone else."

"I guess he's handsome," Stewart said, "but looks aren't everything. How do I compare, I mean, looks wise, to Brian?"

"Don't worry about it Stewart, for a nerd you're a real stud."

"Snort ... well that's another story Joyce, snort, snort."

Stewart had gotten what he wanted, a complement from Joyce and then, the two of them completed the procedure on Tyrone.

The brain assembly skills were now implanted into Tyrone's brain. Joyce and Stewart took him into the Brain Assembly Room and he started working.

"Well, I'd say that Tyrone's brain transplant was a success!" Stewart boasted.

"Most definitely," Joyce agreed as they watched Tyrone assembling the artificial brains like a pro.

Now with the time consuming job of brain building taken

care of, Joyce and Stewart were free to pursue other things and they were both feeling good about their accomplishment.

Joyce took a deep breath, the lab was nice and quiet, for now. But, she was waiting for the shit to hit the fan, when Brian came back with Tache'.

"It's nice, just you and me together, isn't it Joyce?" Stewart said sweetly.

"Yes Stewart it is, enjoy it while you can."

"Well, technically we're not alone Tyrone is in the room with us, but he doesn't count, we are still alone."

"Yes, that mindless drone, Tyrone, is going to contribute something to society, whether he likes it or not," Joyce said firmly. "Now that we've got him working on the brain assembly, we'll need more supplies. I'm going to check our stock and place some orders. Why don't you go relax, stretch out for a while and take a nap or something, you've been working too hard."

"You're right Joyce, I was up all night monitoring Tyrone; I think I will take a nap. But don't hesitate to call me if you need me for anything."

"Don't worry Stewart, I won't need you. You go take it easy."

Stewart left the room thinking about Jody. He flushed with lust, as he thought about her ankles and painted toenails. He decided to go to the Observation Booth and spy on her. Stewart quickly zeroed in on Jody, in Brian's office, and found her standing and reading Brian's awards, hanging on the walls. "Oh there she is," he said panting, "oh, she looks good."

Stewart began to sweat as he zoomed up on Jody's ankles. "Yes ... yes, just keep standing right there."

When Jody moved, he adjusted the camera. "What I would give, just to rub myself on those ankles," he whispered under his breath.

Jody walked across the room and sat behind Brian's desk. This frustrated Stewart, frustration almost beyond his control.

"Gosh darn it Jody!" he shouted. "Well, it's all ruined now! Geez, would you just get up?!"

While Stewart struggled with his disappointment, he decided to switch security cameras. "What's going on in the back alley? Nothing. Switch to my office … nothing. Switch to my room, Hi Einstein. Switch to parking lot … Oh, Brian and Tache', are back … let the show begin!"

Stewart watched as Brian gathered packages full of beautiful things for Tache'. "That's a lot of packages," he said. "Mmmm hmmm, I'll bet there are some sexy short skirts in those bags, maybe even an ankle bracelet!"

"Hmm … what's Tache' doing?" Stewart wondered, and then he zoomed up on her bending over. "She must be getting something out of the back. Oh my, she certainly is reaching far, so far that I can totally see her panties! Snort, snort!"

Brian walked up the ramp to the lab door, "It's me, Brian, we're back!"

Brian's hands were full and Stewart got on the intercom and answered him, "Okay Brian I can see that your hands are full of packages, I'll let you in."

"And Stewart, wait for Tache', she may be a few more minutes."

Brian walked into the lab and Jody immediately spotted him. She ran down the hall to greet him and tried to give him a hug. But, Brian held the bags in front of him and pushed her back.

"Brian! I love you baby!" Jody yelled. But, Brian didn't respond much he just looked at her and smiled.

Jody became angry and she shouted at Brian, "Joyce told me that you were with someone else. Who is this bitch!"

"Yes it's true, I am with someone else. She's very special, her name is Tache' and she's not a bitch, she's a very fine lady. She'll be right in, she broke a nail and she's trying to find it."

Jody couldn't believe her ears and she became frantic. "Brian, we need to talk!" she sputtered, trying to fight back the tears.

"Okay," Brian calmly replied, "let me put these bags in the office and we can talk there. But, it can't take long, Tache' and I are going to have a fashion show!"

"What?" Jody said with her mouth hanging open.

"We are going to have a fashion show," Brian said louder.

"I'm not deaf and I know what a fashion show is Brian," Jody said looking closely into Brian's eyes. "What the fuck is wrong with you?"

"Nothing, I'm fine. How are you? I'm excited I got my wife a gift! Do you want to see it?"

"Your wife? You don't even like your wife."

"Oh, you're so wrong. How could you even say a thing like that? My lovely wife, Peggy, is my soul mate." Brian paused for a second, "Oh, I thought that I heard Tache'. I must have been wrong. I wonder what's keeping her? I wish she'd hurry, I'm anxious for the fashion show to begin. I can't wait to see her in all of the lovely sexy things that I bought for her. Nothing but the very best, everything imported from Paris; accept for the shoes, they're Italian. She's so gorgeous; this will definitely be a fabulous show!"

With that, Jody was seething with anger. She paced back and forth in the room, mumbling about how she was going to attack Tache' as soon as she entered the building.

Stewart was having fun spying on them, "This is Slewin' Stew, watching you. Now I'm a super spy," he snickered to himself.

Minutes later, Tache' found her fingernail and was standing at the lab door. "Oh hi Tache', come on in," Stewart happily greeted her, and then pushed the door release. "Let the fireworks begin!"

Tache' entered the building and came into Brian's office, holding up her fingernail, "I found it!" she said smiling.

"Oh that's great, Tache'!" Brian said with glee. "I knew you would! And let me introduce you to my friend Jody. Tache' this is Jody, Jody this is Tache'."

"Hi Jody nice to meet you," Tache' said in a friendly tone,

and then she reached out to shake Jody's hand. Tache's hands were big and even with the fancy manicure Jody could tell that these were the hands of a man. Jody then realized that Brian had been with a transvestite.

Tache' noticed Jody's hesitation to shake her hand and apologized, "Oh, you'll have to excuse my hands I need to put my nail back on."

Jody slowly looked up at Tache's tall muscular frame and realized that there would be no eye scratching. She relented and shook Tache's hand, while she looked at Brian with tears in her eyes. Jody knew that there was no competing this time and she ran out of the office.

"Oh my," Tache' said concerned, "I better go see what's wrong."

Tache' left the office with Brian following right behind her, "Don't worry about her Tache', let's just get on with the fashion show!"

Jody ran to the big steel, exit door, of the laboratory and tried to get out, but she found it locked. She was crying and turning the door knob, when Tache' approached and offered to help. "Brian, I don't have a security clearance to open the locks around here yet. Why don't you let Jody out?"

Brian acted as though Tache' hadn't said a word to him about opening the door. "Why don't you model this one first Tache'," he said holding a silk negligee.

"Brian open the door," Tache' said grabbing his hand and trying to press it against the security pad.

"But, Brian pulled his hand back, "Here, let me give you a better look at it, it's beautiful." Then he held up the negligee with both of his hands.

Realizing that it would be a wrestling match to try and force Brian's hand on the security pad. And that it was senseless to try and talk to him about anything but the fashion show, Tache' decided to look for Stewart. "Hold on a minute, Jody, I'll be right back with Stewart, he can open the door for you. Don't go nowhere now."

Brian started to follow Tache' and complain about the postponement of the fashion show. "Come on Tache' let's get the show started!"

"Brian we'll get the show started as soon as I unlock the door for Jody. Now you stay here and keep her company, I'll be right back."

Brian reluctantly stayed to wait with Jody. "Isn't Tache' great?!" he said with a big dopy smile on his face.

"Brian, what's happened to you?" Jody asked through her tears. "You're not acting like yourself. Are you on some kind of drug?"

"No, no drugs, I'm just high on love."

"You're in love with Tache'?"

"No, of course not! I'm a one woman man."

"Yes … and …?

"It's different with Tache', she makes me laugh. She's a lot of fun, as a matter of fact, were besties! Oh, and Jody, you said that you were in love with me, but let me make this clear, my wife is my only true love."

"You fucking dick!"

"Oh, this is getting good!" Stewart said and then snorted again.

"There's no need for profanity," Brian scolded.

"No need for profanity?! I think there's definitely a need for profanity!"

"Now Jody, all you need is a man that will treat you right. Stewart for example, he's intelligent and very caring. I think that he would make you an excellent husband! Just a minute, I think I can find him, Oh Stew…art."

"Now I know you've lost it!" Jody said disgusted. "How many times have we made fun of that nerdy weirdo, snorting and pushing up his glasses. Get real Brian, he looks like a lizard in a lab coat!"

"I remember of saying no such thing. I would never make fun of a fine man like Stewart!"

Stewart became angry that Jody was making fun of him, "That wasn't nice, that wasn't nice at all!" he said through clenched teeth.

"Let me refresh your memory you fuckin' idiot!" Jody screamed. Then she lost control, she pushed Brian and began to scratch and hit him.

"Stop! Help!" Brian screamed as he backed away.

Tache' heard Brian's calls for help and came running back down the hall. She saw Jody scratching and beating Brian and grabbed her from behind and restrained her. Brian took little notice of the situation, and upon seeing Tache' said, "Oh boy, time for the fashion show?"

"Not yet Brian, I need to handle this situation."

"No Tache', I'm tired of waiting, I want to see the fashion show, now!" Brian grabbed Tache' by the arm and pulled her toward his office. "Come on Tache', let's go!"

Jody took advantage of the situation and managed to break free. She ran down the hall, looking for another way out of the laboratory.

"Oh good she's gone," Brian said happily, "now we can have the fashion show!"

"Brian, you sure have a one track mind," Tache' said shaking her head.

"Let's get you set up for the fashion show in my office, then you can walk down the hall, like it's the runway."

"Okay Brian, why don't you go through the packages and put the outfits together, while I find Jody."

"Okay sounds good," Brian said happily, and he began to go through the packages and plan the fashion show.

Jody was running frantically through the laboratory, desperately trying to find someone to help her. She opened a door and found Tyrone busily at work. She seductively approached him to get what she wanted, like she always did from men. "Hello," she said sweetly, "would you mind helping me out?" When she got no response, she walked closer to Tyrone. He was busily assembling a brain and she gently touched his arm. "I'm trying to find an exit around here, do you mind showing a little girl the way out?"

Tyrone looked directly at Jody with blank eyes, "Brain

107

number six, point two five ... circuit complete." Then he looked back down at the slimy artificial brain and continued working.

Jody was afraid, "What the fucks going on here?"

"Brain number six point two six, circuit ... complete."

"What kind of a freak are you?!" Jody shouted. She looked around the room and saw human brains in specimen jars, on the shelves surrounding Tyrone. She stumbled and then fearfully ran out of the room.

Joyce was in the Stock Room next to the Brain Production Room. She heard the commotion and went to check, "Did you say something Tyrone?" she asked.

"Brain number six point two eight, circuit complete."

"Okay, good," she said to Tyrone. Everything looked fine, but she wondered why the door was open. "Talk to Stewart about doors," she noted on her pad, and then went back to work.

Jody was getting desperate, "Stewart! Stewart! Honey, where are you?" she called to him as she raced down the halls. "Are you in your bedroom? Better not let me in your bedroom, I might not want to come out."

Stewart was watching, "I don't like you anymore, Jody. You are ankle-less to me now."

Jody checked Stewart's bedroom and found that it was empty. "Where is that weirdo when you want him!" she shouted in frustration, stomping her feet.

"Jody, I'm not helping you, I'm not helping you, la, la, la, la, laaaaa," Stewart sang as he watched her every move.

Stewart saw Jody running toward the Observation Booth. He quickly stepped out and slyly stopped around the corner, where Jody ran, right into his arms.

"Oh Stewart, thank God you're here, finally my big strong man to the rescue!"

"No need to bring God into this Jody," Stewart said, as he tightened his grip on her. "And don't you mean, lizard in a lab coat?!" he grunted, and shot Jody in the neck with a hypodermic needle.

Jody went limp in Stewart's arms, and he calmly dragged her into his experiment room and strapped her on a gurney.

"Okay Jody, now let's put in your I. V." He smiled and whistled as he pierced the needle into Jody's hand.

Tache' was still looking for Stewart, so he could let Jody out of the lab. "Stewart, where are you boy?" he heard her call from the hallway.

Stewart quickly covered Jody with a sheet, and stepped out of the room, before she could see what he was doing. "Yes Tache'," he nervously answered, "What can I do ya for?"

"Have you seen a lady running around back here? Jody?"

"Yes, I did see Jody, and I let her out of the building."

"That's good, I'm glad to see her go. That bitch attacked Brian. She better not come back here again."

"Nothing to worry about Tache', I handled everything to perfection. She was one of Brian's girlfriends, you don't need to worry about ever seeing her again."

"Well, that's good," Tache' said in approval. She turned to walk away, and then paused and turned back around. "Hey, Brian and I are having a fashion show. Would you like to come?"

"Sure, I'd pay to see that!"

Tache' smiled at Stewart's enthusiasm, "No cover charge," she said. And then she noticed tubing, running to a draped figure, lying on the gurney and stepped into the room. "What ya working on Stewart?" she asked.

"I'm keeping a liver and some other organs hydrated, it's an experiment," he stammered.

"Yuck! Don't wanna see that!" Tache' said and backed out of the room. "Anyway, Brian and I will be waiting for you in his office."

"When's the fashion show?"

"Now, let's do it now, Brian's driving me crazy!"

"I'll be right there, I don't want to miss any of the show!"

Tache' left the room, and after Stewart made sure that Jody was sufficiently drugged, he followed close behind her.

The fashion show was about to begin and Brian and Stewart were chanting, Ta … che', Ta … che', Ta … che', as Tache' dressed for her first walk down the "runway." Finally, she burst out of the office, walking like a high fashion model. Up and down the hallway she went with Brian and Stewart vigorously applauding and cheering.

"You really bought Tache' some sexy clothes. Good job Brian," Stewart praised.

"Thanks Stewart, but I think that all of the credit goes to Tache' she can really rock a short skirt."

The two men laughed and whistled, and Brian turned up the music.

The fashion show was beginning to get out of hand, and when Joyce heard the commotion, she went to see what was going on. When she walked into the hallway, she found Brian wearing Tache's orange dress and strutting around like a chicken, to the beat of the loud annoying music.

Stewart was sitting down, he was cheering, clapping his hands and tapping his foot, but, as soon as he saw Joyce, he stood up. "Joyce, I think there's a problem with Brian's programming, he's been doing some outlandish things during the fashion show. I believe some fine tuning is in order."

"I believe your right," Joyce agreed.

Stewart and Joyce took Brian to the Computer Room to adjust his brain program. Stewart watched as Joyce pushed in the password assigned to Brian. "Oh that's right, I need to give you the password," Joyce said.

"I already know the password Joyce."

"Oh really, what is it then?"

"Derek, of course."

"Smartass."

Joyce used the special tool to make the adjustment, and when she was done, Brian got up and went back to his office. He took off the orange dress and put his suit back on. Joyce was happy that that Brian had transitioned so smoothly. "Well Brian, why don't you go home to your wife," she suggested. "Did you get her a gift?"

"Yes, and she's going to love it, it's just beautiful!" Brian answered enthusiastically. "Where's Tache'? She's got it in one of the packages."

Tache' went into the office, and came back with a gold ring. It had an enormous purple stone set in it and she flashed it under the light.

"I can't take credit for it," Brian said. "This was Tache's favorite; she's the one who picked it out,"

"That's a beautiful ring," Joyce agreed. "And why don't you go home now to your lovely wife."

"There's nothing that I would like better, thank you Joyce."

Brian calmly placed the ring back in the velvet box, said his good-byes and then, left for home.

"I had to correct his program a bit," Joyce explained to Tache'.

"Thank God you took out that over-the-top-personality! He was even making *me* uncomfortable!"

"Well, tomorrow is the big day," Joyce said," it's Dan's execution. Are you two fully prepared? Or do we need to review the plan again?"

Tache' and Stewart both confirmed that they were fully prepared for Dan's execution.

"Okay, I'll see you in the morning. And Stewart, be sure to shut Tyrone down for the night, I don't want him to overuse his muscles."

Joyce nodded goodbye and then headed for the back door. Tache' followed her, "Joyce, before you leave, I have something to say to you."

"Certainly, Tache', what is it?"

"I just wanted to tell you how grateful I am. Today was one of the best days of my life, and I owe it all to you." Tache' threw her arms around Joyce and held her close. "Thank you so much Joyce," she said, and then she looked deeply into Joyce's eyes, "I love you Joyce, I love you with all of my heart."

Joyce was a bit taken back, no one had told her that they loved her since her mother was alive. Tache' was tree to

111

express herself and Joyce envied that freedom. She wanted to tell Tache' that she loved her too, but she just couldn't get the words out. Joyce started tearing up and gently pulled away. "Good night, Tache', you're a sweetheart," she said and then quickly went out the door.

Tache' went into the lobby and found Stewart there, looking at one of the dresses that Brian had bought for her. "You didn't get the chance to model this one, Tache'."

Tache' laid down on the sofa. "I'm afraid that the fashion show is over for tonight Stewart. Maybe another time, I need some sleep, all this action is tiring."

"Tell me about it sister," Stewart said trying to be cool. "I'm going to hit the hay myself. I've got the execution tomorrow. Executions usually don't bother me, I just go in and do it, it's just a job. But tomorrow will be complicated."

Tache' wearily closed her eyes and Stewart whispered goodnight, and then left her alone. But as Tache' was falling to sleep, Stewart's night was just beginning........

STEWART'S REVENGE

Stewart started snorting with delight as he glided down the hallway to deal with Jody. He sailed into his experiment room, where he was holding her, and lifted the sheet to take a look. He stood over Jody, staring at her and scratching his head. "What to do? What to do? Shall I let you live or die Jody? Let's see here, ideas Stewart, ideas! I could make you my girlfriend. No ... you don't deserve me. I'm too good for you. Let's face it; I'm too much man for you, Jody. Will anyone miss you, family, friends? I doubt it. Where's your purse? Oh, there it is. Let's see here ... oh good, your cell phone ... contacts. A lot of men ... that want to get rid of you, I'm sure. Who have you been calling lately? Brian ... Brian ... Brian. Kind of boring isn't it Jody? No mother, no brother, no father ... interesting. Sister maybe? No, nothing but men, men, men. You are a loose woman, aren't you

112

Jody? Nice ankles, but your privates must be overused, to say the least. Your medication should be wearing off about now."

Stewart waited and it wasn't long before Jody started to come to. "I'll just grab my handy dandy duct tape, no worries," Stewart said and pulled a strip of tape from the roll.

Stewart taped Jody's mouth shut before she could utter a sound. Her eyes became huge with fear as she saw the needle in her hand and realized that she was restrained to a gurney.

"That's right Jody, be afraid, be very afraid. The lizard in a lab coat is in control now!"

Jody struggled, but couldn't break free. "I guess the new restraints that I installed are working perfectly. Wouldn't you agree, Jody? Admit that the restraints are working perfectly!"

Jody nodded her head, yes. She was completely terrified and realized that there was no charming her way out of this one. No come-hither smile, no flashing of leg, or bending over to reveal her cleavage. She was completely at the mercy of the angry lizard in a lab coat, and whatever he wanted to do to her!

Stewart checked Jody's phone one more time and then ran to see if Tache' was asleep. He peeked into the lobby, "Oh good, she's sound asleep … and snoring; snort, snort, Tache' snores."

Pleased that Tache' was asleep, Stewart went back into the room with Jody. He found her struggling to free herself from the restrains and trying to scream. Stewart stood over Jody and looked into her face, "It is futile to resist Jody, you aren't that strong. Let me think … should I let you live?"

Jody heard what Stewart had said and she vigorously nodded her head yes.

"Or, should I kill you?"

Jody turned her head back and forth and tried to scream … NO!

"Or maybe, a brain transplant?"

Jody was desperate, she didn't know what a brain

transplant was, but it sounded better than dying, so she nodded yes.

"I can't decide right now, but while I think about it, I'll take care of some office work. I don't use a paper shredder, I'm an old-fashioned kind of a guy. I like fire, there's something wonderful about it, it's all consuming, so purifying. Let's go into the Incineration Room together ... shall we Jody?"

Stewart wheeled Jody into the Incineration Room and placed her by the furnace. Just hold on now Jody, I'm going to have to leave for a minute, but don't worry, you won't be alone for long, I'll be right back.

Stewart went into the closet in Joyce's office and picked up a box of old papers that were marked for shredding. He peeked in on Tache' again, "Still snoring, isn't that wonderful that she sleeps so soundly. She looks like an angel lying there." Stewart took a moment, and he watched lovingly as Tache' slept. "Oh Tache', you're so much fun!" he said quietly, then he headed back to the incinerator carrying the heavy box. "Coast is clear! Tache's asleep ... snort, snort. Oh, gosh darn it, my glasses are slipping again." Stewart stopped, he put down the box of papers and pushed up his glasses. "Oaky doky, here I come Jody." Stewart picked up the box and raced down the hall. He entered the Incineration Room, and smiled fiendishly at Jody, "I'm baaaack, I hope that you didn't miss me too much."

Jody looked at Stewart and tried to smile with her eyes, she nodded her head as if she were happy that he had returned. Her heart was racing, she was shaking and perspiring heavily.

"Oh it looks like you're a little nervous, Jody," Stewart said sarcastically and then he pulled his handkerchief from his pocket and gently wiped her face. "Now you just be patient, I need to double check these documents before I destroy them. It doesn't happen very often, but once in a while Joyce misses something important and it ends up in the wrong pile." Stewart held up a paper, "Here's one, right here, this is a keeper. See what I'm saying Jody? As brilliant as Joyce is, she can be a ding head at times, thinking of other things besides paper work. Details are very important, and that's where I come in. I'm a detail man."

Stewart enjoyed watching Jody suffer in the fear and agony of wondering what he was going to do to her. He slowly and methodically went through every piece of paper in the large box. If the paper was to be incinerated he carefully placed it on top of Jody and secured it with a strap.

"Oh look at the time," Stewart said glancing at his watch. "I've got to finish up here and get some sleep. Got a big day tomorrow! Only two more documents to go. But, it seems like I'm missing something Jody. What could it be? Well, I guess I'll have to think about it while I'm burning papers. First, I'll take this small pile, down here by your feet." Stewart took the pile by Jody's feet, pulled it from under the strap, and tossed it into the furnace. There we go, watch it burn, yes ... yes. Thank you for helping me Jody."

"Next pile? Hmmm, the one here, on your chest." Stewart loosened the strap and picked up the pile of papers that he had placed on Jody's chest. He looked closely at her breasts. "Are those natural? Joyce says that they're artificial. Of course I wouldn't know that." Stewart looked away and then threw the pile of papers in the incinerator. "See how much more fun it is to burn papers than it is to shred them? Fun, and a real time saver too, in just a few minutes, the job is completed."

Slewart shut the incinerator door and thinking that his cruel game was over, Jody sighed in relief.

Stewart left Jody on the gurney and started to turn the furnace down. "It seems a shame that I can't remember the missing item." But then he paused, "Oh, I remember now! I didn't think that I could be losing it at my age. Thanks for reminding me Jody. I knew you were trying to tell me something."

Then Stewart opened the incinerator door, and without hesitation, he pushed Jody into the furnace. "Now it's full blast time!" he giggled as he turned the furnace on the highest setting. "Wait for it ... wait for it, okay!"

115

Flames blasted from the furnace and Stewart screeched with delight. He danced as jig as Jody's body burned into ashes. "Oh my gosh, I got a little over zealous. I hope I didn't wake Tache'."

Stewart closed the door to the Incineration Room and ran to see if he had awakened Tache' with his celebrating. He peeked in the room again and saw that she was sound asleep. "She's still snoring, the sound she makes is so cute. I wish that I could sleep like that."

Stewart glided back to the Incineration Room. He found that Jody had been thoroughly destroyed; burnt to a small pile of ashes. "Very good, fire is so thorough and complete. Now, I can get some sleep. Stewart shut everything down, knowing that all of the evidence had been destroyed.

DAN THE DEVIL'S EXECUTION?

The next day, Stewart was in a wonderful mood. After burning Jody to death, he had slept better than he had in months. He did his Tai Chi to center his mind, he had to be prepared; this was a day that he had been looking forward to, the day of Dan's execution.

Once Stewart was ready, he woke Tache'. "It's time to prepare for the heist," he told her. "Put on your driver's uniform, and hurry!"

"Okay, okay Stewart, I just need some coffee."

"Here, have a cola," Stewart said as he handed her a bottle. "It doesn't have to be prepared. It has caffeine, plus sugar to give you a lift. The formula is perfect for your activities today."

"Okay, Stewart," Tache' agreed. Then she opened the bottle of cola and quickly got ready.

A short time later, Joyce arrived at the lab. "Is everything ready Stewart?"

"Of course everything's ready, I'm Stewart. Any real questions ma'am?"

Before Joyce could think of another question, Tache' entered the room, wearing her driver's uniform. She had on the distinct cap with her curly hair fluffing out the sides. She had on full makeup, false eyelashes, thick eyeliner and shadow with bright red lipstick. Her large earrings sparkled as she moved her head.

Stewart looked at her surprised, "I don't remember that uniform having a mini skirt and high heels."

"I gotta be me baby."

"She looks great Stewart," Joyce said defensively. "And now that we're all ready to go, let's get on with the plan."

The three of them climbed into the science van and Tache' drove to the prison. They went through security and then dropped Stewart off at the entrance to the Death House. Joyce wanted to go in and help him, but she had never attended an execution before and she was concerned that her presence would arouse suspicion. So, she and Tache' waited nervously at the loading dock.

One of the Correctional Officers noticed Stewart walking down the hallway. "Hey guys," he said to his fellow officers, "he's here, that weirdo, Dr. Whitehead, the executioner. I swear he loves this stuff." Stewart was so gleeful, that he couldn't hide it, and after observing him, all of the officers agreed that he must enjoy the executions.

Stewart walked into The Execution Chamber, as he had done so many times before. There was a heaviness, and a pain in the room, that was nearly debilitating, but it didn't affect him.

Stewart went to the computer to make certain that everything was in order. "Yes, everything looks fine. Now I need the final paperwork. The papers please men ... chop, chop."

The orderly handed Stewart the final paperwork, approving the lethal injection. "Excuse me, but where are the documents for the organ donation? That's very important."

The orderly went to the office to check the file and Stewart was getting nervous. If the papers weren't available he wouldn't get the body. He wondered if the organ donation had been stopped for some reason. He waited, anxiously tapping his foot.

The orderly came back, a few minutes later, with the papers in hand, "Here they are sir, it was just in the wrong file."

"Oh, it was just in the wrong file, you say that as though it's not very important. Mistakes like this should not happen on my watch, men."

The mistake had noticeably thrown Stewart and he was beginning to sweat. "Let me get the chemicals ready. Give me some time to myself men, without any distractions ... Thank you."

The guards left the room as Stewart had requested. Noticing that he was uneasy, a guard commented, "Maybe we were wrong about weirdo, Dr. Whitehead, he might have feelings after all."

Stewart was alone, he knew the position of the surveillance cameras and avoided detection as he quickly switched the lethal drugs for the death mock formula that he had prepared. Stewart wasn't the one who would pronounce Dan dead. It was the prison doctor that would check his vitals and Stewart hoped that his formula would fool him.

"Oh geepers, I hope this works right," Stewart said to himself. "The doctor is just a doctor, he's no scientist, it should be easy to pull one over on him."

"It's ready now men," Stewart called to the officers. "And I will remind you that I have my science van, at the ready, to bring the body to the lab and extract the organs. We must hurry, it is vital that the body be fresh to preserve all organs and aspects of the human chemistry. No dilly dallying now!"

Stewart heard the warden announce, "We are bringing the prisoner into the execution chamber."

Dan entered the room, he looked at Stewart and then quickly glanced away. He knew that he had a chance to live, but that was all it was, a chance and nothing more.

A guard opened a curtain, and seated behind the glass barrier, were the victim's families, the usual officials and

118

approved members of the press.

Dan stood in front of the victim's families, and looked them in the eyes. They hated him and he didn't blame them. He thought about saying that he was sorry, but stopped himself. "It's easier for them this way," he reasoned. "Let them know what a monster I am. Soon it will be over, one way or another, and I will no longer want to kill."

The warden addressed Dan, "Dan Luger Harris, do you have any last words?"

"Fuck no!" Dan fiercely shouted. "Only that I wish I could have killed more of you skanky bitches!" Then he spit on the glass barrier.

The correctional officers wrestled Dan on the execution table and strapped him down.

Stewart looked sternly at Dan, and Dan winked at him, "See ya on the other side Doc."

Stewart started to snort, but quickly turned it into a cough. He gained his composure and then inserted the needle into Dan's vein.

When it was the correct time, the warden gave the signal and Stewart, flipped the switches to administer the drug.

Enough time had passed and Dan should have been "dead," but he was still conscience. Stewart felt like he was going to pee his pants. He checked his watch and then the prison doctor stepped in and questioned him. "Why is this taking so long? What's the problem?"

Stewart was on the defensive, "First of all, don't ever question me Doctor. Get out of here, I'll let you know when it's time to call it. He's just a big man with a high tolerance."

Stewart didn't want to inject Dan with more of the death mock drugs. It was risky, but he had to take the chance of killing him, and he injected Dan with more of the formula.

Soon, Dan's eyes grew heavy and then, he flat-lined.

Stewart quickly called for the doctor. "Okay, he's dead! He's dead everyone!"

The doctor started to exam Dan's body, but he was moving slow and it irritated Stewart. Stewart knew that he had injected Dan with what should have been a lethal dose of the drugs, and if he didn't revive him within minutes, it would be too late.

"Hurry, you fool!" Stewart shouted at the doctor. "I must have these organs immediately!"

The doctor was angry that Stewart had been so rude to him and he moved even slower. "Hold on now Dr. Whitehead, I need to thoroughly examine this man."

Stewart thought that he was going to go crazy. Perhaps the prison doctor wasn't so stupid after all and he had realized that Dan wasn't really dead! Just when he thought that things couldn't get any worse, one of the guards asked the prison doctor a question about the procedure and the defiant doctor explained it, in detail.

Stewart was beside himself, "He flat lined let's go! He's dead already!" he shouted.

"Let's call it," the doctor finally said, and then he looked for his pen. "I seem to have lost my pen."

Stewart grabbed several pens from his pocket protector and threw them at the doctor.

"Oh my, Dr. Whitehead, you certainly are in a rush. There's still plenty of time for you to harvest the organs. I've never seen you so tense. You better come in for an exam."

"I don't need an exam, all I need is for you to sign the gosh darn papers!"

"What's the date?" the doctor asked looking up from his clipboard.

"The twenty seventh you fool!"

"One more crack out of you, Dr. Whitehead, and I'll have you locked up for a seventy-two hour observation! Now get the body out of here."

Stewart pulled the I.V. from Dan's arm; he transferred him to a gurney and hurriedly pushed him to the loading dock where Joyce and Tache' were waiting. Joyce saw him approaching and pushed open the back doors of the science van.

"It's been too long, it's been too long! I don't know if he's going to make it!" Stewart shouted as he loaded Dan into the van. Joyce gave Dan the antidote shot and tried to revive him, but it wasn't working.

"Stewart, he's not responding. What happened in there?"

"He's too big and I had to give him more of the formula than I wanted to."

"Tache'," Stewart yelled, "get us back to the lab … pronto!"

Stewart didn't have to repeat himself, Tache' was ready, to go. She hit the gas pedal and took off like a flash, her fluffy hair flying as she turned her head while she drove. "Hold on ya'll," she shouted, "I'm taking this turn like a cop after a drug dealer."

Tache' drove the van like a racecar, her high heels performed like champions.

"Great Tache', go, go, go!" Joyce urged her on. "We've got to get him to the lab before it's too late!"

"Yeah baby, I know how to get movin' when I have to!"

"Good job Tache'" Stewart said, and hung on for dear life.

Joyce kept working on Dan, "Stewart, I have a heartbeat!" She held Dan's hand as he fought to come back from death's door. "Dan hang in there you're going to be fine," she said.

Then Dan spoke, "Don't lie to me Joyce, I know the odds aren't good, too …. ma … ny .. in ..jec ..tions."

"Don't give up Dan, I'm not going to and either are Stewart and Tache'."

Dan lost the fight and fell backward towards death. "Stewart get him back, get him back!"

Stewart found that Dan's heart was no longer beating. It was all over, but he decided to take a chance and inject Dan with more of the antidote.

"No Stewart, we've tested the antidote and what you propose to do is fatal!"

"It's the only chance we have to save him Joyce, it's worth a try!"

Joyce held her breath as Stewart gave Dan the injection

that she knew to be a lethal dose. But, afterwards Dan moved his fingers and tried to squeeze her hand. "Stewart he's responding, he's responding!"

Stewart used the limited techniques available to him in the science van as they bounced and slammed against the sides of the van during the high speed ride.

"Joyce he can hear you," Stewart said. "You have to stimulate him, talk to him, say something to get him back!"

The only stimulating thing that Joyce could think of was Tache'. Tache', will have dirty sex with you!" she awkwardly said to Dan. "Talk to him Tache'!"

"Okay Dan baby, I'm gonna hit you so hard, that you'll explode all over me!"

Dan managed to get out the words, "Who's Tache?"

"She's a very sexy, dirty girl."

"But what about you Joyce?"

Joyce wasn't sure how to respond, but suddenly, she heard herself say, "Okay, I'll do you too. We'll have a threesome!"

Stewart was monitoring Dan's vitals. "Okay, that's enough girls, his vitals are beginning to stabilize. Dan's a fighter and he just might make it, if we can get him to the lab in time. Joyce he just might make it!"

The tires squealed as Tache' made the last turn to the lab and started to pull up to the loading dock.

Joyce pushed the door open before the van had even stopped. She ran to the lab door and unlocked it as Stewart and Tache' rolled Dan inside.

Immediately, Joyce put Dan on life support and flushed the toxic drugs from his system.

"He's responding nicely," Stewart said.

"Yes," Joyce agreed, "but, the antidote may have done irreparable harm. We'll have to do more testing. We can't attempt the brain transplant until we see what we have to work with."

"Is he gonna make it?" Tache' asked in a shaky voice.

"We'll know in a few minutes," Joyce answered.

Stewart continued to monitor Dan's condition. He

examined and tested all of Dan's organs and functions. "Joyce, Dan's organs are still intact, but the drugs have had an unforeseen effect and are causing the brain to produce a toxic chemical that's destroying his body. We have to do the brain transplant immediately before the contaminated brain completely destroys him!"

Joyce and Stewart thought that they were going to get a break before commencing with the surgery. They both needed time to regroup, but they summoned the strength to move ahead with the brain transplant.

When Stewart had Dan prepared, Joyce began the surgery. She cut into Dan's head and opened up his skull. She found that Dan's brain was extremely large as she and Stewart struggled to get it out. There was a suction sound as the brain was finally removed.

Joyce and Stewart looked at the brain in amazement. "My gosh this brain is huge!" Stewart said. "I hope the artificial brain doesn't rattle around in there!

"Don't worry Stewart, it will be perfectly fine. The tissues of the Living Artificial Brain will expand to fit the skull.

The transplant went perfectly, and as always, Stewart closed.

Now, it was time for the implantation of memories and responses. Joyce and Stewart reviewed the information that they had been able to save from Dan's original brain.

"Now, Dan specifically asked to retain all of his memories," Joyce said, "even those of the murders. All we are going to do is remove the evil impulses and the desire to kill and rape. He will still be the same person, minus the murderous evil drives."

"Yes I know Joyce," Stewart answered. "I've already removed the brain damaged material and now you need to create the program that we will implant in the new brain."

"Okay, this is the tricky part, Stewart. The murderous impulses and drives should appear in red. But, because of the damage to Dan's natural brain, we're not getting the proper readings and we're going to have to wing it!"

Joyce did her best to decipher the warped readings that she had to work with. When she was satisfied with the program she had created, Stewart implanted it into Dan's artificial brain with the special tool.

Joyce was worried, she questioned every decision that she had made, replaying it over and over in her mind. By creating the program for Dan with warped readings, she feared that she may have created a monster!

"Stewart, maybe we should destroy him. I'm not confident that the program is correct. With all the drugs and the damage, he could be ... well anything!"

"It's okay Joyce, just hang in there. Why don't you go home, I've got this."

"No Stewart, I can't leave until I know what the outcome is."

"Are you sure? It took Brian quite a while before he came out of it, and he didn't suffer near the trauma that Dan did."

"I know, I know, I don't care. I have to see this thing through."

Joyce anxiously waited for Dan to respond. Hours passed and nothing changed. She and Stewart closely monitored him, testing and checking and rechecking, but most of their time was spent just staring at Dan and wondering what he would do.

They waited through the night, and the next morning when the sun began to rise, Dan's eyelids moved slightly. Joyce and Stewart leaped up and observed. Dan moved his head from side to side and Joyce grabbed Stewart's hand.

"Stewart do you have your hypo ready? He may be raging when he comes to."

Stewart reached into his lab coat and pulled out his trusty hypodermic needle. "Got it right here ma'am, as usual, I'm ready for any emergency!"

Dan's eyes slowly opened and Joyce and Stewart were both amazed by how gentle and calm he looked.

"He's peaceful Joyce, it's looking good!"

Dan moved his hand and then his foot. Joyce and Stewart

had restrained him to be certain that he didn't hurt himself, or anyone else.

"Stewart, he's trying to say something!"

Stewart turned on the recorder and then Dan spoke his first words with his new brain, "Am I alive? I must be, I have to take a piss."

Joyce and Stewart were elated that Dan was actually able to move and to speak, but they paid no attention to what he had actually said.

"I said, I have to piss!"

Joyce finally got the message, "Stewart, get the man a urinal!"

"I don't want a urinal, let me up!"

Joyce and Stewart made a bold move and they removed the restraints from the massive man.

"I'm not afraid of you anymore!" Stewart told Dan.

"I'm real happy for ya Stew, but why don't you help me up and tell me where the can is."

Stewart and Joyce both jumped to assist Dan. He was a little stiff, and they supported him as he stood up and walked across the floor.

Both Joyce and Stewart entered the lavatory with Dan and he glared at them. "You two gonna hold my dick for me too? How about some privacy."

"Okay Dan, but Stewart will be right outside the door, in case you need assistance," Joyce told him.

Joyce walked away, happy that the brain and body were functioning.

A few minutes later, Dan came out of the lavatory shouting for Joyce.

"Yes Dan, what is it? Are you having a problem? Do you need something?"

"No, I don't need anything; I just want to thank you. Thanks Joyce, for saving my life and giving me a second chance."

"Don't forget Stewart and Tache', I couldn't have done it without them."

"Yeah Stew, she's right, thanks dude, thanks a lot. And

where's Tache', I want to thank her too."

Stewart and Joyce took Dan to the lobby where they had last seen Tache'. She was still there, but she was sound asleep on the couch. Her makeup was smeared, her nails were broken and she had one leg up on the back of the couch and the other down, sprawled out with her panties showing.

Stewart closely observed while Dan quietly sat on the other end of the couch, next to her. "Look at me," he said, "I'm sitting next to a beautiful woman."

"That's a stretch," Stewart quietly snickered.

"I can appreciate her, but I don't want to kill her. I can't even remember the last time that I looked at a woman and didn't want to kill her, or at least rape her."

"That's wonderful Dan," Joyce said. "How do you feel otherwise?"

"I feel like myself, but without the evil, just like you said I would."

"Yes Dan, against all odds, it appears that your brain transplant is a success. When you've fully recovered, we'll do some plastic surgery on your face and give you a new identity. You'll have to stay here for observation and fine tuning for a while and then, if all goes well, you can get on with your life."

"That's great Doc," Dan replied.

"You must be hungry. Can I get you something to eat?" Joyce asked.

"No thanks, the last time I ate, I ate like it was my last meal."

Stewart snorted, "I didn't know that we made him into a comedian."

"I think it's great!" Joyce commented. "Now maybe his true personality will come out."

Joyce examined Dan, one more time, "You're doing wonderfully Dan, I couldn't be more pleased. I hope you won't be offended, but we're going to have to keep you locked in the Interview Room at night, just in case you have a

126

malfunction."

"That's alright with me Joyce, I understand," Dan said as he entered the room. "At least this time when I'm locked up, I have something to look forward to … a normal life."

Stewart set up a rollaway bed in the Interview Room, and Dan snuggled under the blankets.

"I'll see you first thing in the morning," Joyce told him, "and Stewart will be checking on you during the night."

"Thanks again, Doc. Good night."

Joyce quietly closed and locked the door of the Interview Room and then went into her office.

Stewart was right behind her, "Anything that I can assist you with Joyce?"

"Oh no, nothing, I just want to make sure that everything's finished up here before I leave."

"Everything's fine, I have everything under control, ma'am."

"If you're sure Stewart, I'll head on home."

"Nighty night, boss."

"Good night Stewart. See you in the morning."

Joyce walked out of her office with a smile on her face, happy with what the day had brought. Dan's brain transplant was a success and she was on her way to saving the world.

Before she left the laboratory she went into the lobby to check on Tache'. She was still sound asleep and Joyce covered her with a warm cotton blanket. "Good night, sweetness," she said and then she kissed her finger and pressed it gently against Tache's lips. "See you in the morning," she whispered, then she tiptoed out and went home.

FEAR AND RESENTMENT START TO BUILD

The next morning, Joyce showed up for work to find Stewart, Tache' and Dan enjoying breakfast together.

127

"Good morning boss," Stewart greeted her, and Tache' and Dan chimed in.

"We're just finishing up here. What's the plan for today?" Tache' asked.

"I thought that we would get you settled in your own room."

"That's okay Joyce, I don't want you to go to any trouble; I'm fine on the couch."

"Nonsense, we can't have you sleeping on the couch with two men staying here at the lab. You need your own space."

"Well okay, if you insist."

"Stewart, you'll have a light day today, monitoring Dan. Would you please clear out the storage room, at the far end of the building? It's large enough to make a nice place for Tache'."

"Joyce, that room is packed, what can I possibly do with all of the things stored there?"

"There's plenty of room in the basement. You can stack it all on the east wall."

"Wow, that's a lot of stair climbing and most of that stuff's heavy. Why can't Tache' help me? After all it's going to be her room."

"Stewart, that's the first time that I've ever heard you complain. Moving heavy things is man's work. Surely you don't expect a woman to handle those heavy boxes. And besides that, I'm taking Tache' furniture shopping. I want her settled in her room by tonight. And once you have the area cleared, don't forget to give it a good scrubbing, that space hasn't been cleaned in years."

Tache' started to clear the table and Joyce stopped her. "Come on Tache', let's get going. It might take all day to select the right furniture for you." She took Tache's arm and they headed toward the door together, "Let's see now, you'll need a bed, and a vanity with a brightly lit mirror for hair and makeup and ..." Then the two walked out of the building together.

"Wow Stew, that was brutal," Dan said shaking his head in

128

disgust. "That Tache' sure has Joyce pussy whipped, and she doesn't even have a pussy!"

"Don't be vulgar Dan, Tache' is a nice person and I'm very fond of her."

"Yeah, I guess you're right, she's okay for a faggot." Dan clenched his fist and cracked his knuckles. "Well, we might as well get to work."

"Oh no Dan, you're not in any condition to be working, not after all of the trauma you suffered."

"I feel fine Stew, and I'm sure as hell not going to let you do all that heavy lifting by yourself."

"Your good intensions are greatly appreciated Dan, but I can't allow it. You shouldn't do much more than sit in a chair today!"

"Okay Stew, you're the boss," Dan agreed, and then he took an office chair and started to push it down the hall toward the Storage Room. "Well, if you won't let me help, the least I can do is keep you company."

Stewart was pleasantly surprised that Dan actually wanted to spend time with him. Usually, people made an effort to avoid him.

Stewart took the chair from Dan and positioned it between the Storage Room and the basement doorway. "There, that should be a good spot for you," he declared. "Have a seat and let me check your vitals before I get started.

Stewart examined Dan, "Everything's A.O.K.! You're looking good ... dude," he awkwardly said.

Then Stewart turned his attention to the Storage Room, the boxes were stacked wall to wall and clear up to the ceiling. He felt overwhelmed as he picked up the first box and he was angry about having to clear the room by himself. "Joyce never took me shopping for furniture," he quietly muttered and then took the box to the basement.

When he came back up the stairs for another box, Dan asked if it was okay for him to check out the lab.

"It's fine for you to walk, as long as you're careful, but only for a few minutes."

With that, Dan got up and started investigating the laboratory. He went from room to room, looking on shelves and digging in drawers. He opened the door to the Brain Assembly Room and saw Tyrone, hard at work. "Hey, my black brother, how's it hangin'?"

Tyrone didn't take his eyes from his work and simply said in a monotone voice, "Brain number, five point three two, circuit complete.

Dan slowly backed out of the room, "Fuck, this place is even freakier that I thought. This dude is a fuckin' zombie!"

Dan went back to where Stewart was working. He was curious about Tyrone and asked about him. Stewart was happy to tell him the whole story. Things that were confidential, things that he should not have revealed. He went into detail about how Tyrone was Tache's pimp, and that he had killed the baby, Qunitsha. "Yes, the punishment for his crime was making him into a brain assembly drone."

Dan was shocked by the story. "Man Stew, that's some heavy shit. I killed a few bitches, but killing a baby... " Dan shook his head, "I'm glad that you and Joyce didn't fuck me up like that Tyrone dude."

"Your situation was completely different, Dan."

"I'm glad that you can see that."

"In fact killing a woman ... " Stewart started to say more, but then he stopped himself and thoughtfully paused, "well ... it depends upon the woman. Not all women are respectable. Respect must be earned, not freely given. Joyce is the only woman that I respect."

"What about Tache'?"

"Tache' doesn't count, she's really a man and deserves respect."

Stewart stopped carrying boxes. "I better check you again and see how you're doing after that walk." He pulled out his stethoscope and listened to Dan's heart, "Hmm, heartbeat, a little fast," he noted.

"You seem shaken Dan, don't be concerned, you and I have more in common than you know."

130

Dan wondered what Stewart had meant by the comment. He looked into Stewart's eyes and felt a cold chill go down his spine. There was definitely something sinister about him and Dan wondered if he had made a mistake. Perhaps he would have been better off going through with his execution. He was beginning to believe that being dead might have been preferable to being at the mercy of two mad scientists and a sex freak.

Thinking that he had reassured Dan, Stewart went back to work, clearing out the storage room for Tache.

And while he labored, Joyce and Tache' were having a fun day shopping. They found a store that had good quality furniture and excellent prices. Joyce bought Tache' all of the furniture that she needed and Tache' happily went along with her. But, when Joyce insisted on a queen size bed, Tache protested, "I don't need a bed that big Joyce, I'll be perfectly fine in a twin."

"I know that you're used to lovely things, Tache', and I want you to be comfortable. A queen size bed isn't that extravagant."

"Okay Joyce, the queen size bed will be fine. And I want you to know that I'm very happy. You've changed my life and I'll be forever grateful."

"That's all I want is for you to be happy. I felt terrible having you sleep out on that couch, with those men peeping at you. Now, you'll have your own room with a lock on the door."

"You're the greatest Joyce."

Joyce and Tache' found all of the furniture that they needed. Joyce paid for it and made arrangements for the furniture to be delivered, that same day.

The girls left the store excited and happy. "And now, for some soft blankets and down pillows and a bright lovely bedspread!" Joyce said.

"Oh Joyce, you're just too much."

The two happily left the furniture store, and went on with the shopping trip. When they had found all of the bedding and other things that they were looking for, they loaded them into the hatchback. "The last time that I put something in here, it was Tyrone," Tache' said. "It was such a horrible time in my life. I was so brokenhearted and afraid, I never dreamed that things would turn around and I would actually be happy again."

"Yes, this is a happy occasion," Joyce agreed, "and just the first of many." Then she gently took Tache's hand and gave it a gentle squeeze.

Joyce and Tache', smiled at each other and then climbed into the car and headed back to the lab.

When they got inside, they found the Storage Room cleared out and scrubbed sparkling clean. "Oh Stewart!" Tache' exclaimed, "It's perfect! Thank you so much!" She bent down, wrapped her arms around Stewart and kissed him on the cheek. "You're absolutely wonderful!"

Stewart blushed at the demonstrative affection and Dan snickered. "And you didn't have to suck cock to get it either," he sneered rudely to Tache'.

"Oh my Dan," Joyce said alarmed. "You apologize to Tache' immediately!"

"No Joyce, it's okay," Tache' said, "I'm used to it. Dan's right, I was a prostitute."

"That's the key word … was. It's in your past and I will not tolerate you being abused by anyone ever again, especially not someone in this very laboratory!"

"Dan didn't mean anything by it, Joyce," Stewart said. "He probably just needs an adjustment."

Dan did not want an adjustment, he was afraid of what Joyce might do to him, so he quickly apologized to Tache'.

Joyce was stunned, not only at Stewart's unusual boldness, but it was also obvious that he had divulged sensitive information to Dan. How else could he have known that Tache' had been a prostitute? There was a strange dynamic between Stewart and Dan, and Joyce was concerned. She decided to restrict Dan's freedom and keep a watchful eye.

The tension in the room was broken when the furniture delivery van pulled up to the loading dock. The furniture was unloaded into Tache's room and she and Joyce put everything in place. "The room looks beautiful," Tache' gasped.

"Yes we made some excellent choices," Joyce agreed, "attractive and very functional."

The door to the room was open and Stewart tapped on the wall by the doorway, "May I have a look?"

"Yes, of course you can Stewart," Tache' said. "Come on in. What do you think?"

Stewart looked around the room. He told Tache' that it was nice and then quickly exited. He was upset about the bed, "A queen size bed, what does she need with a queen size bed?" he mumbled to himself. "I've been sleeping on an old, worn-out hospital bed for years now, and Joyce never cared enough to buy me a queen size bed."

Stewart decided to go into the Observation Booth and spy on Joyce and Tache'. He sat down in the chair and switched to the camera in Tache's room. Stewart was thrilled when he saw Tache' stretched out on the bed and stroking the satin pillows. "Oh yes Tache', that's right, roll over now and let me see those ankles, snort, snort."

Stewart's perverted fun came to an abrupt halt when Joyce disconnected the camera. "Gosh darn it Joyce, can't a guy have any fun around here?"

Once the camera was disconnected, Joyce changed the lock identification so that only she and Tache' could open the door. In the past, Joyce had always allowed Stewart access to everything in the lab. But, when he defended Dan after he had insulted Tache', she wasn't about to allow him access to her room.

"Everything looks fine Tache'," Joyce said. "I'm going to leave here with peace of mind tonight. Now you be sure to keep this door locked. Your thumbprint has been entered into the security system and you now have access to every lock in the laboratory."

Joyce left Tache's room and looked for Stewart. He had left the Observation Booth, by this time, and was with Dan, relaxing in the lobby. "Stewart," she said, "I'm going to go home now, let's get Dan settled in the Interview Room before I leave."

"That's okay Joyce," Stewart answered, "I'll lock Dan up before I go to bed."

"No Stewart, I really have to draw the line here. Under no circumstances will I permit Dan to be released from the Interview Room when I am not present. Do I make myself perfectly clear?"

Stewart was angry, but he got up to follow orders, "Come on Dan, you heard the lady." With that, Dan got up and went to be locked in the Interview Room.

After Joyce had left for home, Tache' went into the make-shift kitchen and started cooking. Stewart smelled the aroma and peeked inside.

Tache' had been watching for him, "Hope you like pork chops," she said.

"Oh, am I invited?"

"Of course you are Suga'."

"In that case, the answer to your question is, yes, I love pork chops."

"That's good, and I'm making three for Dan, he's so big, I figure that he must have a big appetite. And I have pie and ice cream for dessert."

Stewart hadn't had a decent meal for years and he was thrilled. "Tache' let me help you," he offered.

But Tache' was wise, if she had learned anything on the street it was how to read people. She knew that Stewart's feelings were bruised and she did her best to make him feel better. "Oh no, this is woman's work," she said. "Now you just sit there and relax. You've put in a hard days' work."

Stewart felt his chest puff up a little and he sat in a chair at the table.

"You know Stewart, Brian has that huge television in his office and I thought that we could watch a movie together tonight."

"Can we have popcorn?"

"Hot popcorn with melted butter, Suga'."

"Wow, this is going to be a great night!"

Tache' served Stewart at the table and then took a plate to Dan in the Interview Room. "I'm sorry that you have to be locked up like this, Dan. But, I'll do my best to make it as comfortable for you as possible."

Dan was terrified of a brain adjustment. He took the plate and instead of saying something vulgar, like he normally would have, he politely thanked her.

Tache' went back to Stewart and found that he had dimmed the lights and placed a Bunsen burner on the table. She was thrown for a moment; was Stewart expecting romance? But, she was relieved when she found that he was merely trying to create a pleasant ambiance. She sat down and they both relaxed and enjoyed the meal.

When they were finished eating, Tache' washed the dishes and then started popping the popcorn. "Stewart, why don't you go get the movie ready," she said. "Men are so much better at electronic things than us girls are."

"Movie coming up," Stewart said and then he went happily gliding down the hall to Brian's office.

This routine soon became the norm. Tache' cooked nearly every night, and then she and Stewart sat and cuddled on the couch together watching movies. "We're besties, aren't we Tache'?"

"Yes Stewart, we are definitely besties," Tache' agreed and then grinned at the strange, frail, little man.

THE BAD APPLE

Brian was making up for lost time and spending every day with Peggy. He hadn't been in to work for weeks and papers were piling up on his desk. Joyce was beginning to be concerned about his lax attitude as she still needed Brian to be there occasionally, in order to keep things running smoothly. Joyce called Brian at home, and asked him to come to the lab to get some work done. An hour later, he happily showed up with Peggy on his arm.

"Hi Joyce," Peggy greeted her. "I hope that no one minds me tagging along with Brian today, but he insisted. He says that he can't stand to be away from me! I'll try not to be in the way."

"No need for apologies, it's always a pleasure to see you, Peggy."

"I just don't want to be a nuisance."

"You could never be a nuisance, Peggy. As a matter of fact, I've been wanting to talk to you."

"It's fine with me, but I don't know if Brian will let me out of his sight long enough ... ha, ha. He's become so possessive."

Peggy told Brian that she was going to talk to Joyce. "Don't be long darling," he said and kissed her before she and Joyce went into the lobby.

Joyce was thrilled that Peggy had come to the lab. It was the perfect opportunity for her to find out if Brian was behaving properly or if he needed further adjustments to his program.

She wasn't sure exactly how she should approach Peggy with her questions. She didn't want to get too personal, as it would be suspicious. "Peggy," she said, "I'm certainly happy to see you and Brian getting along so well."

"Oh yes Joyce, it's been wonderful and you don't have to be secretive with me. I know that you have something to do with it."

Joyce was alarmed, she didn't know how much Peggy knew. "What do you mean Peggy? I didn't do anything. I'm sure that Brian simply realized what everyone else has known all along, that you're the best thing that's ever happened to him."

"Joyce, don't be concerned, you can count on my discretion. You just keep on doing whatever it is that you're doing. Drugging him or whatever it is, I don't care. I'm the happiest I've ever been in my life and I don't want it to end."

Instead of a threat, Peggy had turned out to be an ally.

"You're right, Peggy, we are using an experimental treatment on Brian … with his permission of course! I would appreciate it if you would check in with me from time to time and let me know how he's doing. The treatment could need some adjusting; it's still in the experimental stages. If Brian does anything that you think is strange, please let me know."

"So far, no complaints," Peggy said. "And now I better get back to my sweetheart. Thanks Joyce, for saving my marriage."

"You just enjoy it, Peggy, you certainly deserve it."

Peggy left the lobby with a spring in her step and went back to Brian's office where Joyce heard him happily greet her. After seeing Peggy abused by Brian for so many years, she was finally happy and Joyce smiled and felt a sense of accomplishment.

Joyce was happier too these days, her research was unthreatened and she was enjoying the time that she worked with Tache'. Tache' was a quick study and had turned out to be an excellent assistant for Joyce. But, nearly all of their time together was spent in the laboratory. Tache' both lived and worked in the lab and Joyce didn't think that it was healthy for her. So one day, she decided to take her to lunch. Stewart, expected to go too, but he wasn't invited, he had to stay behind and observe Dan.

"Left out again, huh buddy?" Dan said to Stewart. "Guess there's no compeling with that chick with a dick."

"Joyce might be able to have Tache' during the day, but every night, she's is mine. We're besties you know!"

Dan just bit his lip and looked forward to the day when he would get out of captivity.

Taking Tache' to lunch turned out to be the highlight of Joyce's day. She had such a nice time that she decided to take her to lunch every workday. Each day, they tried a new restaurant, and each day, Stewart was stuck at the lab watching Dan.

Weeks went by, and seeing Stewart as his only ally, Dan tried to befriend him, complementing Stewart and building up his ego.

Dan did not trust women and Joyce was no exception. He always presented himself as cheerful and well-adjusted in her presence, but in reality his hatred and resentment were growing. Joyce was a powerful woman, one who held Dan's fate in her hands, a woman who could make him into a Tyrone, if she wanted to.

Joyce and Stewart continued to observe and test Dan daily, and he was becoming more anxious and fearful.

Feeling that he had been successful at befriending Stewart, Dan decided to try to enlist his help. "Come on Stew, you've got to get me out of here dude. How many tests do you need? I'm telling ya, I'm ready to get the fuck out of here!"

"Perhaps you're correct Dan, I'll speak to Joyce about taking the next step."

"What do you mean, the next step?" Dan asked fearfully.

"Your new face."

"Yeah, a new face, that's cool."

The first chance he got, Stewart talked to Joyce about Dan. "I think that it's time we take the next step," he told her. "When can we schedule Dan's plastic surgery?"

"You're right Stewart, Dan is stable enough, let's get it done this morning. Do you have anything else scheduled?"

"Nothing is more important than Dan. I'll begin the preparations."

Stewart went back to talk to Dan. "Well ... dude, get ready, we're going to do the surgery right away."

But, Stewart didn't get the response that he had expected, Dan wasn't happy, he was nervous. "I don't know buddy, that Joyce, I don't trust her. I killed her mother and I think that she might get her revenge and make me into a freak!"

"Don't worry Dan, Joyce isn't that way."

"Will you be there, buddy?"

"Yes, I'll be assisting."

"Okay man, you watch out for me and don't let her fuck me up!"

Stewart had always been in Joyce's shadow. Now, things

were different. Dan was actually depending on him to see that she didn't do something wrong, and Stewart felt important.

"I will … man," Stewart said.

Stewart had Dan lay on a gurney and he wheeled him into the O.R. Joyce joined him there and the two worked on Dan's ugly face to make it beautiful. "What do you think Stewart, one more nip off the end of his nose?"

"Oh yes, just one more nip and his nose will be perfect!"

When Joyce and Stewart finished the surgery, they were both excited. "I'm looking forward to viewing our work when the bandages come off," Stewart said.

"So am I, I'm certain that he won't be recognizable, even to his own mother."

Dan was terrified of what he would find when his bandages came off. He waited anxiously and when he had had sufficient time to heal, it was time for the unveiling.

After the bandages were removed, Joyce and Stewart gasped at the sight and Dan was screaming for a hand mirror. He was a little swollen, but even so, Dan was now a handsome man.

"Excellent job Doctor," Stewart said, shaking Joyce's hand.

"Excellent job Doctor," Joyce said back to Stewart. "It's incredible, even if I do say so myself! Especially if I do say so myself!"

"Will somebody get me a fucking mirror!" Dan shouted in frustration.

"I'll get one from my room," Tache' said and ran to get her mirror.

When she got back with the mirror, Dan yanked it from her hand and looked at himself. He ran his fingers gently over his now smooth skin. It hurt a bit when he smiled, but he was pleased. "Thanks Doc, this is the first time that I ever looked in the mirror and liked what I saw!"

"Yes, your life will be very different now," Joyce said. "Research has proven that attractive people get much more favorable attention." Dan didn't answer her, he just kept staring in the mirror in disbelief.

MERCY FUCK

"Now that we've completed the facial surgery," Stewart said, "it's time for the next step in Dan's rehabilitation. It's time for him to get a job and function in society.

"How can I get a fucking job without an I.D.?" Dan said still admiring himself in the mirror.

"Yes, you're right Dan, that does present a problem," Joyce agreed. "And I'm not sure how we'll handle it. But don't worry, we'll find a way."

"No need to worry," Tache' said. "I can go see my friend, Ray Ray. He makes identification, that's his thing."

"I'm not crazy about you contacting a conman from your past," Joyce interrupted.

"It won't be a problem," Tache' said, "Ray Ray, he cool."

"How do you contact … Ray Ray?" Joyce asked. "And how long does the process take?"

"I can just stop by his work shop, he won't mind. And Ray Ray got skills, it only takes a few minutes."

"Is it safe?" Joyce asked.

"Oh sure, Ray Ray and I go way back. He was my best friend in the joint. He's a real standup guy, helped me out of a jam."

"Well, if we're going to do it, let's get it over with," Joyce said and then reached into her purse for her car keys. "I'll go get the car."

"I'm sorry Joyce, but I'll have to go alone. Ray Ray won't like it if I bring a stranger to his shop."

"It's out of the question then, I'm not going to put you in jeopardy."

"Joyce, are you forgetting who you're talking to? Believe me, I know how to handle myself."

"No, I'm not forgetting who I'm talking to. I remember a very frightened girl running for her life, and not too long ago, I

140

might add. I won't allow it, we'll just have to find another way."

Tache' was grateful to Joyce and she wanted to help her out. Laws governing identification were strict and people like Ray Ray were hard to find. She knew that Joyce wouldn't be able to obtain the identification that she needed for Dan. If she didn't come through with Ray Ray, the "Dan experiment" would be at a standstill. Tache' thought about it for a moment and then made a suggestion. "Maybe it would be okay if you dropped me off a few blocks away; I could always walk up and Ray Ray wouldn't know the difference."

"I suppose that would be alright, as long as you have Derek with you and I know exactly where you are."

"Oh, Ray Ray loves animals, I'm sure that he'll get on fine with Derek."

Joyce and Tache' went by Joyce's house to pick up Derek, then they headed deep into a dangerous neighborhood. They were sitting, in the car at a stop light, when a crazy man came up to the car with a hammer in his hand. The man raised the hammer and Derek immediately leaped on the window snarling. Seeing the fierce, huge rat, the man ran screaming down the street in terror. Joyce and Tache' started laughing and Joyce was happy that she had her protector, Derek, by her side.

About ten minutes later, they were getting close to Ray Ray's shop and Tache' had Joyce pull into a gas station. "Wait here Joyce," she instructed, "I'll be right back."

"Are we near Ray Ray's?"

"Yeah, but just hold on a minute." Tache' went inside and talked to the attendant and then came back to the car. "The guy that works here is a friend of mine. He'll watch out for you while I'm gone."

"How long will you be at Ray Ray's?"

"Not more than an hour, Ray Ray's high tech."

"What's the address there?"

"It's the only blue building on the next block. But don't worry, there won't be a problem."

"Derek," Joyce said, "you go with Tache' and make certain that she's safe."

"Derek climbed out the window and onto Tache's shoulder. "Oh Derek," she giggled, "you're so silky and soft, but I know that you can kick ass too!" Tache' gave Derek a kiss on his fuzzy nose and the two of them started down the sidewalk.

Joyce watched as Tache' walked away in her short skirt and high heels. The cars passing by honked their horns and wolf whistled at her. "I should have had her change her clothes," she whispered shaking her head.

Tache' got to Ray Ray's door and knocked. She heard some rustling and then Ray Ray's voice, "Who's there?"

"It's me, Ray Ray, Tache'."

"For real?"

"Yes baby, it's really me."

Ray Ray unbolted the door and flung it open. He started to rush and give Tache' a hug, but then he saw Derek glaring at him. "Wow, now that's a big rat," he said.

"Yes, this is Derek."

"Well, hello there Derek, aren't you a big razzle dazzle?"

Ray Ray's voice was friendly and kind so Derek knew that he wasn't going to be facing him in combat.

"Is he friendly? Can I pet him?" Ray Ray asked.

"Sure, he's friendly, as long as you don't do anything weird."

"Don't be afraid Derek," Ray Ray said and then slowly reached his hand out for Derek to sniff."

"Tache' chuckled at the thought of Derek being scared. "Don't worry, Derek's not afraid, he's got skills."

"Oh, so you're a bad boy huh?"

Derek let Ray Ray stroke his fur and then Ray Ray asked if he could hold him.

"That's up to Derek," Tache' said. "Derek, is it alright if Ray Ray holds you?"

Derek looked at Tache' questioning her. "It's alright Derek, Ray Ray's cool."

With that Derek reached his paw out to Ray Ray, and he took him from Tache's shoulder. "Oh, I think he likes me!" Ray Ray said with a big smile.

Ray Ray knew all of the good places to scratch him and Derek was enjoying the attention. He felt so comfortable with Ray Ray that he even let him hold him in his arms and rub his belly. "Oh, there you go now, Ray Ray knows what feels good."

"You sure do have a way with animals Ray Ray."

"That's why I have a way wit' *you*, you a wild thing. What's going on anyway? I haven't seen you in a few months; everything alright?"

"Everything's fine Ray Ray, I just need you to make me some I.D."

"Who for?"

Tache' reached into her purse and pulled out a picture of Dan. "For this guy. Can you do it right away? It's important."

"Of course I can, anything for my sex machine. I'll get started on it right away."

Ray Ray placed Derek in a comfy chair, "There you go boy, you wait here, Ray Ray's gonna get you some nice juicy grapes."

Ray Ray went into the kitchen and got a bowl full of grapes and gave them to Derek. "There you go Derek, you munch on these while I get this job done for my black velvet, sex machine."

Derek pulled a grape from the vine and tasted it. "This is excellent," he thought. "I wish that Joyce would get grapes more often."

Ray Ray went right to work and made the identification for Tache'. When he was done, he gave it to her and then sat next to Derek and started petting him again.

"I'm impressed," Tache' said as she looked over the workmanship, "it's perfect! How much do I owe you?"

"Now you know that I can't charge you *baby*, I can't charge my sex machine. You do me all kinda ways!"

Tache' knew what Ray Ray was angling for and she didn't

like it. "I really do want to pay you Ray Ray, my boss gave me the money."

"Your boss? I thought that Tyrone left the country or was dead or something?"

"Not that boss Ray Ray, I have a real job now."

"It don't sound too legitimate. Why you getting' false I.D. for a legitimate boss, in a legitimate business? You full of shit girl!"

"It's legitimate Ray Ray, just take my word for it."

Tache' put the cash on the table and walked to the door. She unbolted it and then called for Derek.

Derek was eating the juicy sweet grapes; and with Ray Ray scratching him behind the ears, he was in no hurry to leave. He simply looked up at Tache' and stayed in the chair with Ray Ray.

"See girl, even your rat don't want to go wit' you. What you got yo'self into? I know you in trouble, and there ain't no trouble Ray Ray can't get you out of. I got connections baby, anything for my sex machine."

Tache' had Joyce waiting for her in the car and she was in a hurry. She didn't have to have sex for money or favors anymore and she was irritated with Ray Ray. "Ray Ray, if you say sex machine one more time, I think I might scream!"

"I'm sorry girl, I didn't know that Ray Ray was such a turn off. I know how ugly I am."

It was true, Ray Ray was an oddity. He had dark skin and bright red kinky hair with freckles across his nose. He was made fun of as a child, but it only served to make him a powerful fighter and to give him compassion.

Tache' felt bad, she was quite fond of Ray Ray and he had always been a good friend to her, so she decided to give him a mercy fuck.

Tache' stepped away from the door and smiled, "I suppose that your sex machine can manufacture a quickie."

Ray Ray flushed with excitement, he stood up, and then he and Tache' shared a passionate kiss. Derek paused for a moment and watched, then he picked another grape from the vine.

Derek watched the kiss then, he watched as Tache' unbuckled Ray Ray's belt. He watched as Tache' unbuttoned Ray Ray's pants, unzipped them and then pulled them down. He watched as Tache' held Ray Ray's penis in her hand and then put it into her mouth.

He stopped eating the grapes for a moment and observed. "Hmm, I've never seen this behavior before. Tache's not being hurt and my new friend Ray Ray seems to be enjoying himself. I don't think that I need to intervene."

Derek resumed eating grapes, and watched Tache' giving Ray Ray oral sex.

In the meantime, Joyce was waiting in the car and getting more and more anxious. It had been over an hour and she was worried that something may have happened to her sweet Tache'. She got out of the car with a scalpel in her hand and walked briskly down the sidewalk, looking for the blue building. She found it within minutes, and was standing in front of the door when she realized that she didn't have a plan. She quickly decided that she would pretend to be looking for the fabric store and had lifted her fist to knock when she noticed that the door was ajar.

Joyce carefully and quietly pushed the door open and stepped inside. With her hospital shoes on, she didn't make a sound and no one noticed her standing there.

Tache' was busy, Ray Ray's eyes were closed and Derek was eating grapes and watching the great entertainment.

Joyce was enraged and she slammed the door, with a BANG! Tache' jumped to her feet, Derek looked at Joyce and Ray Ray reached in the drawer for his gun.

Tache' grabbed his arm, "It's okay Ray Ray, it's my boss, she cool."

"She don't seem too cool to me baby, you sure?"

"Yes, Ray Ray I'm sure, just back off!"

Tache' pulled herself together and she and Joyce walked out of the building. Derek nodded good-bye to Ray Ray, and then he pulled a few grapes from the vine and ran to catch up with the girls.

"I'm sorry Joyce," Tache' apologized.

"Don't apologize Tache', you have nothing to apologize for. This whole affair is Derek's fault!"

Joyce stopped for a moment and looked back for Derek. Derek touched her leg and wanted to climb up on her shoulder, but Joyce was not having it. "I lay this at your doorstep Derek! You were supposed to protect Tache'. And what did you do? Watch! You were eating grapes and watching while she was being molested!"

"Don't blame Derek, Joyce. It wasn't his fault, it's my fault."

"I certainly do blame Derek. This is exactly what he was supposed to protect you from. And just like every other man, at the first sight of sex, all of his training goes right down the toilet!"

They quickly reached the car and Joyce opened Tache's door and helped her in, then she went to the driver's door and opened it. Derek jumped inside and looked back at Joyce with a grape in his mouth. "Enough with the grapes already!" Joyce said disgusted. Then she climbed in the car and they drove off.

When the three got to the lab, Stewart was waiting at the door. "Were you successful?" he asked.

"Well, we all didn't come out unscathed, but yes we were successful," Joyce said.

They all went to the Interview Room and Tache' handed Dan his new identification. "I asked Ray Ray to give you the same first name," she explained. "I've changed my name a few times myself and it isn't easy to get used to. Daniel's a nice name and Ray Ray was able to do it for me."

"Thanks Tache', you really done me a good turn, getting me identification."

"Yes, this has truly been a team effort Dan," Joyce said. "And now, if all goes well, the next few months, we'll bring our experiment to its completion and send you out into society!"

"Don't worry Joyce, I won't fuck it up."

146

As it turned out, everything did go well. Brian came by the office occasionally to sign papers and make calls to keep the lab going. And Peggy reported to Joyce, that Brian was doing great. Dan never malfunctioned and Tyrone continued to build brains, just as he was programmed to do. All subjects who had received the Living Artificial Brain were functioning exactly as they should.

With everything going so smoothly, the day finally came when Stewart and Joyce decided to complete their experiment. They would release Dan into society and find out if he could live outside the protection of the lab, hold down a job and deal with the stresses of normal life.

With his great looks and winning smile, Dan quickly landed a job as a used car salesman. He found a modest furnished apartment, in an old brick building, on the fourth floor and Stewart helped him move in.

Dan started work, the next day, and had a very successful morning. He sold an expensive sports car and the owner of the dealership was thrilled. Dan had earned an honest dollar and he was quite proud of himself.

Now that he was handsome, Dan enjoyed the way that people treated him. Instead of looking away and being afraid, they were actually attracted to him. Dan was having a great time, talking to the customers and being charming for the first time in his life.

Late that afternoon, the car lot became very busy. A customer, named Daisy Butterfield, came in to pick up her car, and her salesman asked Dan if he would take care of her.

Daisy was thrilled to have Dan, the big handsome man, take over. She was infatuated, with him and flirted shamelessly. This was something that Dan wasn't accustomed to and he wasn't quite sure how to interrupt it.

"Now Dan," Daisy said, "there was a problem with the

brakes and that's why I couldn't pick the car up last week. Why don't we go on a little test drive, I couldn't possibly take the car unless I know that it's safe. You wouldn't mind goin' with little ol' me for a test drive now, would ya?" Daisy looked up and smiled at Dan as she ran her fingers up and down the lapel of his jacket.

"Why certainly we'll take the car for a test drive. I wouldn't feel right letting a pretty lady like you, drive off in a car that I didn't check out myself."

With that, the two got into the car and Dan suggested that they go for a drive in the country. "In the country, you won't have to concern yourself with traffic," he explained. "You'll be able to speed up and stop quickly and really give those brakes a good test."

Daisy happily drove the car out to a country road. She was thrilled, thinking that such a handsome man found her attractive.

Once Daisy and Dan were in a secluded area, Dan heard something amiss in the engine. "Something doesn't sound right," he explained. "You better let me in the drivers' seat, so I can check it out."

Daisy happily agreed to change seats with Dan, and once he had control of the car, the devil got the best of him. He slowly reached for the child lock button and pushed it, trapping Daisy inside the vehicle.

Dan was now alone with a young woman, an attractive woman who had been flirting with him. "I know you want me," he said loudly as he strongly grabbed hold of Daisy.

Daisy's infatuation soon turned into fear, as the huge man pushed her down on the seat and began to tear at her clothing. She screamed in terror, and right in Dan's ear.

Finding that Daisy didn't want him, Dan was furious. "What kind of a fucking game are you playing with me cunt?!"

Dan became filled with murderous rage; he grabbed Daisy by the throat and began to tighten his grip and strangle her. He unbuckled his pants, prepared to enjoy the sick pleasures of his past, a brutal rape and then … the kill. But Daisy had a surprise of her own. "This isn't the first time that one of you dicks have tried to rape me!" she screamed. Then Daisy reached into her bra and pulled out a switch blade. She flipped it open and fiercely rammed the sharp blade into Dan.

Dan was stunned, as Daisy unlocked the doors and jumped out of the car. She ran just as fast as she could into the safety of the woods.

Dan had never had a woman do more than scream and scratch when he attacked her. He couldn't wrap his mind around the fact that this tiny woman had gotten the best of him. He laid in the car, holding his side and moaning.

Dan was bleeding, but he managed pull himself together and somehow drive the car to his apartment building. He got inside, took the elevator up to the fourth floor and then stumbled into his apartment, unnoticed.

Dan realized that he would soon bleed to death. He was afraid to call for an ambulance, he thought that his true identity would be found out, and he would be sent back to death row.

He couldn't face prison again, and decided that it would be easier and faster, if he just killed himself. Dan staggered to the window and opened it, and then he leaned on the sill and looked at the long fall and hard cement sidewalk at the bottom.

Still determined, he tried to climb out on the ledge. But with blood streaming from his body, and pooling on the floor, he slipped on it and fell.

Dan sat on the floor and stared at the fluid flowing from his body. He became hysterical and started laughing wildly and rubbing his hands and wrists in his blood.

Dan paused for a moment, as if he had remembered something. He pulled himself up in the window, and then, as if he were painting, he started to smear the sill and window frame with red blood.

A man on the street looked up and noticed Dan, ranting and "painting" the window frame. He was a cruel man and shouted up at Dan, "Why don't you just jump asshole?"

Another passerby looked up to see what the commotion was and he began to shout, "Jump you coward! JUMP, JUMP!" Soon a crowd gathered and all chanted together, "JUMP, JUMP, JUMP, JUMP!"

Dan became enraged and somehow he still had the strength to scream back at the crowd, "Shut up you fuckers! I'll show you!" Then Dan put one of his legs out the window.

Joyce and Derek were on their way to Dan's apartment to check on his welfare. And when they got close to the building, they saw the crowd gathered on the sidewalk and heard the chanting. Joyce jumped out of the car and quickly looked up to see Dan, bleeding and climbing out of the window.

"Dan, get back inside," she pleaded. "Please don't do this!"

"There's nothing you can do for me Joyce, just let me die!"

"You're wrong Dan, I can fix this!"

"No you can't, no one can fix me. I killed your mother and I enjoyed it! She cried and begged me to let her live, because of her little girl, and it only made it better for me! Did you hear me, Joyce? It only made it better!"

Joyce gave no credence to what Dan was saying. She believed that he was trying to shock her into a rage, so that she wouldn't interfere with his suicide.

The savage crowd continued to chant and Joyce was outraged. "Stop it, stop it all of you! Can't you see that he's a sick man?"

"Stay out of the way Joyce! I'm going to kill myself and end this misery!" Dan shouted. "EVERYONE WATCH ME! COME ON CHANT ... CHANT FOR ME, I TELL YOU!"

The crowd chanted wildly for Dan, "JUMP, JUMP, JUMP, JUMP, JUMP!" screaming louder and louder.

Joyce was getting nowhere shouting up to Dan from the street. She knew that she would have to enter the apartment and confront him, face to face. It was dangerous, Dan was a murderer of women and he was in a frenzy, but Joyce summoned her courage. Knowing that Dan would need treatment, she reached into the car and grabbed her medical bag. "Derek, Dan's brain has malfunctioned and I must intervene! I'm going up to his apartment."

Derek squeaked his disapproval, but Joyce didn't listen to him and turned and ran into the apartment building.

Derek knew that Joyce was in danger. He jumped from the car, ran across the sidewalk and then he leaped high onto the building and began to climb. Derek scratched at the hard brick with his claws, clinging tightly to every nook and cranny as he climbed higher and higher. It was like a wind tunnel between the tall buildings on the street, and strong gusts slammed into Derek, nearly knocking him down. With each gust of the powerful wind, Derek stopped and held on with all his might. He looked down at what would be a fatal fall, but he was determined to reach Dan and save his beloved Joyce.

Derek didn't falter, and continued his heroic feat. Higher and higher he climbed, hoping that he would arrive in time.

Joyce reached the fourth floor of the building and frantically ran down the hall to Dan's apartment. She tried her key and the door unlocked, but Dan had placed a chair under the doorknob and she couldn't get inside. Joyce pounded on the door, demanding Dan to open it one minute, and begging him to the next. But, it was hopeless, she couldn't get into the apartment.

Outside the building, Derek continued his treacherous climb; he fought his way past the first floor, the second, and then the third. But when Derek reached the ledge, just beneath the fourth floor, he was blocked. The ledge was smooth and decorative. It ran the length of the building and projected outward, above his head. Derek was determined, and with total disregard for his own safety, he stretched as far as he could, leaning perilously away from the brick wall, trying to reach the top of the ledge. Balancing himself, and clinging to the brick, with only one of his back feet, Derek managed to get a grip on the edge of the ledge above him.

But, when he jumped, and tried to pull himself up, Dan's blood ran beneath his paws and he slipped. Derek scrambled, scratching desperately to get a grip and found himself dangling, from the ledge, by only one paw, twisting and being blown about by the powerful wind. He was high on the fourth floor of the tall building struggling to hang on, when Dan's blood ran over the edge and into his eyes. Derek could barely see, he shook his head, trying to clear his vision as the blood continued to run and cover more and more of his face and body. A strong gust of wind hit him hard, but Derek kept holding on as the wind tossed and beat him.

Derek's paw was cramping and he knew that he wouldn't last much longer; he had to get past the barrier, and quick. He swung his body to the side, away from the streaming blood. Scratching and kicking, fighting to get a grip with his back legs, hoping with everything in him that that part of the ledge wasn't covered in slippery blood, as well. After a fierce struggle, Derek got a grip with his back claws, and pulled himself up. He was safe for the moment, but now he planned to confront Dan. He was just under the window, where Dan was ranting and screaming at the crowd below. Derek placed his paw on the window sill and Dan spotted him. "Get the fuck out of here, rat boy! Move! I'm going to jump! If you don't get out of the way, I'll take you with me you overdeveloped freak!"

Grasping firmly to the window sill, Derek fearlessly held his position. He locked eyes with Dan and stared at him intensely. Looking into Derek's entranced eyes, Dan became weak and collapsed on the floor.

Immediately, Derek jumped through the window and into the apartment. Suddenly, there is a loud boom, as if a bomb had exploded and the building shook violently. Undeterred, Derek rushed across the floor to the door, as the building jolted from side to side. He wrapped his whip-like tail around the chair leg and yanked it from under the doorknob.

Joyce burst into the room, "Dan, thank goodness you let

me in!" she shouted. But, she was shocked to find that it was Derek who was the one who had let her inside.

Joyce and Derek heard sirens approaching and they stopped and looked fearfully at each other. "It might be over Derek, but we've still got to try and get Dan out of here! There's certain to be an autopsy and the Living Artificial Brain will be discovered! I don't know what Dan's done, but whatever it is, I'm responsible for it."

Derek and Joyce were determined to get Dan out of the building before the police arrived. But he couldn't be moved until his bleeding was under control. Joyce ripped open Dan's shirt and examined the wound, then she quickly cauterized the bleeding blood vessels. "Okay Dan, I got the main vessels, but that's all I can do for now. It's just a quick fix and we've got to hurry and get you to the lab."

Joyce looked at Dan covered in blood. "We can't take you outside looking like this! I'll have to cover you somehow!"

Joyce rifled through Dan's apartment and found a raincoat in the closet. When she tried to get Dan into the coat he fought her. "Get the fuck out of here, bitch! It's too late, there's nothing you can do! Let me die!"

"Dan we aren't leaving without you, we can't! Now quit fighting me!" Dan relented and he tried his best to get into the raincoat, but even so Joyce still struggled with the huge man. Finally, the coat was on and Joyce pulled Dan's arm over her shoulder and tried to get him to his feet. "Come on Dan, you've got to help me ... stand up!" she grunted.

Dan summoned all of his strength. Leaning on Joyce, he stood and then they tottered out of the apartment.

Joyce was concerned about the cruel crowd that had been gathered on the sidewalk, coaxing Dan to jump. She didn't know what this mob was capable of. But, when the elevator door opened, the crowd was running away and thick black smoke filled the air.

Joyce didn't know what catastrophe had befallen the city, but she was glad that the crowd was leaving. Joyce could hear police sirens blaring, heading right toward her. She tensed up and stood with Dan slumped over her, trying to figure out what she would say to the officers. She began to perspire and her heart was pounding wildly. She was relieved when the police cars raced right by, not even looking in her direction.

When the police were out of sight, Joyce opened the back of her car. "I don't know what's happened to the city," she said, "but whatever the catastrophe is, it's been a blessing for us." Joyce laid Dan inside the car, and then covered him with the sleeping bag.

"Come on Derek, let's get out of here!" she said, and then she and Derek jumped inside the car and raced off, with Dan moaning in the back.

Traffic was jammed; firefighters and all emergency personnel were out in force, while Dan was in the back of the car dying. The pressure was on, the police were stopping traffic and firefighters were fighting a blazing fire. Joyce and Derek were struggling to breath in the choking smoke. "Derek, go check and see if Dan's breathing," Joyce commanded.

Derek hopped over the seat into the back of the car and saw that Dan was barely breathing. He looked at Joyce and from his expression, she knew that Dan was fading fast.

Joyce tried to hold it together as she slowly crawled along in bumper-to-bumper, stop and go traffic. Police officers were going down the line of cars and questioning each driver. The disaster that had befallen the city was of little importance to Joyce, as she feared what would happen to her and the dying man in the back of her car.

A police officer signaled for Joyce to roll down her window. It appeared to her that he was looking for terrorists. "Is it chemical warfare?" Joyce asked him. "A terrorist attack?"

"Never mind that, who are you, and where are you going?"

"Dr. Joyce Picard," Joyce said as she showed the policeman her identification, "and I'm trying to get to my laboratory on Cherry Street, it's at the edge of the woods."

The officer signaled ahead, "She checks out, let her through!" Then he waved for Joyce to make the turn and get out of the area.

Derek jumped over the seat, he stood beside Joyce and put his paw on her shoulder. "Derek, we've come so far. I just can't lose Dan now, not when we're so close!"

Derek didn't think that losing Dan would be such a horrible thing. But he moved closer to Joyce and leaned against her arm and held her close.

Joyce looked ahead and she could see the tall trees near the laboratory. "We're getting close Derek, we just might make it!" she said stroking Derek's head.

Joyce pulled up to the loading dock and honked the horn. "Stewart! Stewart!" she yelled.

Joyce jumped out of the car and opened the back, wondering if Dan was still alive. She was terrified to find him lying in a pool of blood and not breathing. She quickly started to try to resuscitate him, but Dan wasn't responding.

"Derek," she said between breaths, "go get Stewart!"

Derek ran to the door of the loading dock and pushed the intercom just as the door burst open. Out came Stewart, pushing a gurney and holding a hypodermic needle in his hand. "Stewart to the rescue!" he said as he rushed to Dan and gave him a stimulant shot.

Derek ran into the lab and got Tache' and the two of them rushed outside.

"Tache' help us get Dan out of the car and onto the gurney!" Joyce said.

Dan was one heavy man and it took all three of them to move him.

Stewart checked Dan's vitals as Joyce and Tache' wheeled him into the laboratory. "He's breathing normally now, but he's lost a lot of blood. We'll need to start a transfusion."

"What can I do to help?" Tache' asked.

"Stewart and I have this, Tache'," Joyce answered. "You just relax, and don't worry. There's nothing that you can do."

Joyce and Stewart worked feverishly on Dan for what seemed like hours, as he passed in and out of consciousness. It was touch and go, but somehow Dan stabilized. "Looks like he's going to make it," Stewart told Joyce.

"Yes, but who knows what condition he'll be in when he comes to his senses, this time. I have to be here. I'll take the first shift."

"Okay Joyce, I'll be in my room. Call when you want me."

THE EVIL SEED IS PLANTED

Joyce sat and watched Dan, she was tense and worried. Several hours later, she remembered that the city was in peril and decided to find out what had happened.

She walked out of the O.R. and saw Tache' quietly sitting by the door. "Are you alright Joyce?" she sweetly asked.

"Tache', what are you doing up? You don't need to be losing sleep over this. I've got everything under control."

"No you don't Joyce," Tache' said as she reached out and wrapped her arms lovingly around Joyce. "How long is it going to take before you realize that I'm here for you?"

Joyce melted into the caring arms of Tache', as she tenderly held her close. "You've been through an awful ordeal today, Joyce. Let's relax for a while. There's nothing more that you can do for Dan tonight. I'll make you something to eat. Why don't you sit down here at the table?"

"Well, I guess I could, eat something," Joyce agreed. "Dan's hooked up to monitors and if something changes, I'll know about it."

Tache' opened the little refrigerator and then began to cook up a delicious meal for Joyce.

Joyce couldn't remember the last time that someone had cooked for her and it made her feel special. "My, it certainly smells good," she commented.

"Oh yes, you're gonna love it," Tache' said as she stirred

and flipped over the food cooking in the pans. And I've got something special for Derek too, his favorite, mini pizzas."

Tache' was a wiz in the kitchen, and it wasn't long before she had whipped up a gourmet meal. After eating, Joyce felt much better and wasn't driven to go back into the O.R. and sit, staring at Dan.

"Why don't we go into Brian's office and watch a movie on the big television?" Tache' suggested. "There's a new release that Stewart and I have been planning to watch, but I'm sure he won't mind if we watch it together."

Joyce was enjoying herself with Tache'. Her sunny personality was overshadowing the horror of the day and somehow Joyce felt like everything was going to be fine. She no longer wanted hear about the catastrophe in the city and decided that watching a movie was a good idea. "Sounds great Tache', it's been a long time since Derek and I have seen a good movie."

Joyce and Derek went into Brian's office to get the movie ready, while Tache' made popcorn. A few minutes later, she came in with a big bowlful. "Can't watch a movie without popcorn," she said in a cheerful tone.

Derek was thrilled, and he enthusiastically jumped up and down.

"Okay Derek," Tache' said, "you get the first handful."

The three of them sat on the couch and snuggled while they watched the exciting movie together.

Stewart was studying in his room and he turned on the radio to listen to his favorite news program, The Babs Maguire Show. Babs Maguire was frantic; an airplane had crashed into the city mall. There was a call for all available doctors to report to the hospital and help treat the wounded.

Stewart bolted from his desk and went to look for Joyce in the O.R., but she wasn't there. He glided from room to room searching for her and when he entered the kitchen area, he found evidence that Tache' had been cooking. "Tache' was cooking and she didn't invite me!" He was outraged. "Joyce must be interfering with my bestie and me!" Stewart walked into Brian's office and there he found Joyce snuggled up with Tache' and watching *his* movie!

He was furious, but he didn't show it. "Joyce, an airplane has crashed into the city mall and there's a call for all available doctors to help treat the wounded! You better get going!"

"Why don't you go Stewart? I'll stay here and monitor Dan."

Stewart angrily clenched his jaw, he wanted to say, "Yeah sure, you'd love nothing better than to stay here and cuddle with *my* Tache' and watch *our* movie," but he bit his tongue. Angry as he was, Stewart managed to keep his composure. "Joyce, you're the one with M.D. after your name, I'm a scientist not a medical doctor!"

"Right again, as always, Stewart," Joyce agreed.

Joyce got up and started to leave the room. "Derek you'll have to stay here with Tache'," she said.

Derek looked over the bowl of popcorn and waved Joyce away. "Okay, okay, I guess it's not a problem."

The minute that Joyce left the room, Stewart snuggled down in the warm place where she had been sitting. "Would you mind starting the movie over Tache'. I've been looking forward to watching it with you."

Tache' started the movie over and Stewart smiled with glee as he cuddled up to her.

That night, Joyce worked feverishly at the hospital and Stewart enjoyed his evening with Tache' and Derek.

In the morning, Joyce came back to the lab; she was exhausted, but wanted an update on Dan's condition.

Tache' greeted her at the door. "How did it go last night?" she asked.

"It was nothing short of a miracle, no fatalities."

Stewart joined them in the hall, "What procedures did you preform, any surgery?"

"Actually, I did have a brain surgery."

"Oh my," Tache' said, looking concerned. "Who needed brain surgery?"

"It was the pilot, he suffered a brain injury in the crash and I was asked to repair it. During the surgery, I found that he had suffered a seizure during the flight, and I concluded that it was the cause of the accident."

"Will he be alright?" Tache' asked.

"Oh yes, he'll be perfectly fine, I was able to completely repair the damage incurred in the accident as well as the cause of the seizure. He should be back to work and flying planes within the month."

"Why Joyce, you're a hero!" Tache' excitedly praised.

The remark struck Stewart to the core. His plan to get rid of Joyce, the night before, had been effective. But now it had backfired and it looked as though Tache' liked Joyce better than he!

"It's not that impressive, Tache'," Stewart said sharply. "I wouldn't exactly say that it makes Joyce a heroine. I can perform that procedure too."

Joyce took no offence. She merely changed the subject and asked about Dan's condition.

"You're here just in time," Stewart told her. "He's about to come out of it."

Joyce was concerned about Dan, he had malfunctioned and she knew that he couldn't be trusted. "He may be violent Stewart, we better lock him in the Interview Room, right away."

Stewart agreed, and the two of them wheeled Dan into the Interview Room. Joyce and Stewart watched as Dan woke up, once again. "Wow Doc, I thought I was a goner for sure this time!" he said.

"Yes Dan, you nearly didn't make it. It's a good thing that Derek and I showed up in time," Joyce said. "I want you to know that what happened was not your fault, it must be a brain malfunction. Until we can remedy the problem I'm afraid that you're going to have to stay locked in the Interview Room again."

Dan did not like being locked up again, but he didn't complain. He was more worried about how Joyce would remedy his brain malfunction. Maybe this would be the time that she would turn him into a Tyrone! Dan thought that Joyce was playing games with him and merely waiting for an excuse to make him into another mindless drone and use him for free labor. He thought that his only chance to avoid this peril, was to turn Stewart against Joyce.

After Joyce went home, Stewart came into the Interview Room and Dan started working on him. "Hey Stew, I'm glad that you're not afraid of me too."

"No I'm not, I understand you Dan. You wouldn't attack another man; it's only women that drive you to kill."

"Yeah, you're my bud, Stew, us men have to stick together. That Joyce is a real piece of work, the way she bosses you around. I don't know how you stand it."

Dan had picked an opportune moment to work on Stewart. Stewart believed that Joyce was interfering in his relationship with Tache'. He didn't want to lose her, Tache', was the sunshine in his dreary life. "Yes, things have definitely gotten worse lately Dan. Last night, Joyce had Tache' fix dinner for her and didn't let her invite me. Then, she made Tache' watch a movie with her, one that Tache' and I were looking forward to viewing together."

"You should just let me off the bitch Stew. Not only is she trying to steal Tache' from you, she's standing in your way. You could run this place so much better without her interference."

Even though Stewart was angry at Joyce, he didn't want to go so far as to kill her. "No Dan, I could never kill Joyce. We've been working together for years."

"Well, you wouldn't have to kill her. What about what you did to Brian, when he stood in your way? You could just give Joyce a brain transplant. That way, she could still work here, but you could program her to take orders from you."

"Hmmm, sounds very tempting Dan, but I don't think that it's necessary."

Dan backed off, he didn't want to push Stewart too hard, too fast. "Yeah, I suppose you're right," he pretended to

160

agree.

"I think that it will work itself out," Stewart said. "I handled Joyce's intrusion, between Tache' and me, last night, by sending Joyce to the hospital. Once she was gone, Tache' and I watched the movie together and had a wonderful time. I believe that I am intelligent enough to ward Joyce off without killing her or performing a brain transplant. She has made many necessary contributions to our research, in the past. I would like to continue working with her, in the same capacity, if at all possible."

"That's cool man, I understand."

Dan hadn't been successful, that night, but he had planted an evil seed in Stewart's mind, and he would wait for it to sprout and grow.

The next day, when Joyce came to work, she was very upset. She had the newspaper in her hand and she called Stewart and pointed out an article and told him to read it.

"Hmm, another command," Stewart thought to himself, "I don't like the way you push me around Joyce."

Stewart looked at the article and read about the attempted rape of Daisy Butterfield. Then he looked at Joyce, "So?" he sharply said.

"What do you mean … so? It was Dan!"

"SO … don't jump to conclusions until Dan has a chance to explain his side of the story. Perhaps there was good reason for what he did."

"No Stewart, no explanations. Obviously it was a mistake allowing him to keep his old memories. As a matter of fact, I've been going over my notes and I don't think that any killer should be allowed to keep any of his previous personality. We completely changed Brian and look how well he's doing."

"You mean that you want to make Dan, like Brian?"

"Absolutely."

"I'm sorry Joyce, but I can't allow you to do that to Dan. He's my friend and he needs to keep his own identity."

"Brian knows who he is, he's just a nicer version ot himself and he's happy," Joyce argued.

"You mean Peggy's happy ... don't you?"

"Stewart, what are you saying?"

"I'm saying that I won't allow you to transplant a brain like Brian's into Dan."

"Stewart, I understand that you have a fondness for Dan, but you have to stay focused on our objective. Our goal is that violent offenders aren't destroyed, but are transformed into healthy minded, happy, productive members of society. That they are no longer a threat and that no one has to live in fear. Ultimately, we'll cure all diseases of the mind and anyone with a mental or emotional problem can have a simple adjustment to be well."

"I know our goal just as well as you do, Joyce, but in Dan's case I just don't agree."

"Stewart I don't want to discuss it anymore. I'm having Tyrone begin assembly on a replacement brain for Dan and that's the way it's going to be."

Stewart was fuming, Joyce had never spoken to him like this before. He remembered what Dan had suggested; a brain transplant for Joyce. Maybe it wasn't such a bad idea after all. Stewart went to his room, he was troubled, but after a moral struggle, he managed to purge the idea from his mind. "I could never tamper with a brilliant mind like Joyce's," he reasonably concluded.

A few minutes later, Joyce came barreling down the hall calling for Stewart and found him in his room. "Stewart," she said, "Tyrone has begun building Dan's replacement brain. How long before Dan will be healthy enough to tolerate the surgery?"

Stewart wanted to stretch things out as much as he could. "He's making progress, but very slowly. I can't predict how long it will take for his recovery this time."

"I'll take a look at his chart myself," Joyce said and then she took Dan's chart. She studied his record, with Stewart looking on and then closed it. "As soon as Tyrone completes Dan's replacement brain, we're doing the surgery. I won't take another chance on him. He would have killed the Butterfield girl, and her blood would have been on our hands. It's just lucky for us, that she successfully defended herself. I don't even like having Dan in the lab in his condition; it's like having a rattlesnake amongst us."

FROM ONE SERIAL KILLER TO ANOTHER

At lunchtime, that day, Joyce took Tache' to a new restaurant and, once again, Stewart was left behind. He was getting more and more resentful of the lunch dates and he decided to go and talk about it to his friend, Dan.

"Yeah I heard Stew, another lunch date and you're not invited. That bitch sure takes you for granted. I don't think she'll ever realize that she can't run this place without you."

"Yes, it's true, I do shoulder a lot of responsibility."

"I don't trust her Stew. Do you know what she plans to do with me?"

Stewart hesitated, he knew that he shouldn't tell Dan, but he divulged Joyce's plan anyway. "I hate to tell you Dan, I consider you a friend, but Joyce is going to transplant brain number five in you, one like Brian has.

"Hell no, I'd rather be dead than be a pussy-whipped wimp like that freak Brian! Just kill me now!" Dan put his head in his hands then he looked up at Stewart with desperation on his eyes. "You can't let her do this to me Stew! You just can't let her do it!"

"There's not much I can do about it Dan. It won't be that bad, Brian's happy. You'll still know who you are, you just won't have any unpleasant memories or desires to commit violent acts."

"I should have known that it would be a fucking bitch, who would get revenge on me. Fuck Joyce!"

"I understand your hatred for women Dan, and I must say that I agree with you, some women do need to be killed."

After Stewart's strange comment, Dan knew something

163

was up, "You killed one of those skanky bitches yourself, haven't you, Stew? Come on, admit it, you know you want to."

Stewart had never told anyone about his secret, and he found that Dan was correct, he did want to tell him about it. "I killed a woman, not too long ago. Her name was Jody, and I did it right here at the lab. She was one of Brian's girlfriends and she made fun of me."

"Yeah, I killed a broad that made fun of me too. Those bitches really know how to piss you off, especially if you like 'em."

"Yes Dan, how did you know? I did like Jody, I thought that she was quite beautiful and even defended her to Joyce. I guess I'm not as unique as I'd like to believe, killing a woman because she made fun of me."

"Who else did you kill Stew?"

"Oh not as many as *you* Dan," Stewart said modestly, "only four."

"Aren't you a freak and a half, here you are studying and executing serial killers and you're one yourself. I got to hand it to ya, Stew you've got quite a scam going here."

It felt good to impress Dan and Stewart went on to divulge more information. "The first time I killed, I was in the second grade. My teacher held up one of my drawings, alongside another students. She praised the other child's artwork and made fun of mine, in front of the whole class! I was so angry that I couldn't get over it. After school that day, I took my father's big hammer, and snuck back into the classroom. Mrs. Classick was grading papers and I snuck up behind her and hit her on the head. Her skull crushed in, and she was dead. It felt so good, that I actually started laughing."

"What did you do with the hammer?"

"I threw it in the river then I burned my clothes and took a swim. I used to wet my pants, so I always carried a change of clothes with me in my backpack. It was really a no brainer."

"Did you get caught?"

"No, no one ever suspected that a little second grader

164

could be capable of such a thing. I got away with it completely unscathed."

"A killer in the second grade, I bow to you, you are truly the master. That's how stupid Joyce is, she doesn't even suspect you, and you committed a murder right under her nose. You've got to admit it Stew, you'd do a much better job without her holding you back. Who better to understand the mind of a serial killer, than another serial killer. She can't possibly comprehend anything the way that you do. You must laugh at her feeble attempts to figure us out."

"Joyce isn't that bad, Dan, she actually does quite well. She has a brilliant mind."

Dan could see that Stewart had had enough and he backed off of Joyce again. "How long do I have before the brain transplant?"

"Don't worry Dan, I haven't given up yet. I'll think of something. I like you just the way you are, and I don't want to change anything about you."

"I'm counting on you man."

With that, Stewart went back to work and as he did, he tried to think of a plan to save his comrade, Dan.

A few days passed, it was Friday and Tyrone was nearly finished with Dan's new brain.

"Stewart, would you please schedule Dan's brain transplant for Monday," Joyce asked. "I've already cleared my schedule.

"Joyce I'd really like you to reconsider. I think that Dan is an exception."

"Stewart we've already been down this road. If you want to know the truth, I've been trying to decide just how much of a liability it is even keeping him alive. We may have to consider exterminating him. Releasing him back into society, under any circumstances would be risky."

At that point, Stewart just turned and walked away. The brain transplant was definitely better than extermination. But, Dan was his friend, the only other person in the world that knew his secret. Stewart thought about releasing Dan and letting him kill Joyce, but his love, and his loyalty to her won out. He had been working side by side with Joyce for so many years that he decided to go along with her, and he scheduled Dan's surgery.

THE SLUMBER PARTY THAT LIT THE FUSE

Joyce worked late that night, and she and Tache' were giggling in her office when Stewart walked in. "What's so funny?" he asked.

"Oh hi, Stewart, we're having a slumber party tonight."

"A slumber party?" Stewart asked. "Sounds like fun. I think that I can find my sleeping bag."

"Oh I'm sorry Stewart," Joyce apologized, "it's just for girls."

"You mean that Tache' and I won't be having dinner together tonight?"

"No, I'm sorry Stewart, but I'll fix you something real special tomorrow night," Tache' said trying to console him.

Stewart wasn't just disappointed, he was seething with anger and jealousy. He silently turned and walked out of the room, while Joyce and Tache' planned the fun party without him.

This was a crushing blow to Stewart; he was an odd little man, and had also been an odd little child. The other children didn't like him and he had never been invited to any of their parties. And now it was happening to him all over again, Stewart the nerd, home alone, while the other kids were out having fun together. Stewart the nerd, always left out.

Stewart was so upset that he couldn't work. He ran to his room and threw himself on his bed sobbing. "I hate you Joyce! And I hate you too Tache'. Pretending to be my friend, and then leaving me here all alone. You'll probably make fun of me at the party too, just like the kids at school used to do."

"But wait a minute, I'm not alone, I still have Dan. Dan the man, he's my only real friend and Joyce wants to change his brain. Joyce will probably program him to be so different that he won't even like me anymore! Joyce is jealous of my relationship with Tache', and now she's trying to take Dan away from me too! Oh, what to do, what to do? I know, I'll release Dan and be free of both of those Benedict Arnold's! That's what I'll do, I'll let my friend Dan, kill the both of them! Only a true friend would kill for you, and Dan is such a good friend, he'd do it for me. Once those two women are gone, then Dan and I can run the lab together and have a great life! Yes, the two of them have to go!"

Joyce and Tache' were so excited about the slumber party, that they left the lab without even saying goodbye to Stewart. He was left alone in his room sobbing, with evil thoughts spinning in his mind.

When Stewart realized that the girls were gone, he got up and started walking aimlessly around the laboratory. He should have checked on Dan, but he didn't. "So unlike you Stewart, not to fulfill your responsibilities, but you can't let Dan see you like this, he'll lose all respect for you."

When Stewart passed Tache's room, he noticed that she had left the door unlocked and he went inside. As he entered, he could smell her perfume and took in a deep breath of it. Stewart raised his arms and began to twirl around, "Oh Tache', your scent is intoxicating!" Around and around he twirled, breathing in the scent of Tache'. "Oh Tache', I love you," he said over and over again, "I could never hurt you. It's Joyce, *she's* the problem, *she's* the one who's trying to take *you* away from me. Joyce, she's the one that Dan must kill."

Stewart opened the top drawer of Tache's dresser and pulled out one of her silk stockings. He held it to his face and rubbed it on his cheek. Stewart laid on Tache's bed and then he decided to climb under the covers. "I wonder what it would be like, lying here under the covers with you, my pretty? Your dark luxurious skin is softer than silk."

Stewart laid in Tache's bed and fantasized about rubbing

her ankles. Surely Tache' wasn't the one leaving him out, she wouldn't do such a thing to him, it had to be Joyce.

Stewart got up from Tache's bed and walked around the lab, trying to come up with a plan. "How to dispose of Joyce? This won't be a simple task, Joyce is a well-known scientist and she'll be missed. And how could I possibly conceal the murder from Tache'? Perhaps if I explain it to her, she'll understand and go along with me. Maybe when she realizes how Joyce is trying to come between us, she'll want Joyce out of the picture too."

Stewart went into Joyce's office and sat down at her desk. He angrily tapped his fingers on her blotter, and found himself looking at a picture of Joyce and him together at their first science fair. They were standing arm in arm and smiling as they held up their trophy. "What's wrong with you, Stewart?!" He screamed and slammed his fist on the desk. "You're planning to murder the best friend that you've ever had, just because you're jealous about a slumber party!"

Stewart was ashamed of himself and feeling remorseful, when the phone rang. He answered it, "Dr. Whitehead speaking."

It was Joyce, "Stewart, I'm calling to apologize. Tache' and I left the lab without even saying goodbye, I'm so sorry." Then Stewart heard Tache' in the background, "I'm sorry too suga', I'll make it up to ya baby."

Then Joyce started talking again, "Tache' is making a menu for a special dinner for the two of you, tomorrow night. I suggested that she make you a cake, you know how much you love the Birthday cakes that I bake for you every year. But, you like both the chocolate and the white cake so much, I don't know which one you prefer. What are you in the mood for, chocolate or white?"

"Well, they're both delicious, that's something you do quite well Joyce, bake a Birthday cake. Either one would be fine, but if I had to choose, I'd have to say that I'm more in the mood for white cake right now."

"White cake Tache', add that those ingredients to the

shopping list."

"With rainbow sprinkles?" Tache' asked.

"Tell her yes, absolutely with rainbow sprinkles," Stewart said laughing.

Tache' and I both feel badly about you not being able to attend the slumber party tonight, but someone has to hold down the fort. You're always so reliable that I think I take you for granted at times, Stewart. But, I want you to know that I greatly appreciate everything that you contribute. We both know that I couldn't get by without good ol' Stewart."

"Oh Joyce, don't be silly, I know that you appreciate me. I can't believe that you girls are making such a fuss over this slumber party thing. What makes you think that I really wanted to come to a female slumber party; that would be ridiculous. All of the giggling and nail painting and makeup tips, I'm afraid that I would find it quite boring. Men don't enjoy those kind of things. You girls have a nice time and I'll see you later."

Stewart hung up the phone and he felt wonderful. Tache' would be home the next day, and the two of them would have a great time together. Eating Tache's special dinner and enjoying Joyce's white birthday cake, with rainbow sprinkles. Things just didn't get any better in Stewart's world. His wonderful friends, Joyce and Tache' hadn't forgotten him after all, and he was on top of the world!

Stewart pulled himself together and checked on Dan through the Observation Booth window. Then he inspected the new brain that Tyrone was building for him. Tyrone was busily at work and it was clear that he would be finished before Monday when Joyce planned the brain transplant surgery for Dan. He thought about interfering with Tyrone's work, perhaps doing something to slow him down or to sabotage him. But then, he decided against it. While it was true, that Stewart did like Dan, and considered him a friend, it didn't come close to how he felt about Tache' and Joyce. He loved them both, just the way they were, and he didn't want to do anything to jeopardize their relationships with him.

After Stewart documented the progress of his current experiments, he felt fatigued. He decided to go to bed early and he soon fell fast asleep.

At the slumber party, things were just warming up and Joyce wasn't prepared for what she was in for. Tache' had brought both her craft kit and her beauty bag. And after having shrimp cocktail and mini pizzas, (Derek's preference, of course) Tache' went into action. She opened her beauty bag and approached Joyce with, hair color, a comb and a pair of scissors. Joyce was afraid, but she decided to throw caution to the wind and let Tache' take over.

Tache' sat Joyce down in a chair by the kitchen counter and pulled the rubber band from her hair. "You have such thick pretty hair Joyce; you shouldn't be pulling it back with this rubber band. It's very damaging. Where'd you get this thing, from your desk drawer?"

Joyce laughed, "You're right, it is a rubber band from my desk drawer.

Tache' shook her head in disapproval and brushed Joyce's hair, "It's so shiny, one of your best features. We just need to get rid of that grey. Tache' applied the hair color and waited the appropriate time. Now let's get over to the sink and give it a good wash and conditioning."

Tache' washed and conditioned Joyce's hair and Joyce enjoyed every minute of it.

"Now it's time for a nice cut. You need some light layers and I'll soften it around your face." Tache' started to cut Joyce's hair. As Joyce watched the hair piling up on the floor, she was terrified, wondering if she would have any left when it was over. Then, Tache' blow-dried and used the curling iron. When she was finished, Joyce wanted to look at her new hairdo, but Tache' wouldn't let her. "No, not until after the makeup," she said. "I have a stunning makeup that I'm going to use on you, one that will accent your beautiful eyes."

Tache' worked on Joyce intently, with liquid makeup and powders and frosts. Shadows and glitters, highlighters and lip liners, things that Joyce had never known existed.

When the stunning makeup job was completed, Joyce was prepared to have a look at herself in the mirror. But even though the makeup was done, Tache' changed her mind. "No, I think that you'll have to wait for the unveiling a little while longer. I want to take a look at your wardrobe first. And we still have to do your manicure and pedicure too; don't forget."

Joyce and Tache' went into Joyce's bedroom and looked through her closet. "Oh my, my, we are definitely going to have to take you shopping girl. This closet is nearly bare."

"I know Tache', there isn't much to choose from. I rarely have the opportunity to dress up. I have plenty of lab coats though."

Tache' gave Joyce a disapproving look and then she pulled a black shift out of the closet. "Now this isn't too bad, I think that I can do something with this dress."

"Yes, that's the dress that I wore to Professor Spits' funeral. I haven't worn it since."

"Now let me see here," Tache' said as she examined the plain shift dress. "A little tuck here and a higher hemline and maybe a slit, up the side. Mmmm hmmm, yes, I can definitely do something with this."

Tache' and Joyce moved into the living room and sat down. Tache' opened her craft kit and Derek took a look inside and pulled out a shiny bead. "Oh Derek likes the sparkle," Tache' said as she looked at Derek admiring the bead.

Tache' went to work, cutting and sewing and then it was time for the finishing touches. Now, this is one thing that I learned from being a ho, men like a little bling. She then proceeded to apply rhinestones and shiny colored beads to the dress and then finished up with a colorful silk scarf.

"We'll put that aside for later," she said. "Now it's time for your nails. Tache' put Joyce's feet into a hot tub of scented water to soak. "You're feet are in pretty bad shape, we'll give them a nice long soak. In the meantime, I'll do your

171

fingernails."

Joyce always kept her fingernails filed and pushed the cuticles back, so it didn't take long before Tache' was ready to polish them. When she reached for her nail polish box, Derek jumped into her lap and held out his paw. "Oh my, look Joyce, Derek wants his nails done too. Oh how cute! Of course I'll do your nails for you Derek, you're my man."

Derek sat patiently as Tache' filed his nails.

"I trim them once in a while," Joyce said, "but he usually wears them down on his own."

"Yes," Tache' said, "Derek's nails look fine. You're all done Derek," she told him.

"And now it's time for your polish," Tache' told Joyce. With Derek still sitting in her lap, she reached for her nail polish box again. Let's see here, we need to select just the right color.

As Tache' looked through the nail polish, Derek politely placed his paw on some sparkly silver polish. "I guess he want's polish too," Joyce said.

"That's fine Derek," Tache' agreed, "I'll paint your nails first."

Derek sat quietly, as Tache' painted his nails with the glitter polish. When she was done, she gently placed him on the coffee table. "Okay now Derek, you sit still for a little while and let the polish dry."

Derek carefully placed his paws on the table and didn't move. "I'll tell ya Joyce, Derek never ceases to amaze me."

"And he never will."

"Now it was time for Joyce to get her nails painted. Tache' tried to talk her into red, as it went so well with the black dress, but Joyce was a little hesitant. "That's fine," Tache' said, "we'll just go with the hot pink." She thought that it was less bold, and that Joyce would feel more comfortable with it. But, the hot pink wasn't any less daring, as far as Joyce was concerned. But, even though she was uncomfortable, she agreed to have her nails painted with the shocking hot pink polish; both her fingernails and her toenails.

Once her nails were dry, Joyce slipped into her newly styled dress and the black pumps that she had worn to the funeral of Professor Spits. Tache' selected some earrings from her bag, a dazzling necklace and about fifteen shiny bangle bracelets. After Joyce put them on, it was time for the unveiling. Tache' stood Joyce in front of the full length mirror with her eyes closed. "Okay now Joyce, you can look!"

Joyce uncovered her eyes and looked at herself in the mirror. And when she saw how beautiful she was, she began to cry.

Tache' wrapped her arms around Joyce, "Honey, honey, what's the matter? Don't you like what I did? I'm sorry, your hair will grow back. Here, come into the bathroom and we'll wash the makeup off. You're okay baby, just calm down. Now where's that rubber band? We'll just put it right back in your hair."

"No, no Tache' that's not it at all, I'm not unhappy with what you did. I'm just in shock, I think that I actually look like a woman. You've made me beautiful!"

"That's right darl'n' you are beautiful, inside and out. And don't you ever forget it."

Joyce kept crying and Tache' didn't know what to do about it. "Now Joyce, you better tell me what's really wrong. Why are you so upset about looking beautiful?"

"It's just that I wanted to be a super model when I was a little girl, and this reminded me of it. The day that my mother was killed, I had fixed my hair in a fancy hairdo and mom told me how beautiful I was. I haven't fixed my hair ever since, and you just don't know how much this means to me."

"I just want you to be happy," Tache' said, "and as long as you're happy, I'm happy too."

"Well, be happy Tache', because I certainly am. You've actually changed my life tonight. You've shown me what it's like to feel like a woman. And from now on I'm going to be a woman, not just a scientist."

"That's great honey, I'm so glad that you're feeling better." Tache' put her arm around Joyce and they walked into the living room together and sat down on the couch.

The two were just relaxing together, when Derek boldly wiggled in between them holding some beads in his paws.

"Oh it looks like Derek would like a little bling too," Tache' said. She was giggling as she reached for her craft kit. She pulled out a piece of elastic thread and began to make a sparkling little collar for Derek. Derek picked out the beads that he wanted and he handed them to Tache', one at a time, as she strung them together. When she was finished, she slipped the necklace over Derek's head and he jumped down from the sofa. Then Derek ran into the bathroom and came back with a comb.

"Oh good heavens, I just don't believe this!" Tache' said surprised. "Okay Derek, it looks like you want a new hairdo too. That's fine with me."

Tache' put gel into Derek's fur, she styled it into a faux hawk and then finished it off with purple hair paint. When it dried, Derek felt his head with his paw and got very excited. He ran down the hallway and signaled for the girls to follow him. When they reached Joyce's bedroom, he viewed himself in the mirror. "Oh, *very* handsome," the two girls said and made a big deal out of Derek's new look.

"This is the cutest thing that I've ever seen in my entire life," Tache' said. "You're absolutely right Joyce, Derek will never cease to amaze me."

By this time, it was getting late and Tache' yawned.

"Yes, I suppose you're right, Tache'," Joyce said, "it has been a long day, but definitely a special one. Why don't we go to bed?"

Tache' took her overnight bag and went into the bathroom to get ready for bed. She put on a silk negligee with matching robe and of course, Joyce, changed into her full-length, flannel nightgown. "I know, I know," she said, when Tache' saw her in the frumpy gown, "we'll have to take me shopping."

"Does your couch fold out into a bed, Joyce? Where am I going to sleep tonight?"

"I don't have any place for overnight guests. It's never

come up before. I'm afraid that you'll have to sleep with me. I hope that you don't mind, but the bed is plenty roomy and we should be fine."

When Tache' realized that Joyce wanted to sleep with her, she was taken by surprise. "Well, here it is … the pay off," she thought. "Everyone wants something from me, and it's usually the same old thing, S .. E ..X." Even though Tache' was disappointed that Joyce was expecting sex from her, she was willing to give her whatever she wanted. After all, Joyce was the boss. As Tache' got into the bed, she whispered to herself, "Tache' the whore, just a whore, as always, nothing more than a whore."

Joyce climbed into bed with Tache', and Derek curled up at Tache's feet. "Wow," Joyce said, "Derek's certainly crazy about you, he's letting you sleep in his spot."

Joyce reached for the lamp, "Good night Tache'," she said, and then she turned the switch. The room was dark, accept for the nightlight, and Joyce rolled away from Tache' and closed her eyes.

Tache' wasn't sure what to do. Was Joyce expecting her to make a move? Would Joyce be offended if she didn't? Or would she be offended if she did?

Tache' decided to at least try, and she placed her hand on Joyce's waist. Joyce rolled over and looked lovingly at Tache'. I've had such a wonderful time tonight, in fact it's been wonderful ever since you came into my life. I could never say it before Tache', but I love you too."

The way that Tache' saw it, Joyce had made her move. But, still unsure of exactly what to do, she simply replied, "You know Joyce, I am a fully functioning male."

"No, I didn't know that, I guess I'm rather naïve when it comes to sex, I've never experienced it. I think that it's fascinating how you can present yourself as a beautiful woman, and also be a fully functioning male. Yes, you are truly an amazing person."

Joyce put her hand on Tache's shoulder and said sweetly, "And when I say that I love you, Tache', I really do mean it. I don't care about your past, who you were, or what you've done. I just want to make you as happy as you've made me."

Tache' was touched; Joyce wasn't angling for sex after all. She just wanted to be loved. She pulled Joyce near and held her close. Joyce rested her head on Tache's chest and the two laid together in silence as the love between them seemed to bloom fill the room.

Tache' knew that Joyce had true love for her, not merely sexual attraction and she felt a peace like she never had before. She wanted to care for Joyce, protect her and love her.

Joyce took the initiative and broke the silence. "Tache' I don't know how you'll feel about it, but I would love it if you would move in here, with Derek and me. We could be a family. I know that you prefer to live as a woman, and it's alright with me. I want you, and I'm willing to live without sex. Just having you close is enough. I want you to be happy and I accept you, completely and in every way.

Tache' was overwhelmed, the love and acceptance that she had longed for was in her arms. She had found happiness with the scientist, Dr. Joyce Picard.

Tache' could barely speak. She nodded her head in agreement, and said, holding back her tears of joy, "Yes, Joyce, yes, I love you and Derek and I want us to live together and be a family."

No more words were spoken as Tache' and Joyce fell peacefully asleep in each other's arms, with Derek cuddling at their feet.

DESPERATE DAN

Back at the lab, Dan was beside himself. He knew that his brain transplant was scheduled for Monday and he had to do something fast or he would end up like Brian. Dan decided that he would try, just one more time, to convince

Stewart to do the brain transplant on both Joyce and Tache'. And if that didn't work, he would kill Stewart and use his thumb for the identification that he needed to escape from the lab.

Dan waited for Stewart to come in and check on him, as he usually did, but Stewart didn't show. Dan didn't know that Stewart had merely observed him through the Observation Booth window and then gone to bed. Dan began to get more and more frustrated and he paced back and forth in the room fearing the fate that awaited him.

Meanwhile, after sleeping a few hours, Stewart was waking up. He stretched and then after grooming, he went to work on a new project. It wasn't unusual for Stewart to get up in the night and work, as he didn't require much sleep.

Stewart walked past the Observation Booth and decided to take a quick peek at Dan. When he did, he saw him pacing back and forth. "Dan, are you alright in there?" he asked.

Dan was elated that Stewart was there. "Stew, I'm having a real rough night. You think that you could come in here with me and talk for a while."

"I can do ya one better," Stewart said. "I'll go get my Scrabble game, nothing like a ripping game of Scrabble to calm the ol' nerves."

Dan couldn't believe that he was going to have to play Scrabble with Stewart and he rethought his plan. Maybe it would be better to kill Stewart right away and make good his escape? But, the laboratory was a safe haven, someplace where he and his buddy, Stew, could continue to commit murders and have the perfect cover. It was a great set up, definitely better than being on the run. So, Dan decided to try, once again, to convince Stewart to see things his way.

Minutes later, Stewart came into the Interview Room with his old, worn out Scrabble game, and set it up on the table.

Dan acted happy about it, "Yeah, this is a great idea Stewart, Scrabble ... love the game."

"Okay," Stewart said, "let's draw tiles to see who goes first."

Stewart and Dan each picked a tile, and Dan got the letter A.

"Looks like you're going first," Stewart said disappointed.

Dan was disturbed about having to play a game, but he tried to hold it together and haphazardly put some tiles on the board. "C..A..N, can … you know shit pot, john."

"I'm afraid that that definition isn't in the dictionary, Dan. Perhaps you should change your position to, a metal container."

"Yeah, sure Stew, whatever you say."

Next, it was Stewart's turn, and he carefully examined the tiles in front of him. "Hmmm, let me see here. Oh, this is a good one, A..B..A..M..P..E..R..E, abampere.

"Yeah Stew, it's a good one."

"Do you care to challenge me?"

"No, I know what it means."

"Abampere is a very uncommon word; don't tell me that you actually know its definition."

Then, much to Stewart's surprise, Dan began to define the word abampere. "The cgs electromagnetic unit of electric current equal to ten amperes. The abampere is the basic unit of the cgs electromagnetic system and is defined in terms of the force,"

Then Stewart finished Dan's sentence, "acting between two parallel conductors when each is carrying a current. I knew that you were intelligent, Dan, but even so, perhaps I have underestimated your knowledge of the English language. It appears that you are going to be a worthy opponent."

Then it was Dan's turn again, "B..R..O..A..D, broad."

"Yes Dan, broad it is a word, but I'm afraid that you're referring to an improper usage again."

"Yeah, yeah, yeah, whatever."

Stewart was anxious to play his next word, F..E..L..S..I..T..E , felsite!"

Dan looked at Stewart, he was disgusted and anxious, and Stewart thought that he was questioning the validity of his word. "Felsite is a word," he said defensively.

"Yes Stew I know, feldspar and quartz in the form of compact mass. I wasn't going to challenge you."

It was Dan's turn again, and he was near wits end, "Hey Stew," he said, placing his tiles on the board. "P..R..I..C..K, prick. I can't keep playing this game, I've got to talk to you man."

"I usually won't tolerate any interference when I'm engaged in a Scrabble game, but okay, we can talk."

"Stew, I've got to tell ya, I'm worried about that fuckin' brain transplant. You know that Joyce hates me, I killed her mother, and who knows what kind of a freak she'll turn me into. I .. I just don't want to be like that fuckin' idiot Brian! Have you figured out how you're going to help me out of this, buddy?"

"Don't worry about it Dan, you'll be fine. You must remember that Brian's happy, and you will be too."

"I thought that you were going to stop this fuckin' thing! Come on Stew, you know that I won't be the same. That fuckin' cunt Joyce doesn't want you to have any friends."

"Please refrain from name calling, Dan."

"Yeah, yeah, you're right, I apologize. Look how Joyce is trying to take Tache' away from you, and I'm the next friend to go. I'm the only one who understands you Stew, the only one that you can confide in, and she wants to take it all away! I won't remember a fuckin' thing, and I'm the only person who knows your secret. You'll be all alone again. Doesn't it feel great to have someone who knows what you are and still gives a shit about you? You certainly couldn't tell anyone else about your killings and be safe. If you told Joyce and Tache', they would turn you over to the authorities in a heartbeat. And you'd end up on death row, just like I was. But, if you do the brain transplant on Tache' and Joyce, you can have everything! You could make sure that Tache' would always be your *bestie*, and Joyce couldn't fuck it up. You know how much you dig your time with Tache'. And what's going on tonight? She's at Joyce's house having a party, and you're not invited. And face it Stew, this is just the beginning, it won't be long before Joyce will have Tache' all to herself, and you'll be totally left out. Think about her delicious cooking and the way that she cuddles with you on the couch, when you watch movies together. And how about the way she smells so delicious. It will all be over with, and pretty quick too! You need to do something about it, while you still can. Just think of it Stew, you could make Joyce your subordinate and you would be the one in charge. You shoulder all of the responsibility around here anyway, but Joyce is the one who gets all of the accolades. And what do you get? You get to stand in her shadow. You could be the boss around here, the big man, and you should be, you know how to get things done."

Stewart liked the idea of being the boss, and he continued to listen to Dan's plan.

"With you being the boss, the lab would move ahead and you'll get the credit that you deserve. You're more educated than Joyce is, and much more qualified. It would be better for everyone, if you took over, even for Joyce and Tache'."

"I have to admit it, Dan, once again, it does sound tempting. But, I wouldn't want to do anything to hurt Joyce or Tache'."

"You wouldn't be hurting them, you said it yourself, the brain transplants are completely safe. They wouldn't even have to know about it. It would make your world a complete euphoria.   And with me by your side; why I'd back you up all the way; I know what a genius you are. You'd be in complete control and don't forget our secret. We could "take care of" all of those skanky bitches that need to be dealt with."

"Well Dan, you do make a great argument and you are definitely intelligent enough to make it work. But, I'm going to have to pass. Joyce and Tache' are trying hard. As a matter of fact Tache's planning a special meal for us tomorrow. You have to remember, Dan, Joyce and I have been together for a long time. I just can't bring myself to betray her, using her own research against her, and for my own personal gain. I'm afraid that you're just going to have to trust me on this one, buddy. I'll take care of you, don't worry."

With that statement, Dan decided to kill Stewart. He stood up and was just about to grab him by his scrawny neck, when Stewart started to speak again.

"I do feel badly about your malfunction. I think that we could have avoided it if I had monitored you more closely."

Dan stopped dead in his tracks, "What do you mean, monitoring me?"

"Oh, I thought you knew. All of the artificial brains are equipped with a tracking device. When I saw you go into the country, when you were supposed to be at work, I should have known that something was amiss. But, like a fool, I waited, thinking that it was just a lengthy test drive. But then, when you went home from work early, I knew that there had been some sort of a problem and I sent Joyce to investigate. I never dreamed that you were suffering such a severe incident. You're lucky to be alive. Now, can we get on with our Scrabble game?"

Dan realized that he couldn't kill Stewart. With the tracking device in his brain, he would never get away with it. But, Dan had two more days and he decided to put them to good use and try to think of another way to avoid becoming a boot-licker like Brian.

"Stew, I'm really enjoying the game, but I'm getting tired now and I think that I can sleep. Thanks a lot for coming in here and spending time with me. If you don't mind, I'll see you in the morning."

"Sure Dan, you should get sleep, things sometimes seem better in the morning."

Stewart got up and opened the door to leave, "And Dan, we can still play Scrabble together, even after your brain transplant."

Dan had all he could do to control himself, but he said goodnight and after Stewart left, he tried to think of a new plan.

The next morning, Joyce, Derek and Tache' awoke in a happy mood, ready to start their new life together. After a nice breakfast, Joyce and Tache' began to clean the apartment to make room for Taches' belongings. Tache' was a neat person and Joyce was happy to have someone help her to get organized. They worked hard all day and were getting near the end of the mess, when Tache' realized what time it was. "Oh my goodness, I have to go and fix Stewart his special dinner."

Joyce was disappointed, "No Tache', I thought that you would move in tonight."

"I'd love to," Tache' agreed, "but what about Stewart?"

"Oh don't worry about Stewart, he's a great guy and he'll understand. We'll just have his special dinner over here, next weekend. We'll make it a celebration."

"Well, if you're sure he'll be okay with it, I wouldn't want to hurt his feelings."

"Nonsense, Stewart will be happy for us. I'll call you a cab and you can go back to the lab and get packed, while I finish up here. I'll come and get you when I'm done."

Tache' hugged Joyce, and then gave Derek a kiss. "Well, this is it, we're going to be a family!"

"Yes, and we're going to be very happy together."

With that, Tache' headed out the door. The taxi picked her up and she arrived at the lab and walked inside. The first thing she did was look for Stewart, but she found him busily working on an experiment. Tache' didn't want to disturb him, so she went straight to the basement, to get some boxes and then began to pack.

Tache' filled about three boxes and placed them in the hall. When Stewart finished his project, he approached Tache's room and saw the boxes. "What's going on Tache'?" he asked.

"Oh Stewart, you won't believe it, the most wonderful thing has happened!"

Stewart smiled and waited to hear the wonderful news. "Perhaps she's going to make her pot roast tonight."

"Joyce and I are in love, and I'm moving in with her and Derek. We're going to be a family! I've never been so happy in my whole life!"

Stewart was shocked by the news, so shocked that he lost his balance and nearly fell backward. "But Tache', what about our special dinner tonight?"

"I'm sorry Stewart, I'll have to cancel for tonight. But, we'll have you over to our place next weekend, for a celebration. I'll make my special ribs, the ones that you like so much, and the white cake with rainbow sprinkles. We'll make a real party of it. Doesn't that sound great?"

Stewart was devastated by the news, his whole life revolved around Tache', and the time that they spent together. And things were even worse than he could have ever imagined. Joyce wasn't just taking her away from him for a lunch date or a slumber party, she was moving her out of the lab and out of his life forever! No more delicious meals by Bunsen burner light, no more cuddling on the couch and watching movies together. No more laughing, no more fun, no more happiness! It was all over!

Stewart was beside himself and he wanted to get away from Tache' before she noticed his distress. "Yes, Tache', I'll mark it on my calendar," he said. "Now I'll just get out of your way and let you resume your packing."

Stewart was in a panic, Tache' was leaving him for Joyce! Dan was his only friend, the only one who understood and cared about him; and Joyce planned to turn him into another Brian on Monday! "Stewart, you must seize control, you must seize control!" he repeated to himself as he quickly glided down the hall to get Dan.

By the time Stewart entered the Interview Room, he was out of breath and near hysteria. He tried to speak, but was unable to.

When Dan saw Stewart in such distress, he sat him down and tried to calm him. "Stew, Stew, what's going on, dude?

183

Take a breath and tell me."

"Dan, Dan! you've been right all along," Stewart managed to say. "I can't stand by and allow Joyce to turn you, my only true friend, into another Brian."

Dan was relieved that Stewart was finally on his side and he anxiously waited to hear what he had to say next.

"I've decided that we will go ahead and perform brain transplants on both Joyce and Tache'."

"Sure, sure man, we can do that. But what happened to change your mind?"

"Tache' came back to the lab and informed me of her intentions; she's moving in with Joyce! They're in love and my whole life is in shambles! We'll have to move fast if we're going to stop this. Tache' is in her room packing as we speak!"

Stewart stood up and started to walk to the door, but then he stopped and looked up at Dan with tears in his eyes. "I can't live without Tache' or Joyce! I have to have things the way they used to be; Joyce as my beloved boss, and Tache' as my bestie!"

"Yeah man, I understand," Dan said, trying not to laugh. "I'm right behind you Stew."

"I knew that you would be Dan, you're a great friend."

"What should we do first?"

Stewart signaled for Dan to follow him and he walked into the Observation Booth. "First step in the plan; block all communication devices coming in or out of the lab. We don't want to be interrupted."

"Yeah, good thinking Stew."

Stewart threw the proper switches and successfully blocked all communication with the laboratory.

"Are all the entrance doors locked?" Dan asked.

"All entrance doors are always secured, to anyone without a security clearance."

"Okay Stew, I'll get the gurney ready, and you do what you do best. Do you have the hypo?"

"Of course I do, I always have one handy; you should know

that by now. I'll call you when it's time for the gurney."

As Stewart approached Tache's bedroom he could hear her singing. "I love it when she sings," he said to himself as he wiped a tear from his eye. Then he arrived at her room and stood for a moment in the doorway and admired her. Tache' had her back to him, and was packing a suitcase that was lying on her bed. Then Stewart decided to make his move, he quickly sidled up behind Tache' and carefully shot knockout medication into her neck.

Stewart had planned to gently glide Tache' onto her bed, but things didn't go that way. Instead of falling forward, as he had anticipated, she slumped over backward. Stewart tried with all his might to hold her up and prevent her from falling and being injured. But, he wasn't strong enough and collapsed to the floor with Tache' on top of him.

Tache' was nearly double his size and Stewart found it difficult to breathe beneath her weight. "Help! Help, Dan! I'm being crushed!" he weakly called out.

His desperate cries for help were unheeded, everything remained silent. Stewart began to panic, "Oh geepers!" he said to himself. "What if Dan has left the building to kill, this was his opportunity. It is a strong desire; maybe he needed to have sexual intercourse. Oh great, Dan, just think about yourself and your own needs. Who cares about good old Stew's requirements!" Then he thought about what would happen when he was discovered. "Tache' will never forgive me. When she wakes up, there I'll be, right under her with no explanation! She's smart she'll figure it out. I'll go to prison! I won't be protected, and my street language will only get me so far! Prisoners have their ways. They'll find out that I'm the executioner and they'll kill me! If that's the case, I hope that I just die right here under Tache'. At least I will be with the love of my life when I pass from this world. Yes, Stewart, it's the end for you, be a man and just die! What was the song that Tache' was singing? Oh yeah, Shall we gather at the ri..ver the beautiful the beautiful ri..ver...that's all I know! Why can't I remember the rest of the words? Tache' sings that song all the time … doggone it! Stewart, remember the rest of that song, will you? This is somehow so important to me now, I must be dying!"

Stewart lay quietly accepting his fate. But then, he heard a squeak … another squeak … more squeak's, repetitive squeak's, coming down the hall!

The sound was getting louder and louder, nearer and nearer. "It's that gurney that's in need of repair; I've got to put some oil on those wheels. I'll be sure to add it to my to-do list. Wait, hold the phone Stewart! Gurney wheels squeaking, means gurney moving! Dan didn't leave me after all! Dan, the heartless serial killer to the rescue!"

Dan entered Tache's room with the gurney. He saw Stewart's predicament and rolled Tache' off of him.

When the weight of Tache' had been lifted from his chest, Stewart gasped for air and coughed loudly. "Dan, where were you? I called for you and you didn't come. I was being crushed to death! I was certain that it was the end for me! Why did it take you so long to respond? I almost died Dan!"

Dan just shook his head, "Well Stew, when I didn't hear you call for me, I waited about five minutes and then decided to head down the hall."

"That is completely inaccurate, Dan," Stewart gasped. "According to my calculations there is no way possible that the timing of five minutes is in any way correct. Why I was nearly suffocated by the time you got here."

"Get over it Stew, just admit it, you freaked out."

"Okay, I'm man enough to admit it. I freaked out. Now let's get back to the task at hand, shall we?"

Dan lowered the gurney so that it would be easier for him to load Tache' onto it. He grabbed under her arms and started to pull her over.

"Watch her head now, Dan, be careful we don't want to hurt her!"

I don't think it's possible to hurt this colossal faggot, but okay, I'll be careful."

"Take that insult back Dan, she's not a colossal faggot,

186

she's a colossal ebony queen! By all means you should be able to move her quite easily. For goodness sake, you're a head taller than her."

"Yeah, but she's solid muscle."

"Well Dan, if you're fishing for some kind of complement, I will say that you would triumph in a wrestling match with her."

Dan smiled and strapped Tache' to the gurney. Then he began to wheel it into the O.R., with Stewart following right behind him.

As he walked, Stewart straightened his lab coat and inspected his pocket protector. He was relieved to find that all of his pens were still neatly lined up as they should be, but his badge needed a little adjusting. Stewart took a deep breath and regained his composure. He pulled out his comb and slicked back his greasy hair as he snorted, trying to clear his sinuses. And as always, he pushed up his glasses.

Stewart was nervous, even though he knew exactly what to do, this would be the first time that he would be preforming a brain transplant without Joyce. The pressure was on, he knew that he had do a perfect job or risk losing his bestie forever.

When they arrived in the O.R., Dan began to prepare Tache' for surgery. With Stewart's direction and Dan's knowledge of surgery, he was doing well.

Dan stopped when he saw Stewart slumped over the counter by the sink.

"Hey Stew what's going on man? You can't wimp out on me now, brother!"

Stewart didn't respond at first, but then he slowly looked up at Dan with a strange stare and glazed over eyes. "Don't you worry about me comrade, I'm in *a zone*."

Stewart had actually frightened Dan, which wasn't easily done. "Yeah, okay man, don't get nuts on me now, let's just do this."

Stewart got his hypodermic needle ready and was just about to add medication to Tache's I.V., when the door opened. It was Joyce with Derek riding on her shoulder. Stewart and Dan had been discovered!

187

When Joyce saw that Dan was loose, and that Tache' was unconscious and strapped to the operating table, she screamed out, "No!! What's happening here?! Stewart what are you doing?! Have you gone mad?! STOP THIS! NOW!! Dan, step away from Tache'!!! IMMEDIATELY!!! Do as you're told!"

Dan roared back at Joyce with his eyes blazing. "I'm done taking orders from you, bitch! It's time I put you into line!"

Stewart grasped Dan's arm and stepped in front of him. "Let me handle this Dan."

Joyce's first thought was for Tache', "Derek," she whispered, "you must free Tache'. I'll divert their attention."

Derek scuttled down Joyce's back and hid under a shelf, in a dark corner of the room. Even with his purple faux hawk and sparkling necklace and nails, Stewart and Dan were so focused on Joyce that they didn't notice him.

"Joyce, don't make this any more difficult than it has to be," Stewart calmly stated.

Joyce was shaking and she slowly backed away, with terror in her eyes. "Stewart, I don't know what has driven you to this, but I'm certain that we can work it out. After all, we're family."

"Oh yes *family*, what a nice charade Joyce," Stewart said with a cocky attitude, "but you see, things they are a changin'. Neither I, nor Dan, want to injure you in any way, just create a more compliant and cooperative Joyce. One that will obey our requests. You see, I'm taking over, and there's nothing that you can do to stop me."

"Yeah we're gonna' put Brian's brain in your head, bitch!" Dan defiantly shouted.

"Well actually Dan, it won't be exactly the same as Brian's brain," Stewart started to explain.

Dan glared at Stewart, "Listen you idiot, what difference does it make?"

Dan and Stewart began to argue and Joyce seized the opportunity and dashed from the room!

"She's getting away asshole!" Dan yelled.

Stewart and Dan raced after Joyce, and the moment that they left the room, Derek leaped into action. He ran out from under the shelf and jumped up on the table where Tache' was strapped down. First he grasped the I.V. and gently pulled it from her hand. Then he began to gnaw at the straps that bound her, but Tache' didn't stir, she was out cold.

Joyce ran desperately down the hall and went into the first room that would lock, the Brain Production Room. She closed the door behind her and then used her top security clearance to override the lock, and keep Stewart from opening it.

Stewart ran up to the door, with Dan right behind him, "Joyce has to be in here," he said breathing heavily.

Joyce could hear Dan and Stewart just outside the door; she was distressed that they had discovered her so quickly.

She picked up the phone and attempted to make a call for help. But, she found that Stewart had blocked all communications with the laboratory.

Joyce tried to think of a plan. Tyrone was in the room with her, assembling brains, but he was a mere drone and couldn't be of any assistance. She needed a weapon of some sort and she frantically began to search the room for something to use to defend herself with.

While Joyce searched, Stewart placed his thumb on the lock pad and found that the door wouldn't acknowledge his identification. "Joyce must have overwritten the door lock."

"Stand aside!" Dan roared and started pounding at the heavy metal door. "Open this FUCKIN' door, you stupid cunt!"

"Now, now brother, there is no need for physical violence. And no more of that foul mouth, please, you know how I feel about that. Perhaps I can reason with her."

Dan backed off and let Stewart give it a try.

"Joyce, listen to me," he said. "It should be obvious to you that your efforts to escape are futile. Now, why don't you come out peacefully and submit."

When Joyce didn't respond, Dan pushed Stewart aside

and began slamming into the door again.

"Dan, Dan stop, you might injure yourself. There's no need to panic, I'm not without resources; I have a plan."

Joyce could hear what Stewart had said, and she wondered what his plan could possibly be. Perhaps he was going to threaten her with harming Tache'. What would she do then? "I can only hope that Derek has freed her by now!"

Stewart coughed to clear his throat and said in a loud firm voice, "Tyrone! This is Dr. Stewart Whitehead, open the door please."

Tyrone, stopped brain assembly and turned toward the door. He took one step and then another. As he got closer, Joyce began to panic, but then she realized that Tyrone was programmed to obey her orders as well. "Tyrone, STOP!" she commanded. Tyrone, didn't listen and took another step toward the door. "Tyrone, please, listen to me!" Joyce cried in desperation. She ran in front of him and tried to physically restrain him, but she wasn't strong enough. She pounded his head and tried to short circuit him, but Tyrone just kept on heading for the door.

Joyce suddenly realized her mistake; she had to identify herself before Tyrone would accept her command. "This is Dr. Joyce Picard, Tyrone, go back to work on brain assembly!" With that, Tyrone, stopped and headed back toward the brain production table.

"I was wondering when you'd catch on Joyce," Stewart mocked. "Duh, snort, snort. Perhaps you're not as intelligent as I thought you were. By the way ah … This is Dr. Stewart Whitehead, Tyrone, open the door." Tyrone put down the brain that he had resumed working on, and once again turned toward the door.

"No, Tyrone! This is Dr. Joyce Picard, STOP!"

Tyrone, stopped, but he became confused and out of sorts. He jerked his arms and head and started knocking things off of the table.

Tyrone, this is Dr. Stewart Whitehead snort, snort. Open the door!"

Tyrone's head and arms were still jerking, but he turned and headed for the door again.

"Stop Tyrone!" Joyce screamed.

Tyrone, stopped, but then he suddenly began to spin wildly around in a circle, violently waving his arms and saying, "Circuit, four two four! Circuit four two four!"

Now, Joyce was afraid of Tyrone, he was strong and completely out of control.

"You forgot to say your name, snort, snort," Stewart shouted through the locked door. "Oh shucks, that was stupid. Stewart where's your brain at?" he questioned himself.

"Enough of this shit!" Dan yelled, "Get away from the fuckin' door Stew!"

Stewart jumped out of the way and Dan took a few steps back.

"Dan, this door is made of metal, I don't think that it's possible for you to ..." But Stewart was abruptly interrupted when Dan rammed into the door, and it came flying off of the hinges.

Dan burst into the room, he was enraged and Stewart was worried. "Don't hurt Joyce! Please don't hurt her Dan!" he cried. "Remember, harming Joyce is not part of our plan!"

Dan didn't listen. "You're dead bitch!" he shouted and fiercely went after Joyce.

Joyce turned the corner, and ran for the back of the room. There the completed, Living Artificial Brains were stored, in heavy glass, specimen jars. Dan ran after her and Joyce quickly picked up a jar and threw it at him, striking him in the head. Dan, was stunned, and covered in the slimy preservative fluid that the brains were stored in. He wiped it from his eyes and kept coming after Joyce.

One after the other, Joyce threw heavy glass specimen jars, fighting to keep, Dan, at bay.

As each jar broke and the brains hit the floor, they were activated and came to life. The brains extended their tendrils and began to move around the room, in the slippery fluid, searching for a host to bind with.

Stewart was standing in the doorway to avoid getting hurt. He tried once again to explain to Joyce, shouting over the screaming and breaking glass. "Joyce, please stop fighting, everything will be fine if you just cooperate with us. We can still be a family. Don't make this any harder than it has to be."

Dan was relentless, Joyce struck him every time she threw a heavy glass jar, but no matter how badly she injured him, he kept right on coming. His resilience was far beyond that of a normal human being, and Joyce realized that the Living Artificial Brain had fortified and strengthened, Dan.

It didn't take long before Joyce ran out of things to throw. She was cornered and she picked up a jagged piece of glass to defend herself with. Joyce swung the glass back and forth in front of her, preparing to strike.

When, Dan, saw what she was doing, he started laughing. "Oh, so you think you can take me down with a little piece of glass, huh? That's the first course I took in prison, 'Everything You Need to Know About Shanks.'" Dan easily kicked the glass from Joyce's hand and now she was defenseless. Fear clutched her heart as she faced the enormous man alone. "Stewart," she cried in desperation, "Stewart, help me!"

"Stewart's sick of putting up with your shit, bitch!" Dan shouted. "And now, it's time to pay the piper!" Dan grabbed hold of Joyce. She screamed and struggled, calling to Stewart, "Stewart, please, please, do something! Help me Stewart!" But Stewart was unmoved.

Dan laughed wildly and raised Joyce up over his head. She looked down and braced herself to be slammed on the hard cement floor.

But suddenly, Tyrone, rushed at Dan, wildly waving his arms and shouting, "Circuit, four two four! Circuit, four two four!" He crashed forcefully into Dan and struck him over and over again with his frantic arm movements. Dan lost his balance on the slime and he and Joyce, both fell to the floor.

When Stewart saw what was happening, he panicked and ran into the room. "Don't damage her!" he shouted. "Dan, I've got everything under control!"

Stewart was holding up his trusty hypodermic needle, prepared to sedate Joyce. But in his haste, he stepped on one of the brains, and skidded across the room. Stewart slammed into a heavy shelf that was fully stocked with glass vials, beakers and specimen jars. The shelf broke loose from the wall and fell on top of him, knocking him down and nearly crushing him. The glass containers shattered and Stewart was severely cut over his entire face and body. Wounded and bleeding, he lay motionless under the weight of the heavy shelving.

The Living Artificial Brains quickly sensed Stewart's blood flowing on the floor. Having found a host, they began the bonding process, attaching to the nerves and blood vessels through Stewart's open wounds and cuts.

Stewart's eyes opened wide when he felt the experience of the brains attaching to his body. "I FEEL ENERGIZED!!! THIS IS EXHILERATING!!!" He insanely shouted and began laughing in delight.

Joyce was stunned from the fall, but she quickly gained her focus and scrambled away from Dan. Dan went after her, and they both struggled to keep their footing on the slimy floor.

Tyrone, was still wandering around, waving his arms, being destructive and adding to the havoc. He came near Joyce, just as Dan was about to catch her. She seized the opportunity, jumped behind, Tyrone, and then shoved him into, Dan. Tyrone was still shouting about circuits and wildly waving his arms. He hit Dan and knocked him back. Dan tried to push Tyrone aside, but then he started spinning around again, striking Dan and blocking his path.

Tyrone had bought Joyce a few seconds. She flashed her eyes around the room and noticed jars of acid sitting on a high shelf. Acid had never been stored in the Brain Production Room before, and she wondered where it had come from. But, she quickly realized that acid would be a formidable weapon and she went after it. Joyce quickly pushed the rolling ladder beneath the shelf, where the acid was, and began to climb. She was injured and frightened and having a difficult time keeping her balance. When she neared the top of the ladder, her foot slipped through a rung and Dan darted under the ladder and grabbed it. He yanked hard and pulled her leg through with such force that it came out of the socket. Joyce screeched in pain and felt herself begin to lose consciousness. She was about to fall backward, when Tyrone started banging a chair on the floor. The loud noise startled Joyce, and Dan loosened his grip on her and turned to see what Tyrone was doing. At that second, Joyce broke away from Dan. She fought the pain and pulled herself up the ladder and grabbed the acid.

She had the jar of acid in her hand, and when Dan looked back at her, she threw it in his face.

For a brief second, Joyce thought that she may have missed her target. But then, she watched in horror as the left side of Dan's beautiful face, the face that she had created, became deformed and sizzled like a piece of bacon.

Dan fell to his knees screaming in agony.

Joyce stumbled down the ladder and shoved Dan out of her way. Then she staggered down the hall to check on Derek and Tache', hoping with everything in her that Tache' had recovered.

When she reached the O.R., she was worried when she found Tache' still lying unconscious on the table. She wondered what Stewart and Dan had done to her. Derek was still by her side, and Joyce asked him if she showed any signs of improvement.

Derek patted Tache's cheeks, with his little paws, trying to awaken her. When he got no response, he gave Joyce a despairing look.

Joyce couldn't be of much help to anyone in her condition; she had to fix her leg. There was a vice-type brace in the O.R. and she painfully locked her leg in it. Then, Joyce summoned all of her strength and courage and forced her leg back into the socket. She screamed in agony and Derek jumped from the table and ran to her. "It's okay Derek," she said. "I'm okay now." Joyce released her leg from the vice and collapsed on the floor. She caught her breath and then struggled to her feet. "I'll lock this door and hold them off as long as I can. You stay here and protect Tache'."

Derek nodded that he understood, he was worried about Joyce and didn't want her to leave. But, he jumped back up on the table with Tache' and Joyce locked the door to the O.R.

Joyce was determined to protect her beloved Tache', who lay helpless in the O.R. She limped down the hall to the kitchen and rifled through the drawers looking for a knife. She pulled out a large butcher knife and looked it over. The knife was very sharp and Joyce noticed that it was an Orto. She remembered the Orto knife from her interview with Tammy, the serial killer. It was the same brand of knife that she had spoken so highly of. "Oh yes, just what I need, superior cutting ability! And now that I've had my first lesson in, 'Everything You Need to Know About Shanks,' perhaps I'll stand a chance." Joyce looked at the knife and flashed the blade in the light. Then she went to Observation Booth, across from the O.R. and looked for Dan and Stewart on the monitor.

She found that they were still in the Brain Production Room, but Tyrone was no longer there. Joyce scanned the rooms and found him in Stewart's experiment room. He was surrounded by Bunsen burners, beakers and test tubes, many filled with dangerous, toxic chemicals. Joyce was concerned about the damage that he could do, but for the time being, she had to focus her attention on the more present danger, Dan.

Joyce shifted her view back to Dan. He was at the sink, splashing water on his face and Stewart was still lying under the shelving, moaning in ecstasy.

"What do I do Stew? That bitch threw acid in my face?"

Stewart was so enthralled with his own experience, that he didn't pay attention.

"STEW, HELP ME!!! SHE THREW ACID IN MY FACE!!"

Dan screamed so loudly that he got through to Stewart, "Use the neutralizer, you're at the first aid station," he told him.

Dan fumbled around and found the acid neutralizer. He applied it to his face and got relief. Then he slowly raised his head and looked in the mirror. What he saw horrified him. Half of his face had been eaten away and part of his skull was exposed. His left eyeball was hanging out of the socket and dangling like a bloody bead on a string. Dan growled like an angry beast and shouted, "JOYCE IS GONNA PAY FOR THIS!!!"

"Dan, I totally understand," Stewart shouted. "But, would you please get me out of this predicament first?"

Dan stomped across the floor, he grabbed the shelf that was on top of Stewart and threw it across the room as he roared.

Dan saw that the Living Artificial Brains were attaching themselves to Stewart. "Oh shit Stew! I'll pull them off of you!"

"Oh no Dan, to the contrary, I will keep them with me always. It's an amazing experience to have the addition of so many brains. It has heightened my intelligence beyond belief! I'm energized and focused! I can see all things! I'M SUPER HUMAN! WITH ALL OF THIS BRAIN POWER, I'M THE MOST MAGNIFICIENT HUMAN BEING IN THE UNIVERSE! Ha, ha, ha, ha, ha!"

Dan pulled Stewart to his feet and Stewart found it difficult to even stand. He had one brain attached to the top of his head and two more on the back. The heavy brains were pulling his head backward and Stewart rested the side of his face on a brain that was attached to his neck.

There was a brain on to the inside of his thigh that bowed his legs out. And his left arm was heavily weighted down from the many brains that were attached to it. It dragged the ground and bent Stewart sideways. His back was completely covered with grey lumpy brains, some closely attached to his body and some hanging loosely from their tendrils.

Dan backed away and Stewart awkwardly limped toward him dragging his left arm and the brains dangling from his back. "It will take some time and conditioning to get adjusted to my wonderful new appendages," he said with a smile. "It might be a slight inconvenience, but well worth it. Don't be alarmed, Dan, my right arm is still functional and I am fully prepared to proceed with the plan."

"Fuck off freak!" Dan yelled. He pushed Stewart to the floor and then left the room, to look for Joyce.

"Dan! Dan! Surely you can see the extreme value of my improvements! Dan, come back!" Stewart shouted. But then Stewart noticed more brains moving toward him and he was delighted. He stayed down on the floor, laughing with glee, "Come to Pa -Pa my babies! The more, the merrier! Go ahead now, don't be shy. Attach! Attach! OH YES, THIS IS EXHILARATING!"

Every brain in the room began to make its way toward Stewart. One after the other, they extended their tendrils and latched onto him. Stewart was completely covered with brains and more were still approaching, piling one on top of the other with Stewart under the mound. He was completely submersed, and went down laughing into the brain meld.

Joyce saw the horror from the Observation Booth and she watched, Dan, stomping down the hallway looking for her. "Come out, come out, wherever you are! I'm a gonna get ya Joyce!"

Joyce held tightly to the Orto knife as Dan methodically checked each room in the laboratory, getting closer and closer to her.

When he reached the O.R., he put his ear to the door and listened. "Joyce, are you in there? I know you're close-by, I can smell your pussy!" Then he started laughing. "You're in there with your faggot friend, now open the fuckin' door!" When there was no response, Dan became enraged, "Okay Joyce, I guess you're gonna make me work for it!" He pounded on the door and then took a couple of steps back like a bull ready to charge. Joyce had seen, Dan, pulverize the door of the Brain Production Room and she knew that she had to stop him before he got to Tache' and Derek.

Joyce got up from the desk, with the knife in her hand. She opened the door of the Observation Booth and lunged across the hall at, Dan, trying to stab him.

Before she could strike, Dan, turned around and saw her swing the knife.

He didn't get afraid, he got excited, "Oh yeah baby, put up a fight. Come on now, show me how bad you can be!"

Joyce kept swinging the knife and trying to stab, Dan, but he was too much for her to handle. After he toyed with her for a while, taunting and making fun of her, he knocked the knife from her hand. Then he grabbed, Joyce, by the neck and lifted her feet from the ground.

Joyce gripped Dan's hands and frantically tried to pry them from her neck. It seemed that she was helpless to do anything to save herself until she suddenly she remembered the weakness of all men. "His testicles! I must kick him in the testicles!"

Joyce aimed and kicked as hard as she could, hoping to hit her target. When, Dan, shouted in pain, she knew that she had made contact!

Dan let go of Joyce and dropped to his knees. As soon as her feet hit the ground, she scrambled for the knife. Joyce picked the knife up and stood over Dan, who was kneeling before her. She had a clear shot to his neck and she raised the blade preparing to sever his jugular.

Joyce knew that she had to make it count. She braced herself and came down hard with the Orto butcher knife.

As the knife swung toward him, Dan, reached up and grabbed, Joyce, by the wrist. He twisted her arm, forcing her to drop the knife as he got to his feet.

"I've had enough of your bullshit!" he screamed and then he threw her hard against the wall. Joyce hit her head and slid slowly down to the floor, she was out cold.

Dan bent over Joyce's limp body, grabbed her by the hair and dragged her down the hallway.

THE BLOODY CONCLUSION

When Joyce came to, she found herself with nothing on, but her panties. She tried to move and realized that she was secured to the table in the Interview Room. Her wrists were locked in the metal cuffs that were used to restrain the serial killers that she interviewed. And her legs were spread apart with her ankles taped to the table legs with duct tape. Pain shot through her entire body and Joyce felt sick when she realized that she was now under the control of, Dan the devil.

Joyce knew that it was useless to try and free her wrists from the metal cuffs. But she thought that she would at least try to get her feet loose.

As she struggled, twisting and turning, she saw, Dan, slowly rising up between her legs, from below the table. She screamed in terror when she saw his horrifying face. His skin was peeling loose from his skull and his eyeball was dangling. He reached over the table, grabbed Joyce by the throat and started to strangle her. She struggled to get air and just before she lost consciousness, he stopped. She coughed and tried to catch her breath while, Dan, pulled down his pants and exposed his raging hard on. Joyce was terrified and, Dan, finally got his wish, he could see terror in her eyes, the fear that his ugly soul loved so much. Fear and terror, the food that the demon inside of him fed on.

"There it is Joyce... fear, the fear that I've been looking for ever since the day that I met you. I smelled your pussy then, and I'm smelling it now, sweet virgin pussy and it's all mine!

Joyce started screaming uncontrollably. "Help, someone help me!"

"Sorry babe, but nobody can help you. We're locked in here, all alone. You see, I have my own security clearance now." Then Dan held up Stewart's severed thumb.

"Oh Stewart ... " Joyce cried, and turned her head aside.

At this point, all Joyce could do was cry and scream while Dan licked her neck and breathed heavy, whispering obscenities in her ear.

It was all over, a serial killer that she had tried to help, was going to torture her and take her life. Her life, it was only just beginning. She had finally found the happiness that she had wanted so much, and now it was being taken away, before it had even started. Perhaps Tache' would never awaken. And what was going to happen to, Derek?

Just when all hope was gone, the door of the Interview Room burst open and standing in the doorway was, Tache'.

Tache' saw what was happening and immediately grabbed, Dan, and pulled him off of Joyce.

Derek ran in, he jumped up on the table and stood over Joyce snarling at Dan.

Dan spun around and looked viciously at Tache', "Well, well, what a surprise, faggy boy is trying to grow some balls. Don't worry Joyce, give me a minute to take care of this interruption. I'll get right back to you babe. Come on faggot, let's get this over with!"

Dan took a swing at Tache'. He hit her in the side of the head and knocked her back, but Tache' didn't go down. She shook it off and went right back at Dan. The two of them wrestled, striking each other, over and over again.

In the struggle, Tache's blouse was ripped off. Her bra was slipping up and getting in her way, so she ripped it off too.

The fighting went on and on, punching and crashing and slamming each other about the Interview Room.

Joyce laid on the table and watched the vicious battle. She was helpless to do anything, but hope and pray that Tache' would be the victor.

Dan threw, Tache', and she slammed into the interview table and landed over Joyce. "You okay sweetheart?" she asked.

"Yes Tache', I'm fine. Just kill him!"

With that, Tache' roared, she rushed full force at, Dan, and knocked him down. She jumped on top of him, and when she did, her skirt ripped up both sides.

Tache' was pounding, Dan. Her head was down and her wig was getting in her eyes. Between punches, she ripped it off her head and threw it across the room.

Tache' was getting the best of, Dan, and it looked like she was going to take him. But, Dan, suddenly realized that he could still see out of his hanging eyeball. The eyeball was stretched out, across the floor, and sitting right in front of it, was a bottle. Somehow, Dan got hold of the bottle and struck Tache' in the head. She fell off of him and didn't move.

When Joyce saw that Tache' was down, she screamed, "No! No! Tache'! No!"

Dan got up and stood over Tache', "I guess I was a little too much for ya after all, faggy boy!"

Dan was out of breath and he turned and looked at, Joyce. "See, Joyce, that's how bad I want you. I fought for your pussy and now I'm going to take it!"

Derek had been trying to release Joyce. He stopped gnawing at the sticky duct tape and shook it from his mouth. He rose to his hind legs, prepared to take, Dan, on. Derek threw his head back and was just about to leap on him, when Tache' jumped on, Dan's, back and got him in a choke hold. She kept jerking her arm and tightening her grip. Tighter and tighter she choked, Dan. And when he started to go out, she choked him all the more. Finally, Dan, collapsed and Tache' dropped him to the floor. But, Dan, had just been acting, and after he fell, he grabbed Tache's ankles and jerked her feet from under her. Tache' lost her balance, and as soon as she hit the floor, she scrambled from the room and ran away.

Dan started to laugh, "Well, Joyce, it looks like faggy boy has had enough." He started slowly walking toward, Joyce, salivating and panting and licking his lips. Suddenly, Joyce saw Tache', standing in the doorway, holding the fire axe in her hand. She wiped the lipstick from her mouth and then raised the axe above her head.

When, Dan, saw the expression on Joyce's face, he turned to see what she was looking at. At that second, Tache' plunged the axe deep into, Dan's, forehead! Blood gushed from the wound and, Dan, turned in a circle, "Joy ... ce .." he said and then collapsed on the floor.

Meanwhile, Tyrone was still running amok. He tipped over two beakers holding chemicals that mixed together and caught fire. The harsh black smoke came billowing down the halls and flooded into the Interview Room.

Tache' ran to, Joyce, "Joyce, Joyce, let me get you out of here. Everything's alright now sweetheart."

But suddenly, Joyce, screamed in terror, she screamed like she had never screamed before. Tache' whipped around to see, Dan, standing behind her with the axe still driven into his skull. "GOOD JOB JOYCE! THE LIVING ARTIFICIAL BRAIN IS STLL FUNCTIONING PERFECTLY!!! Ha, ha, ha, ha, ha!" Dan grabbed hold of the axe and yanked it from his head.

Immediately, Tache' jumped into action, she rammed into, Dan, with all her strength, driving him out of the room and across the hall into the Operating Room. The two of them fought, slamming into the tables and monitoring machines. Everything in the O.R. was on wheels and moving about. Dan swung the axe at Tache' and she jumped out of the way and found herself backed up against the wall. There was an I.V. stand near her, and just as Dan was about the strike, she picked it up and used it to deflect the axe. Dan was brutal, he swung the axe over and over again, and Tache' battled him with the I.V. stand.

The battle raged through the laboratory. Joyce could hear the destruction, the crashing and the crushing blows. Her precious Tache' was battling a monster, one that she had created. She held her breath with each blow that she heard, hoping that it wasn't Tache' who was being hurt. Every time she heard, Dan's, voice, she cringed. And each time she heard, Tache', she rejoice that she was still alive.

Tache' had been knocked down, she was on her back and exhausted. Dan raised the axe above his head, prepared to deliver the fatal blow. He lunged forward, but at the last second, Tache' swung the I.V. stand up in front of her and thrust it into his stomach. Dan was still on his feet, but he had the breath knocked out of him and was stunned.

Tache' jumped up, she yanked the axe from Dan's hand and then she took a mighty swing and chopped through his neck, severing his spinal cord. Dan's head hung forward and then he collapsed on the floor. Tache' stood over him and chopped and chopped with the fire axe until, Dan's, head was completely severed.

She stood panting, covered in blood and looking down at the headless creature lying on the floor. It was over. But now, she had to free Joyce and escape the laboratory fire.

She raced to the Interview Room and when, Joyce, saw that it was Tache', she was overjoyed. Tache' bent over, Joyce, and kissed her on the lips. "It's over Joyce, you're safe now." She stroked Derek's coat, "Good job protecting, Joyce, boy. Now let's get out of here!"

Tache' went into the Observation Booth and released, Joyce, from the cuff restraints. Joyce rubbed her wrists and slowly sat up. The smoke was getting dense and it was harder to breath. Tache' rushed back into the Interview Room. "Tache'," Joyce said coughing, "we must get out quickly or we will soon be overcome by the smoke!" Joyce tried to stand, but she became dizzy and started to fall. She grabbed onto the table and, Tache', picked her up in her arms. Derek jumped on, Tache's, shoulder and she walked through the dense smoke trying to make it to the exit. Tache' could barely see, she was nearly blinded by the harsh chemical smoke. But she kept moving ahead, struggling to find the way. She turned left, thinking that it was the right direction, but, Derek squeaked and signaled for her to go the other way. Tache' trusted, Derek, she turned right turn and was glad that she had, there it was, the exit door! She placed her thumb on the lock pad and the door opened into the fresh air. She carried Joyce and Derek to safety and stopped at a pile of large rocks and boulders. She gently placed Joyce down on a rock. It was dark by this time and, Joyce, was wearing nothing, but her panties, so Derek quickly sat in her lap to keep her warm. The three of them were injured and covered with black soot and smoke, but still their joy overwhelmed them and they embraced and cried in happiness and relief.

Inside the lab, Dan, laid dead on the floor, his head completely severed from his body. But the head slowly started turning as the tendrils of the Living Artificial Brain extend from the neck and crept across the floor. The tendrils attached to Dan's body, and once the bonding process was completed, he began to move his arms and legs. Dan's eyes came to life again and his body crawled to his head and grasped it in his hands. Dan stood up, holding his head in front of him. He was confused at seeing everything upside down and not quite sure how to function. But minutes later, he adapted and started walking for the exit, still obsessed with killing Joyce.

Joyce, Derek and Tache' were still sitting on the rocks, trying to recover from the ordeal, when they heard, Dan, shouting. "I'M ALIVE! GOOD JOB JOYCE! THE LIVING ARTIFICIAL BRAIN IS INDESTRUCTIBLE! I'M GONNA LIVE FOREVER!!!"

They saw, Dan's, headless body, standing in the doorway of the lab, smoke billowing around it. He started to walk toward them, holding his head in his hands and moving it about to see where he was going.

Joyce screamed, at the gruesome sight and Tache' and Derek stood side by side, in front of her preparing to fight the revolting monster.

Tyrone was still in the laboratory, turning levers and knobs, "Brain number, twenty-five point five … ABORT! … ABORT! … ABOR." Then he pushed the lever that turned on the gas! There was a huge explosion and the entire building blew up! Flames shot high into the night sky and Derek, Joyce and Tache' ducked behind the rocks. They watched as the building burned.

Tache' rose to her feet, she took off her high heels, and then ran and threw them forcefully into the fire. She turned and stood looking at, Joyce, the woman that she loved. And what, Joyce, saw at that moment, was a beautiful, strong, black man.

The tattered skirt that he wore hung loosely on his slender hips and his muscular body glowed in the light of the flickering flames. Joyce was in awe of the majestic being standing before her. "Tache', you're incredible!" she said breathlessly.

Tache' responded in a low, manly voice, "I'm Jamal, Joyce, and I'm your man. I came back to life today because of you. I love you Joyce."

With that, Jamal, pulled Joyce up into his arms. He gave her a long passionate kiss and the torment departed from his soul. Jamal picked Joyce up and Derek jumped on his shoulder. Carrying his true love in his arms, Jamal, walked away from madness and into a life of love and perfect happiness.

The lab continued to burn, it was located dangerously close to the woods, but with the concrete surround, the flames were contained. Dan had been thrown in the explosion. His body and head smoldered, and lay chard and black, unrecognizable that it had ever been a human being.

Then, there was a slight crackling sound coming from Dan's remains. The cracking got louder, and suddenly, Dan's, head popped open and the Living Artificial Brain burst from the chard skull and scurried into the woods, under a pile of leaves...

THE END?

This book was brought to you by:

GALVANIZED GROUP INC.

Thank you for buying our book!

Galvanized Group Inc.

Like us on Facebook

Follow us on Twitter

We would love to hear from you!

galvanizedgroupinc@gmail.com